Hardened by Steel

STEEL CORPS-BOOK TWO

BY J.B. HAVENS

J.B. Havens

HARDENED BY STEEL

Copyright (c) 2016 J.B. Havens

All Rights Reserved.

Hardened By Steel is a work of fiction. Names, characters, businesses, organizations, places, events, and incidents either are the product of the author's imagination or are used fictitiously. Any resemblance to actual persons, living or dead, events, or locales is entirely coincidental.

No part of this book may be reproduced, scanned or distributed in any printed or electronic form without permission. Please do not participate in or encourage piracy of copyrighted materials in violation of the author's rights. Purchase only authorized editions.

Acknowledgments

With this, the second installment of Steel Corps, the list has grown. Writing is the most fulfilling and challenging thing I've ever attempted outside of raising my children. Here are the people that helped bring this dream to fruition:

My husband, Mike, my partner in life. I love you. Thank you for being who you are and loving me in spite of my many faults. Without your encouragement and support I wouldn't be able to do this. Thank you for your suggestions and for always listening to me and embracing my crazy.

To Connie, my editor and cheerleader. Thank you for pushing me and shaping my stories into something worthy of the light of day. I've become a better writer because of you; thank you for all that you do.

To Mom, there aren't words to express this. You've given me the strength and tools to shape myself into who I am today. Thank you for everything and for everything you have yet to do. I know your support and love will continue. I hope I've made you proud.

To Aunt Linda, the inspiration behind Aunt Beatrice. Your strength guides me on this journey. I hope when you turn these pages, you see pieces of yourself. I love you.

To Casey. Fellow author and coffee slut. Thank you for Rook. He's who he is because of you. Thanks for reading the countless screen shots and being my sounding board.

To Eric, thank you for your unending critiques and support; for always being willing to be my second set of eyes. Without those videos, your medical expertise, and cartel insights, this book wouldn't be what it is. Thank you.

To Anna and Tim, your story has been a huge inspiration to me. Thank you for allowing me to take pieces of it and shape it into my work. Jackson and Beatrice thank you. P.S. You're never too old for love.

As always to my cousin, Nobel Havens, Retired United States Army Sergeant. Thank you for your continued help and for always answering my odd random questions. These books wouldn't be what they are without your help and support. Thank you.

To my children, my wonderful children. Always for you, everything that I do, is for you. I love you.

Dear Reader, thank you for picking up this book. Without you to read my words, this would all be pointless. I hope you enjoy the journey Mic takes you on. I endeavor to be a writer worth reading. As Mic would say; buckle up buttercup, the fun is just beginning.

PLAYLIST

"Crawling" - Linkin Park

"Mad World" - Gary Jules

"Down with the Sickness" – Disturbed

"Second Chance" – Shinedown

"Killing" – Korn

"Physical (You're so)" – Nine inch Nails

"Bittersweet Symphony" – The Verve

"Don't Fear the Reaper" – Blue Oyster Cult

"Remedy" – Adele (Jordon and Mic's song)

"Green Fields of France" – Dropkick Murphys

"Dragula" – Rob Zombie

"Wrong Side of Heaven" – Five Finger Death Punch

J.B. Havens

ALSO BY J.B. HAVENS

Core of Steel: Steel Corps Book One

It is recommended that the Steel Corps Series be read in order.

J.B. Havens

Chapter 1

The crack of a palm striking my face exploded throughout the room. The burn and sting came seconds after as furious tears of anger streamed down my cheeks. I held up my arms, trying to protect myself, taking the blows that were raining down upon me with my body instead of my head.

"No! Stop!" I screamed, twisting and turning, frantic to escape. Terror gripped my small body in a vicious steel band of shock and panic. I had to get away, but I couldn't. I kicked and thrashed against the arms holding me down. A giant hand gripped my throat and squeezed... pressing down, while laughter assaulted my ears.

I jerked awake, all my senses on full alert; my heart slammed against my ribs. Even after all these years, the dream never changed; a decade of torment beating me down in my sleep. I looked over at my bookcase at the phone hidden there. I wanted to call Aunt Beatrice now more than ever. She had always been able to chase the nightmares away.

Instead, I stood and stripped off my sweat-soaked sheets. Dawn was beginning to breathe light into the night sky. The blackness was giving way to dark blue and inky purple. The light just beginning to seep around the edges of my curtains.

"May as well get up." I spoke to myself more and more all the time. Ever since we got back from Colombia, and Phillips had been killed, I had these old recurring nightmares, when I did manage to get some sleep. Dreams I hadn't suffered since I first joined the Army.

Stepping into the shower, I locked my past away where it belonged and got ready to deal with the day. It had been two months since the night Diego and his men infiltrated our compound. Two months of waiting for another mission. Jackson had given us all a reprieve; we had needed the time to heal and mourn. The wait was over.

I got dressed in my standard uniform of tactical pants and a fitted t-shirt. I strapped on my KA-BAR and M-9. The boys kept ragging on me to upgrade to something better. There are tons of high-quality tactical pistols out there. Browning and Sig Sauer in particular make fantastic military-grade weapons. I couldn't bring myself to part ways with it, though. This pistol had been my sidearm since it was first issued to me. Maybe I was like a little kid, unwilling to let go of my favorite blanket; but I didn't fucking care.

Walking past my bookcase on the way out the door I looked up, like I had been doing every day for two months. Resting on top of the bookcase was the machete: Mateo's machete. The one that was used to kill Phillips; which I had also used to kill Diego. I'm not sure why I recovered it from the field that night. I'd cleaned the blood from it, oiled it, and sharpened it to a razor edge. Next to it, resting on its unused case, was Phillips's Sig Sauer. It was all that was left of him. Just like the machete, I couldn't let it go.

"Get your shit together, Michaels," I said, as I shrugged into my jacket and walked out the door. A light was on in Jackson's cabin.

The remnants of the lingering fog swirled around the compound as

I walked the short distance to his cabin. Fall was almost over and winter fast approached. The leaves had changed to a glorious riot of color, but had long since fallen away, leaving the trees bare and skeletal looking. There was a bite in the early morning air, you could almost taste the snow that would soon blanket the compound. The grass was slick with frost, crunching under my boot heels. My breath was puffing out around my face in soft grey clouds.

Lights were popping on in the rest of the cabins; the team was waking and gearing up for the day, same as me. Today was special, which was why I needed to speak with Jackson before I saw the rest of the men. Stepping onto the small porch, I knocked on the heavy door. It was more of a courtesy than a necessity; he knew I was here.

"Come in, Mic," he said, voice still thick with sleep.

I stepped into the cabin and was welcomed by the comforting aroma of coffee. Standing at his small counter, he held a cup out to me. "Thanks, Master Sergeant," I said, as I accepted it gratefully.

"A little early isn't it?" He asked, filling his own cup.

"Yes, but I just want to get started. Get this over with." It was time to move on and today was the start.

"The file is on the table. Read up; I need to change."

I just now noticed that he was wearing only pajama bottoms. Damn, it was early. "Shit, sorry."

He waved me off and left to change.

I slumped into the chair, the folder weighing on me heavily. I had seen this exact file before. Even read it already, but now it was real. Rubbing my thumb-nail down the tab, I opened it.

His photo was paper-clipped to the front flap; he looked remarkably similar to his cousin, given that Matthew was half Cherokee. Dark hair just long enough that it brushed his forehead, and grey eyes. There was a scar bisecting his right eyebrow. Other than that, he had no identifying marks, no tattoos, or anything that set him apart; provided you discounted his strong jawline and all-over tan skin. He was quite handsome in a rugged way, with his impressive bone structure and carelessly attractive expression.

"What do you think, Mic?" Jackson said, startling me.

"Same as before. This might work, but it's going to be rough. The men are going to flip the fuck out. I wish you had let me tell them, give them time to get used to the idea."

"Your protest has been noted. And I've overridden it."

The soldier's name was typed on the tab in heavy black font: Riley, Matthew, CPL.

"When does he get here?" I asked before taking another sip of coffee. The warm rich brew was flavored with vanilla. Perfection in a cup.

"Any minute. I'd get your ass to the hangar. We'll finish all this later." He pointed at the other thick file. The bright orange folder telling me all I needed to know: orange was for Top Secret. The mission was coming down.

"Copy." Looking longingly at my unfinished coffee, I did as Jackson said, I got my ass to the hangar.

****

Somehow the others had beaten me to the hangar. They were lifting weights and warming up, getting ready for their daily run. Little did they know, they wouldn't be getting it in today; well, there was always tomorrow. If they took notice of the missing jet, they weren't commenting on it.

"Steel Corps, attention!" I shouted. Without question, they all stopped what they were doing and formed a line in front of me. Each of them would stand there at rigid attention until I told them otherwise.

"At ease." I could hear the jet now; my time was running out.

"I've got news. Our new member arrives any minute." They were not going to like what I had to say next. I debated even telling them, but I knew if I let this surprise hit them, they would not take it well. "You're not going to like it, but it's out of my hands. Just try to make the best of it and don't kill him."

Flynn raised his hand. "Flynn, you don't have to raise your hand. Just say it." Jordon rolled his eyes. He must be spending too much time with me.

"Who is it, Mic?" Flynn asked as the noise increased significantly. The jet was landing behind us. No way could I shout over the noise of the engines. Looks like my time to explain was up.

We all stood and watched the sleek black jet taxi, the engine noise dying down and slowing, before stopping all together. The steps came down and a lone man exited. He was in standard BDUs with his duffle slung over his shoulder. His cover was pulled low over his eyes, and what you could see of his face was creased by deep furrows. Being pulled out of bed and forced to make life changing decisions was enough to exhaust anyone.

"Corporal Matthew Riley reporting for duty, Staff Sergeant!" he said, as he dropped his bag and saluted.

"What the ever loving fuck?" Flynn furiously shouted, losing all military bearing in a single moment of pure rage.

I spun on my heel and addressed the men, ignoring Riley, who was standing dumbfounded behind me.

"Shut it!" I shouted. "This was not my choice, but it's out of my hands. Nut up and fucking deal with it or you can go get your walking papers from Master Sergeant Jackson. Those are your choices. What's it going to be, boys?" No one made a sound.

"I'm not going anywhere," Jordon spoke breaking the suffocating silence that permeated the hangar.

"Jones?" I asked him.

He crossed his long arms over his chest. "You know me, Mic, I'm Steel for life."

"Pierce?"

"Do you really need to ask?" He raised an eyebrow at me.

"Flynn?" He was nearly shaking with rage; his face was a livid red. I'd never seen him like this. Flynn was always so easy going and laid back, it was a shock when he displayed strong negative emotions.

"I'm not leaving, but I want an explanation. We deserve a fucking explanation."

"You're absolutely right. And you'll get it." Jackson's deep voice broke in, taking me by surprise. He stepped around me and faced the men.

"Corporal, take your place beside Flynn," Jackson said, his tone allowing no room for argument.

"Yes, Master Sergeant." Riley followed his order and took his place among the men. He fit well in appearance; whether he fit mentally remained to be seen.

"Now listen up. I know I usually let Mic run the show, but in this case, I thought I'd better step in." I did everything I could to swallow my shock and keep my composure. Jackson spoke to me, then I spoke to the men, that's how it worked. I could count on one hand the number of times Jackson had spoken to the men in this way. "Phillips is dead. It's hard and it fucking sucks, but we have to deal. We need another team member and I chose the man that I felt was most qualified."

Flynn's face was nearly purple with rage. If he didn't calm down, he was going to blow a gasket at his superior and get drop kicked.

"Now. I expect you men to treat him no differently than you did Jordon. That being said I am not an insensitive prick. But before you write him off, remember this; don't visit the sins of the father onto the son; or in this case, the cousin." With that he nodded to me and left the hangar without as much so a backward glance.

"Right; you heard him. This is Corporal Matthew Riley." I motioned him to step forward. "He's a former Marine. Did a couple tours in the sandbox, saw some heavy combat in Baghdad and in the north with the Kurds." I could recite his file from memory; I had read it so many times just trying to figure out how we would get past this hurdle.

Pierce was the first to step forward and shake Riley's hand. "Welcome." He said no more before stepping back with the others. One by one, they came forward to shake hands until only Flynn remained. I let it go for now.

"I think it's in everyone's best interest for the moment to just call you Matt or Matthew, unless you have a nickname you'd rather go by?"

"Rook. People call me Rook, Staff Sergeant." His voice was deep and smooth.

"Why do they call you Rook?" Flynn snapped the question at him.

"I like chess." His strong Native American features gave nothing away. The man seemed completely stoic. I could live with that; I had enough drama queen to deal with in Flynn.

"Okay then, Rook it is. You'll be bunking with Jordon and Jones. Boys, show him where he'll sleep. I want everyone in the training yard in one hour. Light gear. Flynn, get your ass over here." I walked away from them, taking a moment to compose my thoughts. I had to handle Flynn just right or this whole thing would blow up in my fucking face.

I briefly considered going into the soundproof room, but we'd have to take Rook in there at some point, so I didn't want to tip him off to its existence. Instead, I headed out into the cold morning air.

I could hear Flynn's boots crunching the grass as he walked behind me. "Speak your mind, Flynn. This is your one chance, so get it all off your chest. Because in one hour, you better stow your fucking attitude or I will do it for you." Pivoting to face him, I clasped my fingers behind my back and glared up at him.

"Mic. It's just so fucked. Every time I hear his name I'm going to see Phillips on his knees, not five feet from where we are standing! It's all his fucking fault!" Flynn's breath was puffing white clouds out at a rapid pace. He clenched and unclenched his fists over and over. I couldn't remember ever seeing him this angry in the five years we had worked together.

"Flynn. It's not. It was Riley, not Rook that betrayed us and got Phillips killed. When shit went down here that night, Rook was ankle deep in blood and sand. He wasn't even in the country. Rook had *nothing* to do with Phillips's death." I kept my tone as calm and even as I could manage. I felt like I was talking a jumper off a ledge; and in a way, I was. If Flynn jumped, he risked exposing us all.

"Don't you think I fucking know that, Mic? God dammit, of course I know it wasn't Matt or Rook or whatever his fucking name is! Doesn't it bother you? Seeing his face? Hearing his name? Or are you really a frigid fucking bitch?" It was my turn to seethe with rage. I stepped closer to him, getting as close to his face as I could.

"Flynn. You get a pass this time. *Once*. Speak to me like that again and you will regret the day you were born." I jabbed my finger into his chest with each word I spit out. "Of course it bothers me. It kills me. Rook will never replace Phillips, but that's not what we're going for here. Our job is to do what Jackson tells us. Nothing more and nothing less. Rook is here. He will have to go through the same training as everyone else before he's part of us. Let the kid prove himself. Maybe he'll surprise us all."

I couldn't speak another word or I would tear him apart. I left Flynn standing there in the cold and went to suit up. Light gear meant a hike and they knew that. It was cold and hypothermia had no sense of humor.

****

Jordon shut the door behind Rook and Jones as they entered the cabin. Jordon didn't know what to make of Rook. On one hand, it was nice not to be the new guy anymore, but it was like getting kicked in the nuts when he heard that name. Riley. The cause of so much destruction and pain for them all.

"Which room is mine?" Rook asked.

"Over here, across from mine." Jordon opened the door and waved him inside. There was nothing left of the man who had called it his home for years. Only the queen-sized bed and a dresser remained. There were dark spots on the walls where posters had hung for years. A set of sheets sat on the corner of the bed, neatly folded and waiting for the new occupant to make use of them.

"Better than a tent and a cot. Or sand and sky." Rook dropped his duffle on the bed and turned to Jordon. Jones leaned his shoulder against the open door. They collectively stared at one another, measuring the other up.

"How many tours?" Jones asked.

"Four. I was about to leave for my fifth when I got the call." Meaning he was probably dragged out of bed by a shouting Gunny Sergeant yesterday morning and had all the details laid out in front of him before breakfast.

"Ever wounded?" Jones was heading to marathon territory for the shortest sentence ever.

"Yes." Rook's bottom-of-the-sea-deep voice gave nothing away.

"Okay then. Light gear means a sidearm and knives. No rifles. Dress warm. We're going into the woods," Jordon explained, leaving the room as Rook began to pull a boxed chess set from his duffle.

Chapter 2

I slipped on my black thermal tactical pants and a matching long-sleeved shirt before threading the strap for my thigh holster through my belt. *It feels good to gear up again*, I thought as I tightened the strap on my thigh. I grabbed a small backpack and loaded it with some goodies for the boys. We had been doing our normal daily PT and training, but not in preparation for anything in particular. The team would be together again, training and sweating together. Two months was a long damn time to be between missions for them. They didn't know what to do with all of this down-time; we would soon be fixing that.

    I paced back and forth in the training yard, waiting for the men to assemble. The sky was fully light now, the sun's weak early winter rays slowly melting the frost and burning off the fog. Just as the last traces of the pink and gold sunrise disappeared the men walked onto the field. Their black tactical clothes were in obscene contrast to the beauty of the morning. They looked like what they were, walking death prepared to fall upon their enemies.

    "Ok boys, time for a hike. We're going to the logging trails. Rook, your training starts now," I said as they assembled in a neat line. "Jordon just went through this, but unlike him, we have enough time to train you properly. Are you ready? Because there are no second chances."

"Yes, Staff Sergeant."

Time to shake him up a bit...

I stepped up to him and checked him over. As he had been instructed, he carried only his sidearm in his thigh holster and a knife. Not the KA-BAR most of us carried, but a shorter tactical knife, with what looked like a bone hilt. Standing in front of him, my head didn't quite reach his shoulder. He was a bit shorter than the others and not as broad. Without taking my eyes off of his face, I slipped his pistol from its holster. He narrowed his eyes and the corner of his mouth tightened slightly at me, but he didn't say anything.

"Nice choice. I'm rather attached to my M-9 and the boys all have Sig Sauers. Why Browning for you?" I asked, as I released the magazine and jerked the slide back. A shell fell at my feet.

The mag was full and he had a round in the chamber?

"This is a little over the top for a hike, Rook. Don't go putting a round in the chamber unless we're on a mission." I slapped the mag back in with a hard smack of my palm, re-engaged the safety, and slipped the pistol back into his holster.

"I like the Hi-Power II. I always have. It may not be the forty-five that they have, but a nine millimeter will always do the job." He snapped the strap on his holster back over the butt of his Browning.

"Good enough for me, Rook." Leading the way, we headed into the woods. He'd done well. I could tell he was pissed, but he didn't rise to the bait.

For Jordon's training, we had skipped ahead and dove head first into the panic room. For Rook we had the time to start at the beginning.

"Ok, boys," I spoke over my shoulder. "We're going to hike fifteen miles today. Jordon, you'll be familiar with this area. We've brought the Jeep up here."

I stepped over rocks and leaves, watching where I put my feet. Rolling an ankle out here would ruin a perfectly good day. For the most part we hiked in silence, with only the wind and occasional curse for company.

"Mic, why are we doing this?" Flynn whined from the back. "It's cold and it serves no purpose."

I stopped dead. Exactly what I was waiting for. We were at about the halfway point of the hike. Just far enough that we were getting a little winded, but not so far that we were dragging ass.

"Flynn, just for that, you get to be first. Get up here." I slipped off my bag and set it at my feet.

"Rook. Front and center." He followed my command without question. No confusion, no questions, just instant obedience. Flynn needed a lesson.

"This is a training exercise to build trust and teamwork. Flynn, Rook, stand next to each other and hold your hands out." Flynn glared at me when he saw me pulling the rope from my bag. There were enough pieces for everyone to pair up. Even me.

"What the fuck, Mic?" Flynn snapped at me.

"Check your fucking tone, Corporal! I've had just about enough of you and your bitching. Do what I say or take your girly ass back down the fucking hill." He clenched his jaw and did what I said. He held his left arm out beside Rook's right. His fist was clenched so tight, the veins in his arm were popping out. I tied them together from wrist to elbow, lashing the rope over and around their thick arms; then I squatted down and tied their calves together as well. This was a fucking sack race from hell.

"Now. You're stuck together. Jones and Pierce you're next. Jordon, you're with me." I tied Pierce and Jones in the same way, while they helped tie Jordon and me which was difficult given our extreme height difference. It might have been better for me to be tied to Rook, but Flynn needed to work his shit out with him. This would force him to do it. Plus, I missed the class-clown-Flynn. I didn't much care for this angry-pissed-the-fuck-off-Flynn.

"Okay, the point of this is to finish the hike to the top and back down without falling. If you fall, get up, walk backward twenty paces, and continue. I'd make you go to the bottom but that seems mean." I let loose my evil smile. The chorus of groans was music to my ears.

"Were you born this evil, Mic, or did something happen to make you this way?" Jordon asked, as we set off, counting "right, left, right, left" under our breaths. So far we were making good progress.

I laughed. "Not sure. You tell me, Jordon." My foot caught a stone and I nearly went down. He jerked hard on his tied arm, keeping me upright, but causing me to fall against him. His scent hit my nose at the same time I realized he'd clasped my hand. My heart sped up, my palm dampened, and my stomach danced with those damn cliché butterflies.

What was I? Twelve years old and excited that the cute boy held my hand? Get a fucking grip, Michaels...

"She was made; the Army makes you into who it wants you to be," Pierce huffed from ahead of us. Jones with his extra-long legs was making it tough going for poor Pierce.

"For some, yes, but not for her. She was spat out from the bowels of hell because Satan couldn't stand her," Flynn chimed in, adding his two cents.

"You're just butt-hurt that I tied you to Rook, flyboy." Flynn detested the name. I only whipped it out when he was being a particular pain in the ass.

"Flyboy, huh? That's one I haven't heard before." Jordon laughed at Flynn's back.

"Fuck off, lover-boy. You don't have any room to talk," Flynn shot back, giving him the finger.

Jones was laughing and not watching where he was going. He tripped while trying to step over a log, and fell sideways into the leaves and dirt with a crash. This caused Pierce to tip over and wind mill his arms, but he still landed on top of Jones in a heap of tangled arms and legs.

"*Oof.* Get the fuck off." Jones shoved at Pierce, but didn't get too far. Pierce fell to the side, but Jones was forced to follow and ended up on top of Pierce.

"Oh, for fuck's sake. Figure it out you two or do you need some alone time?" I tried to snap at them, but my laugher made it difficult to sound too authoritative.

Flynn was finally laughing, tears streaming down his face. It was the first time he'd laughed this hard since before Phillips had died. Progress. Who knew that rope would be the cure?

"If you fuckers are done having your fun, help us up, dammit!" Pierce grouched. He was shoving at a cursing Jones and had finally managed to get them both flat on their backs.

"Nah. Looks like you got it from here. Work together and you can stand," I said. Laughter made it difficult for me to talk.

Jordon chose that moment to lose his footing. He teetered backward and to the right. I pulled hard on my arm and leg trying to keep him upright, but gravity did what gravity does best.

"No! Dammit!" We landed hard. I hit his chest, knocking the air from his lungs with a *whoosh*. I tried to recover my dignity while Jordon tried to make his diaphragm work.

"Oh Christ. Come on... dammit!" I felt Pierce's pain. This was extremely awkward; my crotch was aligned with his, my legs spread onto either side. The rope binding our legs together kept my tied right leg uncomfortably straight.

"Mic. Stop fucking moving, dammit. Just let me lift you off." I was quickly realizing that my wiggling around, trying to get up, was having a noticeable effect on Jordon. A very noticeable effect.

"Fuck. Shit... sorry." I was stuttering like an idiot. I froze when he grabbed my hip in his free hand, squeezing hard with his long fingers.

"Just stop fucking moving." He slid his big hand over my ass, grasped the cheek and lifted up, pushing at the same time. I ended up in the dirt, a sharp rock stabbing into my back. Leaves were falling onto my face and I stayed there for a moment, trying to recover what little dignity I had remaining.

Someone, I couldn't see who, was laughing so hard that he was gasping for breath. Flynn probably.

"Well, that was entertaining," Rook said. Without an ounce of laughter in his voice.

"Don't you know how to laugh?" Flynn asked him, through gulps of air.

"Yeah. I do."

"Do you talk?" Flynn kept at Rook.

Jordon and I looked at each other, sharing the same thought.

What was happening here?

"When necessary," Rook said. With his left hand, he pulled out his knife and cut the ropes tying them together. Bending down, he cut Jordon's and my ropes as well.

"You two, also?" Rook asked, pointing the black blade at Pierce and Jones.

"By all means, my friend." Pierce held his and Jones's arm up.

And just like that, my exercise was over. The ropes were cut, but new bonds were formed. Rook was finding his place among the others and Flynn was laughing again.

"You ready to get up, Mic, or are you going to grow roots?" Jordon asked, reaching a hand down to me. The others had continued on up and around the curve in the trail and were no longer in view. Jordon and I were alone, with only the sounds of the few remaining wintering birds to keep us company.

"Funny. Thanks." I took his hand, and he pulled me up faster than I expected, smacking me into his chest again. I seemed to be ending up there a lot lately. I flashed back to the one kiss we shared in Colombia, the one moment we allowed ourselves to indulge in this crazy attraction going on between us.

"Jordon. No... don't look at me like that." He was inching closer to me. I tried to pull back, but his hands tightened on my arms.

When did he grab my arms?

"Bea." That's all he said, just my name. He let go of my arms and wrapped one hand around my waist and buried the other in my hair. I was trapped. Trapped in his arms. Staring into his eyes, I saw the truth reflected there. This was not just a simple chemical attraction for him. This was something more. A much bigger *more*.

"Chris..." His name was a plea on my lips. A plea to stop, a plea not to.

The *crack* of a branch breaking somewhere nearby in the forest jerked us apart. I stood there staring at Jordon, and for the first time in a long time was unsure of what to do or say. He disarmed me completely; he stole my words as he stole my breath. Reason and thought slowly returned with my air.

"Fucking hell, Jordon; this is not happening! Do you hear me?!

This can't happen." I pointed back and forth between us. I was angry beyond words; angry at him, but mostly at myself.

"I know. You just... you're so..." He ran his hands through his hair, pulling at it. I could almost hear him mentally berating himself.

"Not ever again. Got it, Corporal?" I knew that I wounded him with my words, but I had to. We had been dancing around each other for months. I was his team leader first and a woman second. I had sacrificed everything for this team; I wasn't about to stop now.

"Copy that, Staff Sergeant," he barked at me and stomped up the trail. I followed, aware that I was the NCO here and I was going to end up being the last to the top... so be it.

****

I sat at the long cafeteria table in the mess hall, staring at my tray of food. We finally have a chef back and the food was getting better. It was identifiable now at least. I looked up as Pierce sat down next to me. "What happened out there today, Mic?"

I picked at my plate of spaghetti, not having much of an appetite. "What do you mean?" I was being deliberately evasive. I knew exactly what he was asking.

"You know damn well what I'm talking about." He shoved some pasta into his mouth, chewing slowly. Wiping sauce from his mouth with a napkin, he was giving me time to decide if I was going to answer or not. I thought back to what had happened after I'd reached the top of the trail.

I walked into the clearing, and saw the men gathered together at the edge of the cliff. They were standing in a line, all looking so much alike and yet they were each so different. Jordon turned to me as I approached. His jaw tightened and he looked away quickly. Nothing like a bruised male ego to cause a temper tantrum.

"What did you all learn today?"

"I don't hate Rook," Flynn said, punching Rook in the arm.

"Hit me again, flyboy, and I'll feed you that arm," the newbie growled.

Flynn laughed. "I take that back. I hate him."

"Shut it, children. She means, did we learn we're still a team? That even when separated, we are still one?" Jones interjected.

"Always the quiet ones…" Flynn's mouth had been out of commission for a while; it sounded like he was making up for lost time.

"Jones is right. Jackson is going to be briefing me on a mission later tonight. We need to be ready. A lot has changed for us recently. We are and always have been a team. Don't forget it." Thinking my speech was over, I walked away. Jordon's furious voice stopped me in my tracks.

"Still have that machete, Mic? Can't let it go, huh? Looks like I'm not the only one who has to let go of lost causes." If words could cut, I would be bleeding out on the ground.

"We all have our demons, Jordon. Each of us deals with them in different ways. Figure it out or go." I left them there on the mountain. I couldn't look at any of them in that moment.

"Earth to Mic, come in, Mic." Pierce was waving his hand in front of my face.

"Knock it off, dammit. I hear you."

Sort of, I thought to myself.

"Do you? You told Jordon to leave. Jordon, of all people; we know you have a soft spot for him. We all know something happened between you two in Colombia. It's coming back to haunt you now, isn't it?"

I knew he was just concerned. I knew he wanted to make sure that I wasn't losing it, that I wasn't going to flip out. This was my business though, and I wasn't about to have this conversation with my Sergeant, no matter how much of a family we were.

"I'm not discussing this with you, Sergeant." I stood, leaving my untouched tray on the table. I had a meeting with Jackson to get to.

Today was going down in the books as nearly a total fail. The only good to come of today was that Rook was being slowly integrated into the team and I didn't think I had to worry about Flynn gutting him or anyone else, anytime soon.

My relationship with Jordon was as complicated as ever. Just when I thought we were going to be okay, friends and no more, he goes and tries to kiss me again. I wanted him to so badly I could taste him. I wanted to feel the security of his arms and the pressure of his lips on mine, but I've spent most of my life wanting things I couldn't have or shouldn't have; no reason to stop now.

I continued to let my thoughts wander as I left the mess hall and walked to Jackson's cabin. I needed to get my shit together before I saw him. He would know right away if there was something wrong with me.

As I walked, I unwillingly remembered my non-existent childhood. The memories were so close to the surface these days that once I relaxed even slightly, they rose to the forefront of my mind. My recurring dreams would not let me push them back down into the past where they belonged.

I remembered the musty smell of the closet, the tiny space and the heavy darkness. I remembered the sting of a slap and a hard shove hitting my narrow back, making me stumble and trip.

Shake it off, Michaels. You don't have time for this. The men need you; get your shit together!

The pep talk did little to help. It's so hard to listen to your own advice, even when you know it's good advice. Practicalities get pushed to the side in the wake of such deep-seated pain.

Before I knew it I found myself at Jackson's door. Waiting inside was the one man in this world whom I respected and trusted totally. Also waiting for me was an orange file with a red stamp. I both relished and dreaded the thought.

Chapter 3

Rook picked up the knight from his chess board, tossing it from hand to hand. Being here was like coming home for him. He wasn't part of Steel yet, but he could see himself being here for a very long time.

He didn't like to talk much, but heard and saw nearly everything. He knew that he made the others uncomfortable because of his cousin. He had been briefed on the whole story prior to arriving. He'd been told about the mission in Colombia and Phillips's death. Jackson had warned him that he might get the cold shoulder for quite a while.

Fact of the matter was, he hadn't known his cousin, hadn't seen him since they were kids. Their parents had not gotten along and they never saw each other beyond the occasional awkward holiday dinner. It had taken him a few minutes to place who Jackson was even talking about when he'd said "your cousin might be a problem".

Flynn was the only one that he felt he had to win over; the rest would follow. With that goal in mind, he gathered his chess board. He stood in the doorway to the living room for a moment before letting his presence become known. Flynn was there, talking with Jordon.

"I get that it wasn't Mic's decision, but you know as well I do that she fucking knew... and didn't tell us." Flynn was pacing back and forth. Jordon was kicked back on the couch, slapping one flip-flop against the bottom of his foot.

"Look man, I get it, but she would have told us if she was allowed to. She has to follow orders the same as us," Jordon said, taking a drink from his beer.

"I don't fucking care, Jordon! She should have told us!" Flynn shouted.

"She was ordered not to," Rook said, enjoying the shock on their faces. He set the chess board on the coffee table, knocking Jordon's feet off in the process.

"What do you want, Riley?" Flynn snapped.

"First off, don't call me Riley. It's Rook or Matt. Second of all, I'm here, and I'm not going anywhere. Get the fuck over it."

Flynn moved to lunge at Rook, but Jordon stepped between them, putting a hand on each of their chests. Though if they really decided they were going to step off and tear each other apart, other than shooting them, there wasn't much Jordon could do about it.

"Knock it off. Both of you." Jordon shoved them, making them take a few steps back. "What exactly is your plan here, Rook?"

"Chess." He bent down and began sorting the black pieces from the white, placing them all in their respective homes on the board.

"Come again?" Flynn was calming down, his voice nearly back to normal. He was like an emotional yo-yo today.

"We're going to sit here and play chess until you realize I am not your enemy." Rook took a seat on the couch, the shiny white pieces facing him.

"What makes you think I want anything to do with you or chess?" Flynn crossed his arms over his chest, staring at the board as if it was going to jump up and latch onto him like a face hugger. *Alien* this was not.

"Because you're Steel and very soon I will be as well. We can go outside and I can beat you into the dirt or we can settle this in a slightly more civilized manner. We may be warriors and soldiers, but we don't have to be animals." He kept his tone level and even; talking to Flynn was not much different than talking a jumper off a ledge.

"You're speaking to Flynn here, Rook; you would do well to remember that." Pierce materialized out of nowhere.

"Who the fuck are you, Houdini?" Flynn kept snapping at everyone like a dog on a short leash.

"Sit your ass down, Flynn. Play chess. Un-wad your thong." Pierce gripped both of Flynn's shoulders and pressed down, forcing him to sit.

"I don't wear a thong, asshole." Flynn was heading into to an epic level-ten pout.

"Excuse me; sorry, I forgot. You wear boy shorts, red lacy ones." Flynn shot his foot out and kicked Pierce in the shin. When he didn't get the reaction he was hoping for, he moved a pawn two spaces forward.

"Chess is the game of gentleman. Disputes have been settled over of a game of chess for centuries." Rook also moved a pawn.

"I am no gentleman." Flynn moved again. The game went on silently after that. Each moving and taking the other's pieces. Soon, they both had a respectable pile of their opponent's pieces.

"Check." Rook sat back and allowed Flynn to think. Over the course of the game, Flynn had seemingly forgotten what he was so angry about. "When I was in Iraq this last time, I was fortunate enough to find a chess board; I kept it in my tent. Every time we made it back to base, my buddy and I would take a turn, but only after a successful mission."

Flynn was trying not to pay attention, but obviously failing. He was staring at the board, looking for a way to move that didn't put him right back into check in two turns.

With a heavy sigh, Flynn moved his queen, in full retreat now.

"Only one day, we were on patrol; normal everyday stuff over there." Rook moved a rook, putting pressure on Flynn's queen. "Our Humvee got hit by an IED." Flynn moved his queen. "My buddy was thrown from the vehicle. We were taking heavy fire. Most of us were wounded or dead. I called in air support and a medivac for him. By the time they got there, it was too late. He was dead. Bled to death in the sand." Rook took Flynn's vulnerable queen.

"We've all been there, Rook. Each of us have lost brothers over there," Flynn said, backing his king up.

"The Apaches greased the fuckers firing on us. I got back to my tent and the chess board sat there. This same board. I never got to finish that game with him. While that was happening to me, you guys were in Colombia. I was over the Atlantic when Phillips was killed."

"It's a sad story, but what's your point?" Flynn moved his king again; Rook was chasing him all over the board.

"I never want to leave another chess match unfinished. I can have that here. So... I'm here to stay, Flynn. Get over it." Rook moved his last knight, cornering Flynn's king. "Check-mate."

Without waiting for a response, Rook gathered his board and went back to his room. Softly shutting the door behind him, he turned the radio on and Jefferson Airplane's, *White Rabbit* came on. It was fitting for the moment, since he felt a lot like Alice right now. Falling down the rabbit-hole and things were getting stranger by the second.

****

Flynn sat back on the couch and stared at the ceiling, counting the tiles under his breath. Jordon and Pierce both stood there glowering at him; as if they were the disapproving parents and he was the errant child.

"Well... that went well," Pierce said.

"I think it did," Jordon interjected.

"He made his point, that's for sure," Flynn said, getting up and grabbing a beer.

"He put you in your place, is what he did," Pierce said, catching the beer his teammate threw at him.

"Yeah, I was there, dick. I noticed." Popping the top and letting the cool beer slide down his throat, Flynn shut his eyes and ears to what was around him. He didn't want to like Rook. He didn't want to let this go.

"Did you?" Jordon asked. Burping and slapping his chest, he pitched his now empty can into the trash. "Two points!" He exclaimed, before standing to get another beer.

Flynn grabbed a second beer and went outside. He wasn't about to sit in there and listen to this shit. He went back to his own cabin and locked the door, giving Pierce a none-too-subtle *"fuck off"*, by locking him out of his own cabin. He flipped them both the bird over his shoulder for good measure; not caring that they couldn't see it.

Chapter 4

I knocked on Jackson's door. The sun was making its way down behind the mountains, throwing strange shadows across the training yard behind me, stretching out long and black as if the night was anxious to descend, and reaching as far as it could to hasten its arrival. Just as Jackson opened his door I saw Flynn going into his cabin alone, beer in hand.

Wonder what that's all about?

I shoved it aside for now. It was a problem for later. I had much bigger issues staring me in the face. A giant, angry-looking one glaring down at me. Jackson was as mad as I'd ever seen him. I had a bad feeling this was all directed at me.

"Master Sergeant," I said, stepping around him into the cabin.

"Staff Sergeant. Sit."

When your superior speaks to you in that tone, you do as you are told. I sat and had to bite words back; now was not the time to break protocol and speak before being spoken to.

"Would you care to explain this?" He dropped a phone into my lap. I recognized it immediately; it was my burner phone. *Fuck fuckity fuck*. My stomach dropped to my feet like a lead weight before flipping over and threatening to expel its contents.

"I have no defense, Master Sergeant." First lesson in taking an ass chewing, make no excuses. Take it on the chin and hope you come out alive.

"Try." His voice was as cold as ice.

"It's mine. I call one person on it; it's untraceable."

"Who?" His voice was cold and tight with fury.

"My aunt." I flipped open the phone with a practiced flick of my thumb and pulled up her number.

He jerked the phone out of my hand and threw it across the room suddenly, shattering it into plastic confetti.

"Why?" He turned his back; seemingly unable to face me while trying to get his anger under control.

"I can't let her think I'm dead. We're all the family the other has. I can't bear to be the reason for her grief." My voice cracked as I spoke the last. My eyes burned, but I swallowed the threatening tears down.

"How long?" We were up to two words now. Making progress in the conversation department.

"Years. We did our first couple of missions, but after the op I did with Liam, when we took down those Nazi freaks, I called her then. I've never spoken to her, I just leave a message on her machine." I didn't try to spare myself, I just laid it all out there.

"God dammit, Bea, do you have any idea what you've done? I should knock your ass back to Private and ship you off to the most miserable shithole I can think of." He used my first name. I could count on one hand the number of times he'd called me Bea, and still have three fingers left over. Both times were when I was wounded and he was patching me up. He finally sat down, clasping his hands in front of his mouth and staring at me.

"Master Sergeant, how did you find out?" I thought I had been so careful, that I had covered my tracks completely.

"Are you fucking kidding me, right now? The NSA is my bitch. I can find out anything I want about nearly anyone in the world. I have suspected something was going on for some time, but I couldn't nail it down. I had them ping off all outgoing calls from the compound for three days after every mission. A call came from an unknown number originating from your cabin. So today when you were on your hike, I searched your cabin. It took me a while to find the phone, I'll give you that." It was sometimes easy to forget that Jackson had once been in my shoes; he had the same skill-sets as me. He could break into and out of just about anywhere.

"What happens now?" I didn't think he would be demoting me and kicking me out of Steel, or he would have done it already.

"Your aunt is in danger. If she didn't need our help so desperately right now, you would be out on your ass." He tossed a folder into my lap.

"What the fuck are you talking about? All she knows is that I'm alive. That's it. I haven't told her anything else. Just that I'm above ground, and more or less okay."

"Just open the fucking folder, Mic," Jackson ordered as he paced around the cabin.

Inside was a picture of my Aunt Beatrice, her dark hair healthy and shiny. She had of course aged since I'd last seen her; she had more wrinkles and worry lines around her mouth and eyes than I liked, but she was as stunning as ever. Her brown eyes sparkled with laugher and warmth, just like always. She had elegant cheekbones and a wide smiling mouth... she was beautiful.

Below her picture was a standard file, outlining her address, work details, and bank account information, along with a few pages of handwritten notes. Someone had been keeping her under surveillance, most likely the NSA. The notes outlined her daily schedule and routines. All very predictable: leaves the house for work at the same time every day, comes home at the same time nearly every weeknight. She has book club on Saturday afternoons. Sundays she stays at home or does her grocery shopping.

"Who's been watching her?" I asked, not looking up from the file. I was starving for this information the same way someone dying of thirst begs for water. Any drip of information about her was refreshing and delicious.

"A friend of mine that I was in boot with, he works for the NSA now. He's been personally doing her surveillance."

"Why is she in danger?" I didn't see much here beyond a normal dossier.

"Flip to the last page." Jackson sat across from me and tugged over his green ash tray then lit a cigar.

There were slightly grainy, black and white pictures of people looking in my aunt's windows. The figures were heavily disguised, their faces and heads covered with tactical hoods. None of the pictures gave me any idea of who they were. They definitely didn't look like your average criminals casing the place though. They were too organized, too well-equipped, to be your average B&E guys.

"Tell me Jackson, please just fucking spit it out," I begged, a cold shiver gliding down my spine.

What have I done?

"Those men belong to a cartel out of Mexico." The shiver turned to a lump of sickening fear in my gut. I didn't like the way this was going. "They're led by a man named Vega, Adolfo Vega. You won't recognize the name, but if Diego was still breathing, he would. Vega is the cousin to Diego's widow. The families are tied together; they worked together moving drugs and weapons. Diego and his father handled the cocaine. Vega and his men control the fields where the poppies are grown, and the villages where the poppies are processed into opium, and finally into heroin. Also, they run guns back and forth between Colombia and the States."

"And what does that have to do with my Aunt Beatrice?" Fear was choking me in a vise-like grip.

"Diego covered his ass. After you killed him, I sent his phone off to the NSA. He made a few calls to Mexico on his way here. He had your name, Mic. The only thing that staved this off until now was that those fuckers had trouble accessing your records because legally, you're dead. Your Aunt Beatrice is listed as your next of kin on your death certificate. That's how they found her."

"We have to help her. They'll kill her to get to me. You know it as well as I do, Jackson, and it won't be a pleasant death. Either you help me bring her here or I'm done. I'll protect her myself." I stood, ready to get in my Jeep and drive to Ohio.

"Keep your pants on, Mic. Of course we're going to go get her. Sit the fuck back down and let me finish."

As badly as I wanted to get to my aunt as fast as possible, I sat again, as ordered. "Okay, I'm listening." My legs were twitching with the urge to jump up and run out. I couldn't let anything happen to her because of me.

"They tapped her phones and listened to your message. They were probably going to go for her anyways, but now that they know you keep in touch, their timetable has been moved up. The NSA tells me that the DEA is working with Mexican Police, trying to infiltrate this cartel. They have a mole inside the Vega family. According to their source, there is a hit out on your aunt."

"When Jackson? Fucking when are they coming for her?" I stood abruptly, it was taking everything I had not to just say 'fuck you, Jackson' go get her.

"Tonight or tomorrow."

I hurried to the door. I wasn't dicking around anymore. I was going to go get her, and fuck the consequences.

Jackson followed me, watching me, and not commenting as I pulled out my phone and set off the tones. Everyone's phone would beep and flash a message to meet in the hangar, ASAP. Ohio was only a four hour drive, but I wasn't about to wait that long. We were taking the jet.

"Michaels. Chill out a fucking minute." Jackson jerked my arm and pulled me to a stop. I could see the others running out of their cabins, heading for the hangar. They would be throwing open their lockers and gearing up. "Go get her, but don't come back here. Go to the other house. She'll be more comfortable there than here and it's more secure. I'm not taking any chances with these guards after what Riley did."

I jerked on my arm which didn't loosen his grip at all; with a heavy glare, he released me.

"Copy that, Master Sergeant." Impatience coloring my tone, I was borderline insubordinate. I turned to go, needing to brief the men. I needed Jones to hack into a satellite and get me some real-time feed on my aunt. I needed to see with my own eyes that she was okay, for the moment, at least.

Jogging down the steps, I quickly cut a path to the hangar. The bay door was rising even as I approached. Jackson's long legs let him easily keep pace with me. "This isn't over. Get her, and I'll meet you at the house; then we'll finish this. Don't think you get off the hook that easily, Staff Sergeant."

"I fucking said 'copy that', now let me go,"

He jerked back like I had slapped him. There was no respect in my voice in that second. I wasn't thinking about how much deep shit I was in with Jackson; I wasn't thinking about losing my command. All I was focused on was Aunt Beatrice and getting her to safety.

"The ice you're walking on is thin and melting fast." He pivoted on his heel and stomped off. He was pissed and I just couldn't bring myself to give a flying fuck right this second.

Pushing all thoughts of Jackson aside, I strode quickly into the hangar, my boots thudding harshly on the concrete. Even my footsteps belied my anxiousness.

"On me, guys!" I shouted. They lined up in a loose formation near the bench in front of our lockers; they were already geared up, looking every inch the bad-asses they were. I quickly jerked on my flak vest and grabbed my MP-5, slipping the sling over my head and across my chest. I was ready to go in less than a minute.

"Listen up. We need to move. As soon as we're in the air, Jones, I need satellite feeds for Ambrose, Ohio. I'll give you the address on the plane. Jordon, you're going in with me. Rook, stick next to Flynn and Pierce." I finished pulling on my tactical hood, which I let hang down off my face and around my neck. Grabbing my helmet, I strode to the jet.

Stepping aboard, I didn't wait for the captain to arrive. "Flynn, now. Get us in the air." He nodded, all business, pushing his normal bull-shit aside. They were all tuned into the urgency that I was exhibiting in my tone and actions. "Sit down and buckle up, ladies. We have zero time. Rook, you ready?"

"Copy," he said, as he sat in the first seat he came to.

"Mic, fucking tell us what we are heading into," Pierce said, as we began to taxi down the runway. The engines roared and we sped up, lifting into the air with ease. "We're flying blind here."

"We're going to get my aunt." I think I heard each and every jaw drop onto the floor.

"Come again?" Jones said, disbelieving.

"My Aunt Beatrice lives in Ambrose, Ohio. She's in danger from the cartel kissing-cousin of Mateo and Diego. They're going after her to get to me. We have to get her first. Period." There was much more to it than that, but I didn't care to explain that right now. There would be time for explanations later, after I had my aunt safe at my side.

"Fuck me," Jordon groaned.

"You sure?" Jones asked; he was typing away, fingers flashing on the keys as the monitors above him sprang to life. Satellite images filtered in popping up in quadrants on the screen one-by-one. "What's the address, Mic?" Jones wasn't wasting time on the 'why' or 'how.'

"64 Elm."

"Really, Mic, your aunt lives on Elm Street?" Jordon forced a laugh, attempting to inject some levity into the situation. There was none to be had.

I sank back into the buttery leather of my seat, breathing deep and trying to calm my racing heart. We were going to get there in time. No doubt we were going to scare her half to death. The last time I saw her was shortly after I graduated from basic training. I had been about to be assigned to intelligence and there wasn't much I could tell her, even then. It was only nine very short months later that I became the first member of Steel. That was five years ago.

"Yes. Now shut up, Jordon." His face fell into a familiar angry mask. Fuck. I was really screwing up with everyone today. "Jones, we need transport as soon as we touch down."

"Copy, already on it." The jet leveled out from its climb, we were at cruising altitude.

Unbuckling, I stood and went into the cockpit, shutting the door behind me. I sat in the co-pilot chair for no other reason than I had never sat there before.

"Flynn, ETA."

"One hour with this headwind." An hour. I could deal with an hour.

"I found a small airport fairly close to the town. Here are the coordinates," he said, handing me a slip of paper. I stood and stepped back into the cabin again.

"Here's where we're landing. I want two SUVs," I said, handing Jones the paper.

"That's going to be a tall order, Mic. This is a small town. I'll do what I can." Translated, that meant if I had one SUV and one sedan, I was just going to have to deal with it.

"Sit down, Mic, relax; tell us what's going on. You're not making any sense." Pierce was right. I was running on an adrenaline high right now; my hands were shaking and fear for my aunt was turning my stomach sour.

"We all remember Diego, right?" Stares of disbelief greeted my question. "Okay then, before Diego came to visit us, he made a few phone calls. He knew my name somehow. He gave it to his tech people and they tracked my aunt down through my death certificate, of all things. I call her after every mission and leave her a message. I tell her I'm alive and no more."

"What the ever loving fuck, Mic!" Pierce shouted at me. "Are you brain dead or something?"

"Okay, I deserved that." I ran my hand through my hair, frustrated. Fuck, did I hate being in the wrong. "Now, after we sent Diego to hell, his widow was pretty pissed. She called out a hit on my aunt. The DEA is working with the Mexican Police and they have an informant in the

Vega cartel. The hit is happening tonight. We have to get there first."

"Then what?" Jordon asked.

"Then we get her on this plane and we go to the Wonka House." Flynn let out a huge "Whoop, whoop!" from the cockpit. Flynn loved the Wonka House, it was like having the best playground around and never being able to use it. Anytime we got to go, he was like a little kid at a free toy giveaway.

"The what, now?" Rook asked. Jordon raised his hand, seconding the question.

"I can't explain. You'll just have to see it." I thought the name was pretty self-explanatory, but who knew? Maybe it wasn't. "Flynn! ETA?"

"Fifteen or so," he shouted back.

"Okay, gear up, check your weapons. Jones, do you have that satellite feed yet?" I pulled the slide back on my rifle, making sure a round was in the chamber. Leaving the safety on for now, I let it hang on its sling.

"Coming online now, Mic." He hit a button and the main screen lit up. You could see my aunt's roof and the surrounding houses. Her car was in her driveway, so it looked like she was home.

"Why don't you call her? Let her know we're coming?" Jordon asked.

"You're right, Jordon! Fuck me, why didn't I think of that?" I glared at him over my shoulder until he got the message. "Yeah, Sherlock, her phones are tapped." I surveyed the screen, looking for any potential threats. It looked quiet and clear with nothing out of the ordinary. Just a normal split-level house with a nice deck. Same as those in half of the suburbs of America.

"Jones, I want you in this tree. Jordon, on my six. Pierce, take the back with Rook. Flynn, you're driving and providing our extraction cover; though once I assess the situation that may change. Got it, boys?"

They studied the live images with me. Seeing what I was seeing, lots of bushes for cover. Deep shadows along the fence, a blind spot under the deck. Just because we didn't readily see a threat, didn't mean it wasn't there.

I checked my watch—it was nearly midnight. She would be in bed sleeping and completely unaware of the immense danger she was in.

"Sit your asses down, we're landing." Flynn hit the fasten seatbelt sign a couple times, making it do that annoying 'ding' sound over and over.

"Fucking Flynn," Jordon muttered.

"Jones, switch to thermal." He tapped the keys and the screen switched from green night vision to grey and white thermal. There was a heat signature in my aunt's bedroom. We had a fairly generous view. As I watched three, and then four, heat profiles popped up in the yards of the neighbors. They fanned out and slowly made their way to her house.

I gripped the back of Jones's chair as we landed and I pulled my hood up over my mouth, pleased to see that my team did so as well. Before the engines were even fully shut off, we were out of the plane and running to the waiting SUV.

"Everybody in!" There was only one SUV waiting, but it was better than no wheels. Pushing Flynn aside, I took the driver's seat. Thankfully the rental company had left the keys in the ignition and I didn't have to fuck around finding them.

I knew these roads and could get us there much faster than Flynn. Luckily, this airstrip was only about a ten-minute drive from her house; I would make it in significantly less.

"Go, Mic, go!" Flynn shouted, as Jordon who was last, climbed in.

I was burning rubber before his door was even shut. The gate for the airstrip was closed, but I didn't slow. I smashed into it doing fifty. The crash shook the SUV, but I didn't let it slow us; I kept my foot down hard on the gas pedal. The gate was hung up on the grill and sparks flew through the air as I drug the gate about a dozen yards before the tough vehicle released its prize.

I was practically standing on the gas pedal, but I didn't care. I was determined that I was going to make it there before those cartel fucks had a chance to touch my aunt.

"Be ready, boys; as soon as I stop I want you out and converging on those fuckers." The clicks and slaps of rifles being readied and double-checked greeted me. "Jones, update." We were almost there; I needed to know the positions of the hostiles.

"Two under the deck, one trying to hide in the bushes in the front," he said, watching the satellite feed on his phone. "Fourth signature is gone."

"Contact local PD. Let them know we're coming in hot; to expect gunfire and prepare for casualties." I didn't care about diplomacy right now. The Vega cartel fucked with the wrong girl. I was determined to grease every last one of these dirt bags.

Jones was rattling off an alphabet soup of information to the local cops. Phrases like 'under control' 'will call you when needed', and 'national security'.

I screeched around the corner onto Elm Street, the speed at which I took the turn and the force of it, throwing us all to the side. I didn't bother to attempt stealth, it would all be over before anyone had a chance to respond.

"Watch your friendly fire, no shooting the civvies." I slammed the SUV into park with a screech of tires and jumped out, shouldering my rifle as I ran. The men fanned out behind me; Jones went to his tree, scaling it like cat. Pierce and Rook slid around back; I signaled Flynn to follow, changing my mind on where he should be. I didn't want them outnumbered.

The man in the bushes stood up and raised his weapon; I fired before he had a chance. I got him with a solid hit to the chest, and he fell backward into the bush with a crash of breaking branches. Lights popped on all over the neighborhood; we were making a hell of a lot of noise. With Jordon glued to my back, I kicked in the front door. Advancing forward with fast shuffling steps, we checked corners and cleared each room. The thermal images didn't show any hostiles in the house, but I wasn't going to be careless.

I heard shots from the back yard and a scream that was quickly cut short. The door to my aunt's bedroom opened and I was greeted by the muzzle of a 357 Magnum.

"Get out of my house!" Aunt Beatrice shouted at me. I dropped my rifle on its sling and raised my gloved hands.

"Aunt Beatrice, it's me. It's Bea," I softly spoke to her. Her hand cannon never wavered from me. She didn't keep it just for show; she was deadly accurate with it.

Looking at her face, I drank her in. I hadn't seen her in five years and the time melted away like it had not ever existed. It was physically painful restraining myself from going to her.

"Bea? Is that really you?" She began to lower her pistol when I realized I still had half my face covered by my hood. I jerked it down around my neck and she visibly paled at the sight of me.

"It is you!" She dropped her gun with a *thunk* and rushed forward, gathering me in her arms. She enveloped me in her scented cloud. *Oh god, she even smelled the same. Chanel No.5.*

"Aunt Beatrice, we don't have time for this." I slid out of her arms reluctantly. I wanted to wrap up in her warmth and stay there for the next year, but I had to get her out of here and on the jet. "There are people here who want to kill you; there's a professional hit out on you. You have to come with us, right fucking now." I was scaring her, but we didn't have time to sugar-coat it.

"You watch your language, young lady!" I felt my face flush and I heard Jordon choking on laughter behind me. I grabbed her and towed her with me, pushing her between Jordon and myself.

"Package is secure, heading out." I pushed on my comm and told the others.

"Copy that," Jones replied, meaning he had us covered and we were good to exit.

"Bea, I need to grab some clothes or something. I'm not dressed!" She was in a nightgown with little dancing penguins all over it and a white robe over-top.

"I'm sorry, there's no time." I opened the door slowly. "Coming out now. Cover us to the vehicle, then roll out. Over." Once again bringing my rifle up, I led the way out. "Aunt Beatrice, get down; stay next to Jordon. Do not fucking move from his side." I ran in a crouch across the lawn to the SUV, hearing Jordon and Aunt Beatrice behind me. He opened the back door and shoved her in, slamming it closed and standing guard. I knew he would take a bullet for her if he needed to.

Shots rang out from the back, bursts of two and three. My men were being engaged again.

"Report!" I shouted into my comm. Not willing to leave Aunt Beatrice unprotected, I made a decision. "Jordon, go!" He nodded and ran off into the dark.

Aunt Beatrice tapped on the window and tried to open the door. I ignored her as Jones shouted his update. The gunfire cut off abruptly.

"Two more hostiles held a defensive position. Third tried to flank us. Threat has been neutralized. Over." I guess that fourth heat signature showed up after all. Jones and the boys left him rapidly cooling on the lawn.

"Copy. Get your asses in the fucking truck, now." I jumped back into the driver's seat and started it up. I had it in drive and was ready to go as they piled in. Blue and red lights were flashing in the dark, making their way closer. Sirens were screaming down on us and I stomped on the gas. I refused to be held up for days with bureaucratic bullshit.

"Bea Michaels, you slow down right now or you can pull over and one of these men of yours can drive!" I nearly swallowed my tongue when Aunt Beatrice whacked me upside the back of my helmet.

Flynn started laughing, getting the others going. I didn't slow down, though, I was nearly to the airfield and I could see the whole town lighting up in my rearview. I would need to have a talk with Aunt Beatrice about dressing me down in front of my men.

"Jones, update Jackson. He'll need to send a mop-up crew in. Anyone wounded?"

"Negative," Pierce said. "I'm Sergeant Pierce." Pierce held his hand out to my aunt to shake. The others all took turns introducing themselves. Rook shook her hand and just said 'Rook'. Her look of confusion did nothing to force him to explain. Later in private I would give her a run-down on each of the men. Jones was last, he gave me a grave look. I would be getting my ass chewed out by Jackson, I'm sure.

I pulled to a stop on the runway, exiting the vehicle, I left the keys in it. Someone would be by to pick it up—at least this time there was no blood on the upholstery. That was always a bitch to clean and we never got our security deposit back.

"Double time; get us in the air, Flynn." I followed him onto the plane. He sat down in the pilot seat and started flipping switches and speaking into the radio.

Aunt Beatrice came up right behind me. I got her settled in one of the soft chairs and stowed my rifle, snapping the clips to secure it to the wall of the plane. I could feel her watching my every move, analyzing me. I took the seat next to her, for the most part ignoring the men, as they too settled in. The fasten seat belt light chimed a couple of times as we began to taxi.

"Ladies and gentlemen, this is Captain Flynn speaking. I'd like to thank you for flying with us today. Here at Air Steel we take your satisfaction seriously and we hope you have a pleasant flight. Do try to keep any blood off the seats and no discharging of weapons inside the jet. We'll be arriving at our super-secret military installation as quickly as possible. Thank you and have a pleasant flight." With a screech the loudspeaker shut off.

"Fucking Flynn," I said, as I stood and went to the cockpit. Knocking on the door, I waited for him to open up. When he did, he wore a smug grin; he must think he was really funny.

"Can the shit and just fly the fucking plane."

"It's a jet, Staff Sergeant," Flynn shot back. I slammed the door shut on his laughing face.

Chapter 5

Sitting next to Aunt Beatrice, I took her hand in mine. It felt so good to be with her again, after all this time.

"Bea, talk to me. What is going on? Why were those men after me?" Her voice drew my eyes to her face. I had to be honest with her, but I was scared. So scared she would be disappointed in me.

"They called out a professional hit on you; they were trying to kill you. They did all of this to get to me," I explained, but confusion colored her face. She still didn't understand. "Those men are from the Vega Cartel, cousins to the remnants of the Fernando Cartel. Two months ago, we had a mission that ended up in us taking out nearly their entire operation in Colombia. They want revenge against us, against me."

Her hands enclosed my face, pulling me in close for a hug. I let it happen; let myself have a moment with her. I knew we wouldn't have much time. Jackson would ship her off to a safe house somewhere, then relocate her after we scrubbed the Earth of the scum coming after her.

"Oh Bea. What do we do?" She was worried, as she should be. They would not hesitate to kill her if they got the chance. It was how these cartels operated. They didn't just kill *you*, they killed your family, your cousins, even your damn dog. Everything you held dear in life, they would wipe it out.

"For now, you stay with us. We're going to our secret compound. Well, correct that; our *more* secret compound. It's hard to explain what it is, you'll just have to see it."

"When did you start all of this?" As usual she pushed the immediate unsolvable problem aside and instead focused on what got us here.

"Aunt Beatrice, it's a long story. I was caught in a nasty situation in Afghanistan. The long and short of it is that I proved my worth, saved my men, and I became the first member of Steel Corps. I lead them now. I can't tell you more than I already have. I'm sorry. They used those phone messages I left you to track you; along with my death certificate."

"That was the worst day of my life. The day those men came to my door and told me you were dead. You weren't even supposed to be in the field! You were supposed to be behind a computer somewhere!" She was shouting now; the men were looking and trying not to. It was a big plane, but it wasn't that big. There was no way for us to not be overheard. All of the men were listening raptly; I could feel it. Until now, they didn't know any of this; they didn't know how or why my aunt was targeted

"I'm sorry." It wasn't enough, but it was all I had.

"Sorry isn't good enough, young lady. Until I started getting those phone calls, I was a mess, sunk into my grief over you. I thought I was going crazy when I heard that first message…," she trailed off.

"I shouldn't have called. All of this is my fault." Guilt was eating my insides like a cancer.

"Don't you dare say that, Bea! Don't you dare even think it! I'm glad you called. Just hearing your voice saved me from sinking into an abyss."

"It's against protocol," I said softly.

"Screw your protocol!" Her beautiful face twisted with anger. I had put her through so much already, and here I was, dragging her down again.

"Aunt Beatrice! There's a reason our families are told we are dead. This is it, right here. So this doesn't happen. The things we do... there is no room for family in our lives."

"How sad for all of you. Good thing I'm here now. I can mother you all." Her voice was firm and resolute.

"Aunt Beatrice, you can't. My Master Sergeant will have you out of here as fast as he can. Don't get your hopes up. Where we're going, we'll have a little time together, then that's it. I'll be gone again. We need to get rid of this threat, then you will *have* to return home." I pointed to the rest of the plane, the team no longer trying to hide their interest in our conversation. "The men and I aren't around enough for you to mother anyway. If we aren't on a mission, we're training for one."

"It's true, Beatrice," Pierce said. "Though, Mic, we do need a cook in the worst kind of way."

"I could be your cook! You know I love to feed people! I would only need an assistant from time to time."

I groaned. Usually it was Flynn getting me into these messes. "Pierce; Aunt Beatrice; no. It can't happen. You'll just be in more danger. Not less."

"I have to disagree with you there, Mic." Jordon surprised me by speaking up. "She couldn't be safer than in the arms of Steel."

I threw my hands up in the air in defeat. "Fine, go ahead. Bring it up to Jackson. I dare you. I want her there more than any of you could ever know, but I refuse to get my hopes up. He won't allow it." I dug my iPod out of my pack and slipped in my ear-buds. It was rude, but I didn't give a crap. I wasn't having this conversation.

Aunt Beatrice smacked my arm, much to the delight of the men. I ignored her. I felt like a teenager again, struggling for my voice to be heard. It was not a feeling I enjoyed. 'Mad World' by Gary Jules washed over me and I let the lyrics carry me away. At least until we landed; then I would be back in the shit and I knew Aunt Beatrice wasn't satisfied with the answers I had given her. I was looking forward to the jog down memory lane about as much I wanted another bullet dug out of me. My leg gave a twitch at the memory.

****

Rook relaxed back into the large leather seat. During his military career whenever he flew, he was stuffed into one of those huge C-17 troop transport planes, packed in like a sardine. This was traveling in style for sure. Plenty of leg room and no one constantly bumping into him. The whole jet was apparently designed for large men and their deadly toys. It was an unexpected and very welcome luxury. Anyone who had ever been crammed into a coach seat on a commercial flight knew this; try doing it five seats deep with smelly, overly loud men. Not something he wanted to do again if he didn't need to.

He took his time observing everyone around him. Mic and her aunt were deep into conversation; Jordon couldn't keep his eyes off Mic. There was something between them—it was obvious to everyone. It was comical how they tried to hide it. Why they even bothered, he wasn't sure.

Jones appeared to be sleeping, though Rook was pretty sure he was faking. He was a sniper; he could sit still for days if he needed to.

There was nothing as calm, quiet, or deadly as a sniper. Rook would do his best not to piss him off; if such worry was even necessary. Jones seemed level-headed, but it was hard to tell with the quiet ones.

As of yet, he was unsure of his place within Steel. But standing shoulder-to-shoulder with Pierce back there had been everything he ever wanted. He had loved the comradery with his brothers in the Marines, but he hated the red tape and bullshit that held them back from being as effective as they could be. Steel unleashed them and let them actually make a difference in the world.

He had been with Steel for only a day and already had been in a firefight. He couldn't wait to see what else they had in store for him. He just needed to be careful to ensure that his past remained secret. There were some things that were better left unsaid.

****

"Buckle up, ladies; we're landing in a few," Flynn said over the loudspeaker.

I held Aunt Beatrice's hand as we began our descent. The Wonka House was the safest place for her and us. It was nearly impenetrable. Like any good soldier, I knew that a breach team could break through just about anything, given enough explosives. However, we could cover and defend every single opening in our fortress. Anyone attacking us would immediately feel the pain of hot lead ripping his body apart.

We landed on a small airstrip at a tiny forgotten airport about fifteen minutes from the Wonka House. We were on the outskirts of Rothenberg, the next town over from our compound.

"Okay boys, let's go. Two vehicles. Flynn, you drive the lead car; Pierce, follow with the second." My orders given we gathered our gear and disembarked.

There were two Suburbans waiting for us, kept here for this

express purpose. We separated into groups and climbed in. We could all fit into one, but it was too tight. The men had bitched enough that we finally ordered a second one.

I climbed into the passenger seat of the first Suburban with Flynn in the driver's seat. Aunt Beatrice got in the back with Jordon and Rook. Pierce, Jones, and all of our gear were in the other one.

"Try to keep it under seventy, Flynn," I said, settling back into the seat. The dark road before us was illuminated by the headlights, twisting and turning through the trees. Houses were few and far between. Large plots kept the neighbors from being too close, which suited our purposes perfectly.

"Bea, tell me about this bunker-thing we're going to," Aunt Beatrice spoke from the back.

"It's a safe house. Which doesn't really explain it at all, honestly. It's so much more than that."

"It's the coolest, most rad, and most intense fort you could ever imagine," Flynn said. "Being in the Wonka House is like a little kid being in a multi-story tree fort with gun turrets."

"While that sounds like lots of fun, Flynn, it doesn't really explain anything," Jordon added.

"I forgot you haven't been there yet." I turned in my seat to look back at him. "You'll like it. It's got a track."

"Our safe house has a track?" His eyes lit up like a kid at Christmas. I really liked how he said 'our.'

"You'll see soon enough. We're here," Flynn said, slowing as he made the turn into the gravel driveway. The stones crunched and pinged under the Suburban as we made our way to the house set at the end of the long lane. It was your standard split-level house, though on the small side. It was blue with black shutters and a red door; very American looking. Nothing set it apart from thousands of other houses all throughout this area, which was exactly the point.

"Doesn't look like much," Jordon said.

"Very observant of you," I replied as I took a small controller from the glovebox. It looked like a small TV remote, but appearances can be deceiving. When we turned onto the lane we had engaged a silent alarm. Right now, there were alarms screaming and screeching in the control room, which I shut off by pointing the remote at the sensor hidden in the security light which was currently blinding us. Four digits later, the light turned off, which was our signal that it was safe to proceed without the other security measures engaging.

I pressed a different set of numbers and the door on the small attached garage rose up silently, the lights inside automatically turning on. We drove into the pool of light as I again entered some numbers on the remote. Flynn stopped with the front end only about half-way inside.

"Now comes the really fun part, Jordon. Aunt Beatrice, don't worry. It looks crazy, but it's very safe." No further words were necessary as the concrete floor just in front of the Suburban began to vibrate and slowly lower. A ramp opened up in the floor of the garage like magic; though magic it was not, just giant hydraulics and damn impressive engineering.

"What the fuck?" Jordon gasped. I knew what was coming as soon as 'fuck' left his mouth. Aunt Beatrice hauled off and whacked him in the arm.

"Watch your language in front of me, young man. Talk however you want when you're alone, but you will keep a civil tongue in your head in my presence." The shock on his face was beyond comical. Flynn was laughing like a mad-man and I just smiled.

"Yes, ma'am," he wisely said, rubbing his arm. There was really no other appropriate response. Only I knew that when Aunt Beatrice was upset, she cursed as bad as the rest of us. This was her way of trying to make up for it.

Flynn swallowed the rest of his laughter and drove us down the ramp. While not overly steep it had enough of a downgrade to make you grab your seat. It was a short ride. At the bottom, the narrow tunnel opened up and there was enough parking for eight vehicles to fit comfortably. Jackson's truck wasn't here yet. Odd that he didn't beat us here.

Everything around us was concrete and recessed lighting. It was what was hidden behind the concrete that made this place so amazing. Thick plates of re-enforced steel surrounded the foot thick concrete. It would take so much more than bunker bombs to breach our house.

We exited the vehicles and quickly gathered our gear. I hit the remote and closed the ramp. The noise from the hydraulics echoed all around; we patiently waited for it to stop before speaking. It was damn loud down here while it closed.

"I get the Wonka reference now. Small on the outside, big on the inside. Clever," Jordon said. Rook didn't say anything. He was silent as ever, taking his time looking at everything. He quickly noticed the only weak point, the elevator.

"What now, Bea?" Aunt Beatrice asked, holding her robe tightly closed against the chill.

"Follow me," I said, stepping over to the elevator. Next to the shiny steel doors was a small recessed panel and a key pad. I entered my ten digit code, a beep sounded and the light flashed green. The door on the small panel slid up and I put my face close to it. A green light beamed out and scanned my right eye, first back and forth, then up and down.

"Holy crap, Batman; enough security measures here?" Rook said.

"Enough, yes," I replied. The pad beeped again, turning the light yellow. The keys slid back and a flat scanner slid out. I placed my left palm on it and waited as I was once again scanned by a green light. Another beep sounded and the light changed to red.

"Done yet?" Jordon asked.

"No. Now shut the hell up."

"Name and rank," an electronic voice asked from the panel. There were a lot of hoops to jump through, but they were damn effective. The chances of anyone getting my biometrics, the codes, and my voice were slim to fucking none.

"Staff Sergeant Michaels," I spoke clearly into the panel.

"Security phrase." I changed this after every visit. I tried to keep with a theme, to make it easier to remember.

"August 26th, a day to remember and one I always forget."

"Welcome to Wonka House. Enjoy your stay, Steel Corps," the voice said before beeping a final time. The elevator doors slid open with a soft hiss.

"What's August 26th?" Jordon asked as we squeezed into the elevator. There were three levels to the Wonka House; we were going to Sub-Level Two first. I pushed the button and the doors slid closed.

"I could tell you, but then….well you know the rest," I said. It was my secret and that is how it would stay.

It was a short ride. The typical elevator bell sounded and we trooped on out.

"This is the level you'll probably spend most of your time on, Aunt Beatrice. It has our quarters, the kitchen, and a common room. Sub-Level One is more for the team, with our war room, a shooting range, and the medical center." I walked her down the hallway. It was carpeted, but that is where the comforts ended. The walls were concrete block, painted a soft grey. "Sub-Level Three houses our weight room, the track, and a decent-sized swimming pool. This is all set up in the event that we need to live down here for years, if necessary. There is a large stock of MREs and canned goods. For now, though, Jordon and Flynn can go to the store to get supplies whenever you are ready. Just give them a list."

"Hope there aren't any zombies…," Jordon said, trailing off. He seemed spooked, looking behind him and all around.

"What the fuck are you talking about, Jordon?" I asked him, truly bewildered.

"Well, it's like *Resident Evil* down here. I feel like I'm in *The Hive*. Where are the bio-labs and shit?"

"They're on Sub-Level Four and only Mic or Jackson can access them," Flynn told him, completely deadpan. Jordon paled and took a step back toward the elevator.

I rolled my eyes. "He's just fucking with you, Jordon. Christ, there are no zombies! No bio-labs. Un-bunch your girly parts and let's get going."

"Bea! Watch your mouth! You've always had a foul mouth, but this horrible." Aunt Beatrice gave me her best mother-glare-of-death.

Just off of the elevator was a hallway with our quarters. Each was a simple room with a small bathroom. Nothing too fussy, but still comfortable enough. At least we didn't have to share bathrooms. That was something I had strongly spoken against when we began the design.

"Here's your room, Aunt Beatrice; mine is right beside you." I pointed to the two doors to our left. "The rest of you guys will just have to check out the other rooms and call dibs."

Aunt Beatrice poked her head into her room and seemed satisfied enough. There was a twin bed and a desk and chair. Along with a dresser and a small wall-mounted TV, those were the rooms' only contents. They were built to be functional and nothing more.

"Follow me; I'll show you to the common room and the kitchen." We continued down the short hallway. It opened up and out into a large room at the end. The common room had thick carpet and even some posters and paintings on the walls to break up the starkness of the blocks. Couches and chairs were arranged in front of a giant flat screen. There was an air hockey table and a pool table.

"Homey," Rook said, flopping down on the couch and quickly propping his boots on the table.

Aunt Beatrice looked as if she was going to say something to him, but I shook my head 'no' at her. There were times to tell the guys off, like she did with Jordon in the car, and there were times when *not* to tell them off. This was one of the latter.

"Over here is the kitchen, Aunt Beatrice. I think you're going to be suitably impressed." I opened the double-hinged door and flicked the light on.

A giant expanse of stainless steel and culinary wonder was revealed. Her gasp of surprise echoed back to us. Long tables and counters were sheathed in gleaming stainless steel, and a giant Viking range with ten burners and two ovens was the focal point of the room. An industrial sized fridge was more than large enough to accommodate the amount of food required to feed these men.

"Bea, this is amazing. I can't wait to put it to use. It looks like it's never been touched."

"It hasn't been much. We haven't had to use this place that often. And when we have been here, it's only been for short periods, when eating MREs was easier than getting groceries and a cook."

She walked deeper into the kitchen, running her hand along the edge of the large table in the middle. She touched each knob and dial on the stove and opened the fridge, only to find it bare.

"I haven't gotten to spend a holiday dinner with you in over five years. Even with all you're going to have to deal with to keep me safe, I'm thankful to be here. I'm making a grocery list. Tomorrow is going to be Thanksgiving."

Chapter 6

Later that night or morning considering the time, I lay in bed staring at the ceiling. Sleep was more elusive than usual tonight. Seeing and being around Aunt Beatrice brought even more of my past to the forefront of my mind. It had already been working its way closer to the surface, and now it was oozing out.

A knock on my door startled me out of my thoughts.

"Who is it?" I called out. I couldn't be bothered to get up right now.

"It's me," said Aunt Beatrice. I should have known this was coming; I had hoped that she would have held off until tomorrow.

"Come in." I sat up, pulling a pillow into my lap. I clutched it tight as if it would protect me. "It's late, why are you still awake?"

"I think you know why, Bea," she said simply, sitting down beside me on the bed.

"Yes. I can imagine," I spoke softly. I didn't want to have this fucking conversation, but Aunt Beatrice was the one person in this world that I couldn't get my way with. If she wanted to talk, we were going to talk.

"I deserve to know why." It was a statement and question rolled into one. The hurt that was laced into her voice caused me near physical pain.

"I know. You're right, you do. It's not like it's easy to explain, though. There is nothing simple about it." I tried to find my anger, but couldn't. The only thing I felt at the moment was intense regret. Not for what I did, but for what my actions had put her through.

"Just start from the beginning, Bea; make me understand." She took my hand and forced me to look at her. She knew this was painful for both of us. Time to rip off the band-aid.

"You know I joined the Army to get away from him. It felt like the safest place for me to be. I would be gone halfway around the world and well beyond his reach." I was choking on the words, but it was like a breaking dam. The words just flooded out, pushed by the back-pressure.

"Two weeks into my scheduled deployment, I received a message. I don't know how he managed to get it to me, but he did. He said that if I didn't come back, he'd find me. He didn't care if I was a solider now, he would put me in my place where I belonged. Stupidly, I believed him." I clutched the pillow tighter, hugging it tight to my chest. "So instead of dealing with it, I volunteered to go on a mission in the field. It was supposed to be a routine patrol and we'd be delivering food and medical supplies to a village for the U.N. It was in an area that was getting hot, but we had my platoon and two others in the area. We thought it would be safe enough." The memories were coming back in a rush, the sounds and smells assaulting me as if I was there. Aunt Beatrice squeezed my hand, anchoring me in the present.

"It went to hell; we were betrayed by a local informant. He gave away our location. My commanding officer was killed in front of me, putting me in charge. I got my platoon out after two days of fighting and retreating. The other two units in reserve weren't so lucky. They were wiped out. After I got back stateside, Jackson, my Master Sergeant, came to me with an idea. I would be the first member of Steel. He laid it all out for me; he told me that I would be declared legally dead. That you would be told I was killed in a training exercise. It broke my heart; but in the back of my head, I just kept seeing his message; that he would find me. I did it because then he would think I was dead, and I would be free." I finally looked at her. Tears were streaming down her face in a steady tide. I had knowingly broken her heart. To save myself.

"I'm glad you did it," she said as she took my face in her hands. I was shocked beyond words. I had prepared myself for her censure and anger. I never expected compassion for my actions.

"Why…" I was lost; I couldn't form a thought or word.

"My brother was an evil man. You were a light that he never deserved to have in his life. When your poor mama died, he went off the deep end. And you suffered for it. I only wish I had known sooner, then maybe I would have saved us both a lot of pain. You never deserved those terrible things he did to you; no child does. You escaped and learned to protect yourself. I commend you for it. You're so brave and strong. That's your mama in you. She was like you, fierce and bold."

"Where is he now?" I asked, trying to change the track of the conversation.

"Dead."

"When?" Relief flooded through me at the news.

"About a year ago. He wrapped his truck around a tree. He was trapped; they told me he died slowly." She stood then, and paced around the room. He may have been an unbelievable bastard, but he was still her brother.

"Good," I said. Maybe I would go dance on his grave.

"It's over now, Bea." She put her hand on the door knob.

"It's been over for a long time. I'm sorry you had to go through all of this."

"I'm not, because now I have you back. I'm not letting you go again, and you can tell your boss I said that." She left my room, softly closing the door behind her.

I believed her. There weren't many people in this world that scared me, but Aunt Beatrice was one of them. When she put her mind to something, she was set, and there was no changing it. I couldn't wait to see the confrontation between her and Jackson. It would be epic. I should sell tickets and popcorn. I'd need to get Flynn right on that.

It was my turn to pace; I was keyed up on the news of my father's death. His demise. His justice. His bite in the ass from karma. Fancy that, trapped and unable to move while he slowly died. Fitting death for the bastard. Quickly changing into running clothes, I went down to the track. I knew I wouldn't sleep tonight; there was no point in even trying.

****

Jordon stood with his back to the wall next to Mic's room. He was floored by what he had just heard. Mic's father abused her? She had never let on even for one second she'd been through something like that. Jordon was hurt and pissed the fuck off. Good thing that old bastard was dead or he would have been tracking him down and gutting him with a spoon.

Why didn't she tell him? Jordon knew about her occasional PTSD flashbacks and her insomnia. Why not tell him this? He didn't know, but he was going to find out.

He was poised to knock when he saw the knob turning, so he

stepped back quickly and around a corner as he watched her leave the room in running gear. So she was going to go run from her feelings?

Not this time, Bea…

****

My feet were slapping against the track, making almost no noise. The vast empty room stretched around me. I hadn't switched on more than the most necessary of lights. Strange shadows cast by my running form twisted around the room as I ran, changing shape and moving with my body. I didn't count laps or listen to music, I just ran. I ran until my breath began to come faster and my heart slammed in my chest. I ran without grace or form, pushing my body to escape my mind. It was futile.

Memories continued to assault me and I just let them come, I gave in, not fighting it anymore, I let them wash over me.

The front door slammed and heavy staggering footsteps came down my hallway. It was late and he was drunk again. Today was Friday and he was always worse on paydays. Both because he got money, and because it was never enough. I hadn't eaten today; the cupboards were bare again. I knew I would not eat this night or tomorrow.

Boom! Boom! My door shook with the force he used to pound on it. I sat on my bed and waited. The door was unlocked, but he was too drunk to reason it out. Locking it never helped. He would just kick it in, and then I would be without a door at all. Finally he turned the knob and I watched him come in.

I could smell the cheap whiskey from where I sat on my worn-out and threadbare bed. His bloodshot eyes found me waiting, which seemed to only enrage him more. I knew by now that no matter what I did, it would be the same. Hiding didn't help, it just got me locked in the closet. I couldn't stand the tight spaces anymore. Instead, I met him head on. I stood as he approached; even knowing what was coming I tensed, fear gripping me in a vicious hold.

"You little bitch...," he screamed as he raised his hand.

A sound behind me jerked me back to the present. I didn't think; I just reacted. Stopping quickly, I pivoted and kicked out without even looking to see what the threat was. My foot connected with a solid mass. I heard a loud grunt and it was then that I saw who was behind me.

"Jordon?" I said, disbelieving. I was on the track. I was not at that house with that man. I forced my mind back to the present.

"What the fuck, Mic?" Jordon shouted at me. I was not in the mood to be yelled at.

"Don't you fucking shout at me! Don't sneak up on people and you won't get kicked," I shot back. My temper was rising and needed an outlet; as usual, Jordon was a convenient target.

"I didn't sneak! I said your name four times!" He advanced on me. He was incredibly pissed.

"What the hell are you so mad about?" His anger was disproportionate to the situation. I was missing something.

"I overhead you talking to your aunt," he said. I retreated a few steps until I realized what I was doing. I stopped and stood my ground, planting my feet both physically and mentally.

"So, not only do you sneak up on people, you listen at doors. What next? You going to sit in a tree outside my window while I get undressed?"

"Dammit, Bea! It's not like that! How could you not tell me!?" He was just as angry now as the night we had tortured him.

"Why? I don't talk about it and I don't fucking want to start now." I turned my back on him and began to walk away. He grabbed my arm, trying to spin me around to face him. Dropping my weight, I spun on my heel and tried to foot sweep him. He saw it coming a mile away and ended matters quickly. He planted his shoulder into my stomach and swung me up and over.

"Put me down Jordon! That's an order!" I kicked for all I was worth, getting a few grunts for my efforts. It about as effective as kicking a tree.

"Fuck your orders, Bea." He marched off with me dangling over his shoulder. I had a perfect view of his ass. Making a fist, but popping the knuckle of my ring finger out into a point, I punched him in the nerve on the small of his back as hard as I could. His legs buckled and he dropped me with a yell. I landed in a heap, my legs tangled with his arms. To say that it was undignified was an understatement.

He was kicking away from me, trying to get untangled. I was doing the same in the opposite direction. I got free and stood, but before I could run, he tackled me from behind. We hit the soft track with an explosion of air from my lungs. I was crushed beneath his considerable weight.

"Get... off." I shoved, but he didn't move an inch. I hadn't felt so physically ineffective in a very long time. I didn't like it one damn bit.

"Not fucking happening." He let me up enough to spin me onto my back, but quickly dropped back down between my now spread thighs.

Great, this just gets better and better.

"What the fuck do you think you are doing?" Balling up my fist, I moved to hit him, but he dodged it and grabbed my wrists. Slamming them down, he pinned them to the track beside my head.

"Whatever I want it seems," Jordon replied. I was pleased to note that he was breathing as hard as I was. Sweat dotted his forehead and ran down his temples. At least it wasn't easy on him, either.

"Get the fuck off me, Jordon. This isn't funny." I saw the intent in his eyes before he moved. "Jordon..." I barely got it out before his mouth crushed against mine.

****

Pierce couldn't sleep and when he passed Jones's room, he could hear the TV with the volume down low. Apparently he wasn't the only one still up. He'd changed and thought he'd go for a run, to try and tire himself out. It freaked him out to be underground. It wasn't really too obvious that he was inside of the Earth, but it was a thought never too far from his mind.

If pounding out a couple miles on the track helped him to sleep, he'd run until he collapsed if he needed to. Cardio was never a bad thing anyway.

****

Jordon's lips were as soft as I remembered; he tasted like coffee and Chris. Such an unlikely, but wonderful, combination. All thoughts of resisting him flew out of my head as soon as his tongue made entrance to my mouth and danced along mine.

"Chris...," I said, catching a breath finally, only to lose it when I saw the intensity of his gaze. His dark green eyes seemed to glow in the dim light, they burned with desire and another emotion I could not name.

"Bea...please," he gasped before kissing me again. He released my wrists finally and I wrapped my arms around his shoulders and head, wrapped my legs around his waist, and held him tight against me. He overwhelmed my senses, his weight, his smell, his taste. I was spinning off my axis, unable to stop it even if I wanted to.

His hand was hot against the skin of my stomach as he slid it up and under my shirt. Slowly... like he was memorizing the feel of my skin.

"You're so fucking soft, Bea," Chris growled, finding his prize, crushing his lips back to mine. I ran my hand down his back, dragging my fingertips over his trim hip and then forward along his stomach, seeking my own prize. Our sighs and gasping breaths were the only sounds in the room, echoing back and all around us.

"Well, this isn't entirely unexpected." We froze, not seeing the source of the voice, but recognizing it all the same. We didn't need to see Pierce. Chris removed his hands from under my shirt, and sat up, pulling me with him. I'm sure I looked just like I felt, a flushed, excited woman who was kissed nearly to death.

"Pierce." It was all I could manage. Speech had yet to fully return. I smoothed my hands over my hair, trying to tame it into something normal instead of the sex-mussed hair I'm sure it resembled. Jordon quickly stood and pulled me up to stand beside him.

"Mic. Jordon. It's obvious what's going on here. But the question remains, what should I do about it?" He strode into the light. He, too, was dressed for running. Apparently none of us could sleep.

"There isn't anything you need to do. This is between myself and Mic," Jordon said. His speech capabilities had recovered quicker than mine.

"True enough. But it impacts us all. If it was only about you two, I'd say go ahead, fuck like rabbits until you collapse. But it's not just about you two. This could be a huge problem for us. What happens if one or the other of you is captured? You're so emotionally involved that you wouldn't be able to make an effective decision." Pierce walked closer with each word until he was seriously invading our personal space.

Seeing his face clearly now, I could see he wasn't mad in the least, only very worried. I side-stepped the hand Jordon tried to place on my shoulder. I ignored him as I steeped farther to the side and I could practically hear his jaw breaking as he ground his teeth.

"You're absolutely correct. This is something I have been telling Jordon for some time now. Since before Colombia." I risked a glance at him and he physically recoiled at my words. "But... as he has said: we're human, no matter how much the military wishes it otherwise. We sometimes can't help the attractions we feel or emotions they bring. I'm asking you to trust us, Pierce."

"Trust you how? To keep it in your pants? Sex is a moot point here, Mic. Whether you do the deed or not is inconsequential. The damage, as it were, is done."

"True enough. I was having a bad day and I let things get out of hand. I am, after all, only human. It won't happen again."

Pierce turned from me and focused his attention on Jordon. "Won't it? Jordon, do you agree to that or are you going to keep trying to kiss her every opportunity you get?"

"I can't really say. I can't help myself when it comes to her." At least he was honest.

"You had better learn to, Jordon. It's her or Steel. You can't have both. In fact, you can only have Steel. Because if you get kicked out of the unit, you won't see her at all. You've painted yourselves into a corner. It's up to you two to decide how to get out of it." With that being said, Pierce turned on his heel and walked away.

"Can't help yourself, huh?" I crossed my arms over my chest.

"No, I can't. You're like gravity; an unstoppable force, pulling me in no matter how hard I resist. And don't cross your freaking arms like that, woman. It makes me stare at your chest and that will only lead to more trouble for us both." He too, turned on his heel and left me.

"Well, you're pretty unstoppable yourself," I said to the empty room. With my words came the realization that I was in serious hot water without even knowing how I got there. I was like a frog placed in cold water, slowly heating and being cooked without even realizing it until it was too late. Chris was the water and I was stuck, unable to jump out.

Chapter 7

The next morning, I found myself standing and staring at my door, almost unwilling to open it and face Pierce and Jordon. Which was unacceptable. I couldn't let them see how much I was affected by that kiss last night. They didn't need to know that I slept without nightmares for the first time in two months. Instead my dreams had been filled with blazing green eyes and strong grasping hands.

Walking into the common room, I immediately noticed Rook and Flynn bent over a chess board. Flynn was taking a long time between moves, but Rook had no such hesitation, quickly advancing and adding to the growing stack of Flynn's taken pieces. I didn't enjoy chess or follow it that well, nor did I care to learn. I left them to it. My target was kicked back watching FOX News.

Grabbing a cup of coffee first, I sat next to Pierce. He looked at me before resuming his brainwashing.

"We good?" I asked simply, taking a sip of my coffee.

"We're good. Leave it at that."

"When is Jackson due to arrive?" I looked around, not seeing my aunt, but judging by the smell of bacon and fried potatoes coming from the kitchen, she had matters well in hand.

"In thirty," he said, again not looking at me.

"Copy," I replied. Giving up on conversation I headed into the kitchen.

"Morning, Aunt Beatrice," I said, kissing the cheek she offered me.

"Morning, Bea. I'm making your favorite." There was a spread the likes of which I hadn't seen in years. Stacks of waffles and bacon, and pan fried ham and potatoes. I wiped my mouth, making sure the drool pooling inside wasn't running down my chin.

"When's breakfast ready?" I asked, peeking around her shoulder to see what she was doing on the stove. She had a western omelet the size of a serving platter in a giant cast iron skillet. How she even lifted the damn thing I will never know.

"Any minute. Tell the boys to set the table." This was going to be fun. They most likely hadn't set a table since before they joined the military. If then.

Stepping back out into the common room, I shouted to get their attention. "Listen up ladies, breakfast is almost ready. Aunt Beatrice wants you to come and set the table. File in!"

"What the hell?" Flynn said, stepping back from the chess board with a sigh of relief. He continued to smart off. "What next? Are we going to be wearing aprons and peeling potatoes?"

"If you keep that attitude up," Aunt Beatrice said, "then yes, and I'll make sure it's a lace one with ruffles. If you want to eat, you help. Since you seem to be so excited for it, you get dish duty, Flynn.". She walked back through the kitchen door, leaving a shocked silence behind her.

"Well, Flynn, I'm going to start shopping for your apron now.

With your mouth, I think you're going to be in constant trouble with Beatrice," Pierce said, shoving Flynn as they walked into the kitchen.

"Fuck you man, you're no angel," Flynn snapped back.

"Make that two days of dishes. The only person who gets to swear in my kitchen is me," Aunt Beatrice said calmly, as she laid the platter with the giant omelet onto the table.

Flynn's face colored, but he shut his mouth. It was a nice change. We should have brought Aunt Beatrice in years ago.

We had just sat down and began to pass the heaping platters of food when a loud buzzer sounded.

"Jones?" I watched as he pulled out his phone and tapped into the live feed of the cameras.

"It's Jackson," he said, turning his phone so I could see our Master Sergeant jumping through all the security hoops at the elevator.

"Let him in." A few taps later, the doors slid open. Jackson got onto the elevator and came our way. "Ready to meet the boss, Aunt Beatrice?" I asked.

She stood and took off her apron, smoothing her already flawless hair into place. She was wearing a pair of my jeans and a soft pink sweater she must have knitted last night or something, I had no damn idea where she found it. "He's a man, Bea; don't worry darling, I got this."

Flynn snorted orange juice up his nose, and was gasping and coughing when Jackson strode purposefully into the kitchen.

"What the fuck is this?" The strain on his face from holding back his drill instructor shout was evident.

"I presume you are Master Sergeant Jackson?" Aunt Beatrice asked, standing and walking toward him with her hand extended.

"I am," he said, shaking her offered hand. The rest of us sat back in stunned silence, watching as the drama unfolded before us.

"This is breakfast; if you are unfamiliar with it, please have a seat and become acquainted."

"Ma'am, I am perfectly aware of what this is, but these men have work to do. They do not have the time to sit and have a leisurely brunch." Jackson looked at each of us in turn, but in that moment I think we were all more afraid of offending Aunt Beatrice.

"Let them eat. They haven't had a decent meal in months. I won't have all my work go to waste." Aunt Beatrice very deliberately turned her back on Jackson and again took her seat. "Will you pass me the potatoes, please?" Pierce startled and handed her the platter. I know I was in shock; Jackson looked like he'd been hit by a two-by-four.

"Don't get comfortable, Beatrice. Your stay will be a short one. Mic, I want you in the war room in ten minutes," Jackson snapped as he left the kitchen.

"So... that went well," I said, stuffing bacon in my mouth.

"Yes, I think it did." Aunt Beatrice stabbed a piece of waffle with undo force. It was not over between them, not by a long shot. I just hoped I was around to see it.

"Jackson is right. We have a lot to do today. Rook?" I got his attention. He had been single-mindedly clearing his plate; he looked up and swallowed quickly. "You'll be doing more training today. Lucky for you, we have facilities here to accommodate you."

"Copy that," He said, before bending back to his task.

"Jones, I want a file on the Vega cartel as soon as possible. Everything you have, I need it. Jackson already has some info; get the file from him and start there."

"Copy." Jones took his plate to the sink and rinsed it before heading off to get to work.

"What about us?" Jordon asked.

"You and Pierce will be with me, training Rook. I have to talk to Jackson first. I'll meet you on Sub-Level Three as soon as I'm finished. Get warmed up; I want to see you spar."

"Forgetting me?" Flynn asked.

"Nope. You have dishes to do. And then you can help Aunt Beatrice. I think she's going to need someone to run to the grocery store for her. You're her errand boy for the day." I smirked at him as I took care of my own plate. Any day I got to stick it to Flynn was a good day, indeed.

****

Jackson entered the war room and sat with a rare and heavy sigh. He would never let onto the others, but he hated this place—this room in particular. Too many painful memories were here for him. He was being hard on Mic, worse than normal, and it wouldn't be long before she called him on it. He was sort of surprised that she hadn't already.

He was just so fucking mad at her. After Riley betrayed them and Phillips was killed, he had never been so glad that the team was all 'dead.' Then Mic had to go and call her aunt and put them all in danger again. Losing Phillips was like losing a limb for them all. Mic had been the first and Phillips had been the second member of Steel. Jackson didn't think he could take losing another team member. He was getting too old to be standing over flag-draped coffins; he had seen enough of them to last him a lifetime.

Beatrice was a huge complication. The men were getting attached to her already; it was so easy to see. The breakfast had made them all feel like a family again, surrounded by friends and good food. It was something not many of them had experienced in a long time. It was a feeling they were going to fight him to keep. He didn't blame them in the least, but if he had to sacrifice their happiness for their lives, he would.

As soon as he was done with Mic, he was going to the kitchen and telling Beatrice the way things were going to go. She *had* to be made to understand that she couldn't stay here. Being with them put her in mortal danger; he wouldn't have more innocent blood on his hands.

****

My orders given, I left the others in the kitchen and took the elevator up to Sub-Level One. Stuffing my hands in my pockets, I passed the dark medical center. The war room was the next door. I stood outside, knowing I had to go in, but dreading it all the same. It felt like I was in high school again and being sent to the principal's office. Sucking it up, I knocked firmly.

"Enter."

I took a seat at the long gleaming wooden table in the center of the room. The walls were concrete block like the rest of the Wonka House, but a little more effort at decorating had been made in here. The walls had been painted a soft tan and framed photos of us all were evenly spaced along one wall: pictures of us in BDUs, with painted faces, on at the compound, in jungles and deserts, and some even in Finnegan's. There were years of memories on this wall. Each picture with Phillips was like a punch to the throat, equally stealing my breath and rolling my stomach over in a nauseating wave.

Forcing myself to look away from the memories, I instead focused on the man impatiently waiting for me to acknowledge him.

"Sit down, Mic," Jackson spoke, clasping his fingers in front of his mouth.

I sat. I had decided before I came in here not to speak until he asked me a direct question.

"I could have you brought up on charges of insubordination, among other things." I just stared at him, not saying anything. He returned my glare. "The only reason I won't, is because I'd have a fucking munity on my hands. If the men didn't love you so much, you'd be out of Steel... for good." His tone was perfectly serious; I knew he meant every word. "Anything else going on that I don't know about?" He continued.

My thoughts jumped to Jordon and the kiss on the track last night. Then to my flashbacks and nightmares. There was nothing I could mention and still remain a member of Steel.

"No, Master Sergeant." I wasn't sure if he knew I was lying and had decided to let it go, or if he actually believed me. Only time would tell.

"Fine. Next is your aunt. She can't stay here and I don't care how good of a cook she is. It's not safe for anyone. Once we deal with these Vega bastards, she's going home. Got it?"

"Copy, Master Sergeant." He looked suspicious, but I wasn't about to defend Aunt Beatrice; she'd do that all on her own. Seeing these two butt heads was going to be worthy of pay-per-view.

"Not going to argue with me?" he asked.

I laughed. "No. She's perfectly capable of doing that on her own."

"I'm sure she is. But the fact remains, her being here puts her in danger not to mention us. I don't know about you, Mic, but I don't care to bury another one of you," He said, pointing to the pictures lining the wall.

"Is that what this is all about? Phillips?" If he was harboring guilt over Phillips, it would explain his behavior of late.

"Follow my fucking orders, Staff Sergeant. You won't get another pass. Train Rook, get as much intel on Vega as you can, and send your aunt home. That's it. Dismissed."

****

Down on Sub-Level Three, I stood back and observed. Rook and

Jordon were sparring, with Pierce acting as referee. Rook was damn impressive. There weren't many people faster than Jordon, but Rook was managing it. Every time I thought Jordon was going to get a solid hit in, he somehow dodged it.

Jordon was going to be a hurting unit tomorrow, I thought, as Rook tried to drive his fist through Jordon's rib cage. I stepped over to Pierce at the edge of the blue mat. Rook hooked an arm around Jordon's neck and dropped him on his back. Quickly moving behind him, Rook wrapped his legs around Jordon's torso and squeezed; at the same time he compressed his carotid artery. Jordon tapped Rook's arm frantically.

"I'd say he gets an A plus in takedowns," I said to Pierce, as Rook helped a coughing Jordon up.

"Agreed," he responded as Jordon and Rook squared off again. "How did it go with Jackson?"

"Well enough," I said, wincing in sympathy as Rook took a solid kick from Jordon.

"That doesn't really tell me anything, Mic."

"I'm well aware of that." At this point both men were sweating profusely and tiring. "How long have they been going at it?"

"Since we came down here, right after breakfast."

"For fucks sake." I stepped onto the mat and shouted to get their attention. "What the hell? You've been sparring for over a half hour? Do you two want to be able to walk and use your arms tomorrow?"

"Has it been that long?" Rook asked, wiping sweat from his brow with the back of his taped hand.

"Go clean up, both of you. Rook, I don't think you need any further training in hand-to-hand combat. Let's go to the range."

A tone sounded over the speaker that was in each room. I went to the panel near the door and pressed a button.

"Yeah?"

"Mic? I have something you all need to see." There was a tone in Jones' voice I had never heard before. He sounded almost... scared.

"What is it?" A shiver of dread slid down my spine.

"I can't... just come up here."

"Copy." My bad feeling only got worse, Jones was unshakeable. For him to be unnerved was very unusual.

"Back up we go boys; meet me in the war room."

Chapter 8

Jackson was hovering over Jones's shoulder, staring at the monitor. Their tense postures didn't bode well for us.

"What's going on?" I asked, sitting at the table. The atmosphere was charged with tension; the very air was heavy with it.

"Wait until the others get here," Jackson said, his voice firm and all business.

I didn't have to wait long. The table quickly filled. Jordon, Rook, and Pierce had taken the time to change, but little else. Flynn came in last, a large wet spot in the center of his shirt. Doing dishes really sucked.

"Jones, put it up." The lights dimmed and the large flat screen on the wall came to life. It showed satellite images of a small town. It looked like Mexico or somewhere similar; basic infrastructure with little in the way of anything modern.

"What are we looking at here, Master Sergeant?" I asked.

The images quickly began to play. The time stamp advanced a few hours before the photos slowed. Jones began to narrate as the images slowed down even more into individual pictures. "This is *Villahermosa*. A small town on the southern end of Mexico and home to the Vega Cartel. Here they grow poppies and process them into heroin. It's an extremely labor intensive process and must be done by hand. Usually done by the local people. It takes thousands of poppies to yield a single kilo." The images showed a mass of about a hundred people being gathered in the town square. Cartel assassins or *sicarios* with AK-47s pushed the people into a tight circle. A man and a woman stood in the center of the circle. The pictures stopped for a moment and Jones kept talking.

"The man and woman in the center are Adolfo Vega and his cousin, Mercedes Fernando, Diego's widow," Jones said.

"Fuck me," Flynn said with feeling.

"What else?" I asked. Jones didn't respond, just advanced the photos a little more. One of the Vega flunkies shoved an elderly man into the center of the circle, forcing him to his knees. An equally old woman off to the side collapsed at the sight. The man folded his hands in prayer and bowed his head. The *sicario* shot the old man in the head, spraying blood and brain matter all over his wife.

"Fuck me," I gasped. I'd seen executions before; hell, I've been the executioner, but defenseless, innocent people being coldly executed was something I never got used to seeing. "Tell me, Jones."

He turned off the screen. "This happened yesterday. A confidential informant within the cartel said the old man was executed because he refused to work in the poppy fields anymore. Anyone who refuses to work is executed, or their families are. Or they starve them. Sometimes a combination thereof."

"We've always known that the cartels are cruel bastards. This isn't news. These fuckers are going to be coming for us," Jackson explained. He stood and began to pace.

"Agreed. What's your plan?" I asked. I was all for raining down hell and burying every last one of those fuckers. We were outnumbered nearly ten to one. We were better trained and better equipped, but sometimes that just was not enough. If it weren't for the innocent townspeople, I would just call in an air strike and be done with it.

"We watch and wait for now. The brass is holding us back on this one. They don't want us to go in too early and endanger the life of the informant," Jackson said.

"We could get him out, do what we did for Linc. Seems to be working for him," Pierce said. We had gotten an update; Linc, now known as Josiah Keen was very happily living out his life in upstate New York.

"They aren't ready for him to be extracted," Jackson said.

"So, our hands are tied? We can't go in there without knowing who this CI is; and if we go in and take them out and he lives, his cover is blown. Fuck," I swore. "So, Master Sergeant, what the fuck do we do now?" I snapped at him. My aunt's life was dangling in the balance. Failure was never an option with us, but the stakes were higher than ever this time around.

He glared at me. "We wait, Mic. We gather intelligence, we get Rook trained. Now is not the time to go in there. We have to wait for the status quo to change."

"I get what you're saying, but I don't fucking like it." I stood up and flung my chair backwards, knocking it over with a crash of breaking plastic. "While we sit around, those fuckers will be killing more innocent people. I have half a mind to tell you to take your status quo and shove it."

"Stop right fucking there, Staff Sergeant." My feet stopped of their own accord. Jackson's authoritarian tone made the trained soldier in me respond. I stood at attention, waiting for the verbal beat down I deserved. He came closer and stopped less than a foot away from me. I didn't look up at him or to either side. I stared straight ahead at his broad chest.

"You *will* address your superior officer with more respect or I'll smoke your ass. Stow your fucking emotions and use the brain the Army gave you. My threat is not idle, Staff Sergeant Michaels. You *will* follow orders or you'll be on the next plane to Alaska as a measly little Private. Do I make myself clear?" He never even raised his voice; he didn't need to.

"Yes, Master Sergeant!" I continued to stand at attention until he dismissed me. The others stared in stunned silence. They had witnessed Jackson reaming me out, but they had never seen him go off like this before. They were frozen, not wanting to move or draw attention to themselves.

"All of you, get the fuck out of my sight." Jackson turned his back on us, staring at the blank TV monitor; presumably lost in thought.

We followed orders and got the hell out of the room in a hurried but orderly manner.

****

Jackson paced the length of the war room. Hours passed and still he had no solution. No matter how many circles he made, he couldn't settle his thoughts. Mic and Beatrice kept swirling around in there, posing impossible questions.

What to do with Beatrice? She couldn't stay, but leaving would keep her in danger. Cartels were notorious for their blood debts and feuds.

Mic was being an unreasonable bitch; there was more going on with her than she was saying. Should he push her and get the answers, even if those answers were things he didn't want to hear?

Jordon couldn't keep his eyes off Mic; it was plain as day for everyone to see. She, on the other hand, ignored him, which told its own story. She made a pointed effort to not be near Jordon. There was something going on, but there wasn't much he could do about it. Strong emotions like love and hate almost had a physical presence. Fighting them often caused more damage than just letting them go.

He wasn't going to find any answers in here. He would tackle these problems like any other: start at the top of the list and work his way down. Beatrice was first.

Jackson took the elevator down to Sub-Level Two. He followed the smells and sounds of cooking. Mentally he told his stomach to shut the hell up. He didn't care how much like home this place smelled; she couldn't stay. Pushing open the door, the heavy scents of cinnamon and apples hit him. His mouth watered at the scent.

There was pastries everywhere; three pies were cooling and Beatrice was filling a fourth with steaming apples. Flour coated her hands and apron, there was even a smudge on her face. A giant golden brown turkey rested on a platter, its stuffing spilling out. Apparently Thanksgiving was in October now.

"Can I help you, Master Sergeant?" She asked, never looking up from the dough she was carefully placing over the pie. She cut the excess off in a swift, practiced motion and slit some holes in the top. He forced himself to stop watching her clever hands.

"We need to talk," he croaked before clearing his throat; his voice felt like it was stuck in there somewhere.

"What about, exactly?" She turned and bent down, sliding the pie into the oven. He quickly snapped his eyes back to her face when she turned around.

Did she catch him checking her out?

"Master Sergeant?" She prompted.

"You can't stay here," he barked out. Anger tightened her face, looking as good on her as the flour.

"Where exactly would you have me go?" Her voice sounded just like Mic's when she was pissed off.

"Not now. When we neutralize the threat, then you have to go. You can't stay with us." He was trying and failing to get his point across. He sounded like an asshole. Fuck, he *felt* like an asshole.

"Oh really? And who is going to make me leave? You?" She placed a flour dusted hand on one hip and stared him down. He'd faced terrorists that didn't scare him as much as this woman. In moments, she had turned his thoughts upside down. With just a few simple words, she was making his decision feel like the wrong one.

"You're a civilian." It sounded lame even to his ears. She flapped a hand at him and turned back to the sink.

"I don't care about that. I am the only family Mic has left, besides you lot. I am going to be here for her. You may as well get used to the idea, Master Sergeant." She kept up her work, cleaning green beans.

Was she making green bean casserole? Oh God, he hoped so.

"Stop calling me Master Sergeant. I am not your NCO. Call me Jackson." This conversation was not going the way he planned. *Try a different approach?*

"I am not one of your soldiers. Either I call you by your rank or your first name. Your choice. You do have one, don't you?"

"No one has used my first name in a decade or more." He gave up the intimidation route and sat at the table, picking up and biting into an apple. The juicy sweetness burst onto his tongue. Beatrice had her chestnut colored hair pulled back and up; a piece fell down and she tucked it behind her ear. He followed the movement with his eyes, brushing over the delicate skin of her neck.

There were a few streaks of grey beginning to show near her

temples, but he thought they only added to her attractiveness.

I bet she tastes like apples...

"How sad for you. Tell me, what is it?" She paused and turned to him, startling him from his thoughts.

"You want to say my name, *huh*?" He couldn't help it, the words popped right out of his mouth before he could stop them. This woman was disarming him. He wasn't sure who was more shocked at his attempt at flirting—Beatrice or himself. From her file, he knew she was two years older than his own forty-eight.

Her shock quickly faded into a smile and laughter, and it was a sight to behold. She was beautiful in her anger, but her joy made her stunning.

"You deserve to have a woman say your name." His face heated like he was sixteen again and talking to a girl for the first time. His brain went on vacation.

"Fisher," he managed to choke out.

"Fisher Jackson. Has a nice ring to it." She was putting the green beans into a big dish and covering them with sauce.

Oh yes...

"Don't tell anyone or use it in front of the team." She stared at him, raising an eyebrow in the same manner Mic did. "Please," he added quickly. While her anger had been beautiful, he didn't want it directed his way. Standing, he was much closer to her. As he moved to toss the core into the garbage, she stopped him with a hand on his forearm. Her skin was naturally fair, next to his darker skin, it looked porcelain and delicate. He tried to only see her hand and not imagine what the rest of her would look like; her bare, white body pressed against his own darker skin. This was Mic's aunt, not someone he should be fantasizing about. He was having trouble focusing on the conversation.

"I won't use your name in front of the others, Fisher. Will you tell me why?" Her eyes burned with curiosity.

"Back before Steel, when I was just a regular Army grunt, the other men called me Fisher King. I was good at tracking and everything that went with it. My name was spoken with fear on the other side of the line. When I was transferred, I stopped using the name." He tossed what was left of the apple into the trash and left the kitchen. He saw where Mic got both her beauty and balls, but Beatrice still had to go. It wasn't safe for her here, or for him. She was entirely too attractive.

****

Jordon tucked his M-4 tight into his shoulder and sighted down range. Here he was, underground in a military bunker the likes of which he didn't think existed outside of the movies. The range itself was damn impressive, benches separated by dividers and equally spaced. The targets were on motorized tracks that could be positioned wherever the shooter wanted. Low lights and sound suppressing acoustics made it a grunt's dream. This was just the range; down on Level Three was the gym area and a freaking pool. He would be partaking of that later tonight. Swimming had a way of sapping every last once of energy. Unless he was fall-on-your-ass-exhausted, he didn't think he'd be sleeping.

Mic was haunting him; he couldn't keep his eyes off her, trailing them over all of the places he wanted to put his hands. The woman had done something to him last night when he'd had her under him, her skin against his palms. There was no going back for him, no matter what he had told her and Pierce.

"Yo! Jordon! What the fuck are you doing man?" Flynn shouted at him, bringing him back to the present. It was then he realized he hadn't fired a single round.

"What?"

"Where are you, dude You sat there on that rifle so long we thought you exchanged rings or some shit. Are you going to fire that weapon, boy-o, or fuck it?" Flynn mouthed off in typical Flynn style.

Jones joined in on the fun in a rare moment of levity for him. "Maybe he will, but I don't think it's that rifle he wants to make it with. I think boy-o here has a thing for Mic."

They all surrounded him, one by one, mouthing off and busting his balls. He didn't bother to defend himself or deny it, it would be as effective as giving an addict another hit. Instead, he pulled back the slide and loaded a round. Tucking the rifle into his shoulder, he stood in off-hand position—right hand on the pistol grip, left hand on the forward hand grip, his feet shoulder-width apart. He balanced lightly on the balls of his feet and rapidly fired.

Not really aiming and not adjusting between rounds, he just fired, one round after another, the recoil knocking into his shoulder, burning slightly and stinging. His world narrowed down to his sights and the target down range. The loud shots echoed even with his ear protection, drowning out his thoughts for the first time that day. His vision continued to tunnel and focus, until he clicked empty.

Empty shells were rolling across the concrete with a soft hollow metal sound and smoke stung his eyes. His world was slowly opening up; he became aware of his breath and heartbeat, and he could hear the echo in his head. Taking his ear plugs out and letting them hang on his neck he returned the stares of the others.

Pierce was the first to speak. "Well. Guess we won't pick on you about Mic anymore, Jordon." Jordon looked at their shocked faces, not understanding the source of it. "What are you talking about? What did I do?" he asked, breathless still.

"Look at your target," Rook spoke up.

Jordon turned and hit the button to bring the little paper man closer. His mouth fell open in disbelief. For not paying attention to where his shots were going, he did a damn fine job. Nearly every round was in the center mass; those that weren't were solid head or neck shots.

"Well, damn. Who are you pissed off at?" Mic chimed in out of nowhere. They had all been so focused on his target, no one heard her come in. On second thought, Rook didn't seem surprised, but it was hard to tell with him. A rock showed more emotion.

"No one. Just practicing," Jordon said. Flynn choked on a laugh, trying and failing to disguise it as a cough.

"Looks like I missed the training again." Mic turned her back to Jordon and focused on the newbie. "Rook, did you have a go yet?"

Flynn came over and patted Jordon's shoulder. Leaning close, he whispered in his ear, "Don't worry, she still likes you best."

Jordon dropped the barrel of his rifle down and quickly knocked Flynn right in the nuts. Clasping his abused jewels, Flynn staggered over a few feet, gasping and supporting himself with one hand on the wall.

"What the hell?" Mic snapped.

"Accident, Staff Sergeant," Jordon said as sweetly as he could manage.

"You going to make it Flynn?" she asked him.

"Copy, Staff Sergeant," Flynn gasped out, bravely standing.

Shaking his head, Rook took his place and began firing down the line. Mic stood back, her arms crossed over her chest. She was watching his form and his aim. He was textbook perfect. The man seemed to be exceptionally proficient at anything he set out to do.

Jordon ground his teeth in irritation.

****

I stood back and watched the men; there was something going on. They had all been very relaxed until I came in, other than Jordon who was flushed and tense. It didn't take a genius to figure it out, since everyone had shut up when I'd walked into the range. They were giving Jordon shit about me. We had a serious problem if the others were all picking up on whatever this was. It was bad enough that Pierce had walked in on us. If the others sensed something was going on, sure as shit Jackson did as well.

I didn't have time for this high school drama bullshit. I had the new guy to train and a cartel to make a grease spot of. Shaking off the thoughts of Jordon and all that he entailed, I focused on Rook.

His stance was perfect, each round going exactly where it should. Nothing seemed to faze him. I needed to shake him up somehow. Knock him off-kilter and see what was really inside him. A plan began to form, but I needed to talk to Jackson first. After dinner seemed like a good time, once he was full of turkey and apple pie.

Chapter 9

Flynn was once again setting the table. Aunt Beatrice had gone all out. What must be a thirty pound turkey took center stage on the table, surrounded by all manner of traditional side dishes. Green bean casserole and sweet potatoes with marshmallows. A gravy boat brimming with golden brown deliciousness. Cranberry sauce and mashed potatoes. Everything we all loved about the holiday was spread out before us on a glorious culinary playground.

"Aunt Beatrice, you've outdone yourself. This looks amazing." I took my seat and looked around, trying to decide where to start. Too much food with too small of a plate.

"We have five years to make up for. This is just dinner; you haven't seen the desserts yet." She smiled so broadly at us that I thought her face would stay that way. I looked around at everyone, seated together, enjoying each other's company, and this amazing meal. We were a family, but this made us really look like one.

"Thank you for this, Beatrice, but you know it doesn't change anything," Jackson said softly. Aunt Beatrice blatantly ignored him.

"I don't know where to start...," Flynn said, looking overwhelmed.

"Start with this." Aunt Beatrice handed him a meat fork and a carving knife, pointing at the turkey.

He looked terrified, but took the tools. He stood and examined the turkey, no doubt deciding how to execute his plan of attack. He moved to stab the fork into the turkey, but before he could, Jackson stood and took the fork and knife from him.

"Sit down boy, let me show you how it's done." Jackson quickly and confidently carved the turkey with precision. Aunt Beatrice sat back and watched him do it, even though I knew for a fact she was perfectly capable of carving a turkey.

Interesting...

Jordon was sitting across from me; Rook was to my left and Pierce on my right. Aunt Beatrice was at one end, with Jackson on the opposite end. It felt like we were in some sort of fucked up, Norman Rockwell painting. All happy family and smiles, except with lots of weapons and proficiency with explosives.

I was savoring a bite of the tender, gravy soaked turkey when I felt something touch my foot. I looked up and Jordon was staring at his plate, not looking at me at all. It definitely came from across the table, not to the side. Flynn was beside Jordon and I almost didn't put it past him to be screwing with me. When the foot trailed up my leg, I knew it wasn't Flynn. Deciding to have a little fun I spread my legs apart a little farther, letting him get to my thigh. Jordon's face was flushing slightly. He was doing a good job of ignoring me, deep in conversation with Flynn about the latest mods available for our M-4's.

Slipping my left hand under the table, I placed my hand on his ankle, just above his boot. I felt his whole leg tense as he froze. He was doing a damn good job of not looking at me, which made this easy and delightful. Quickly palming an ice cube from my glass with my right hand, I ran my left hand slowly up and under his pant leg. I could feel the hair there tickling my palm. His skin was very warm and firm under my hand. When I had his pant leg pushed up high enough, I slid the ice cube under the edge of his boot and made sure it stuck on the sensitive skin near his ankle. He jerked back sharply, but I held on to his leg, pushing the cube down deeper from the outside of his boot.

I stared at him, letting my smile stretch my face. I let go of his foot and picked my fork up again. Returning to my turkey, I enjoyed seeing him turn beet red and quickly excuse himself. Mark one in the win column for me.

Pierce was looking at us sideways, taking in my satisfied grin and Jordon's sudden exit.

"Something happen, Mic?" he asked me.

"Not a thing, Pierce, not a thing." He didn't look like he believed me, but I didn't really give a crap. I was done with this day.

It was then that I noticed the looks passing between Jackson and my aunt. If that wasn't a case of two people making eyes at each other, I didn't know what was. I felt like the whole unit was turning into a soap opera and I was not a fan.

Just as Jordon returned to the table, an alarm began to sound on Jackson's phone. The high-pitched screech was broken up only by shrill beeps.

Seemingly not worried about the alarm, Jackson calmly checked his phone, ending the grating noise with a practiced swipe.

"We have incoming. Beatrice, go to your room and stay there until I come get you." His possessive tone had us all raising eyebrows. He gave us no time to comment.

"Mic, we need to get the room downstairs prepped for a visitor. Get the team on it. You're coming with me to greet our guest. Jordon, you too." Jackson stood and walked out of the room. We did what any good soldiers would do: we followed.

****

After giving the others their instructions, I geared up and waited just outside the elevator in the parking area with Jordon. We both had our tactical hoods on, covering our faces except for our eyes; our helmets covered the rest of our heads. We were dressed the same, with no skin or identifying marks showing. Jackson had only said this visitor was being delivered by the local PD on orders from the DoD and that we needed to be anonymous.

Jackson had quickly put on his BDUs with his rank displayed. Jordon and I flanked him, looking every bit the black ops assassins we were. With gloved hands clutching our MP-5s on their slings, the matte black weapons and our black clothes would be enough to intimidate nearly anyone—which was precisely the point.

"Don't speak. I'll handle the exchange. Mic, do you have zip ties ready? They'll want their cuffs back." I showed him the plastic strips I had in my pants pocket. "I know you want to know what's going on, but there's no time to explain. Just stand there and look scary."

"Copy." I muttered into my hood. Jordon echoed my response. Using the remote, Jackson lowered the floor of the garage and we walked up the ramp. Once we reached the top, he raised the floor back up, quickly hiding the entrance. After this, the locals would know that that was a safe house of sorts, but they didn't need to know all of our secrets. Pressing the button on the wall, Jackson raised the garage door and we waited. The cold night air hit us in a chilling blast. It was raining steadily, making the cold worse with the dampness. The only sounds were our breathing and the rain on the metal roof of the garage.

We didn't have to wait long. Headlights shone through the darkness, coming steadily closer.

"Show time," Jackson spoke over his shoulder at us. Jordon and I raised our rifles, the effect more for appearances then any real threat.

The standard police cruiser pulled to a stop, splashing muddy water across the gravel as it hit a puddle. Two sheriff's deputies exited the car: one was older and obviously in charge, the other was young and fresh looking with just enough shine worn off to make him dangerous. He looked like someone who was willing to do whatever he needed to do to make a name for himself.

Opening the rear door of the cruiser, the younger deputy pulled out a hooded and handcuffed man who was bandaged in a few places and walked with a heavy limp. He was on the short side and a little soft around the middle. Otherwise, there wasn't much to note about him. Judging by the little of his skin I could see, he was Mexican. The pieces began to fall into place in my mind like dominos.

"Here's your delivery. I want to state for the record, we do this under protest," the younger deputy gruffly said. Someone had their panties in a wad today. Guess he wasn't used to dealing with terrorists or drug dealing scum-bags like we were. I decided to cut him some slack based on his inexperience.

"Tie him." Jackson waved me forward. Slipping the zip ties from my pocket, I turned the man around so his cuffed hands were facing me. He began to struggle when I slipped a tie around his wrist.

"Hold him," Jackson said to Jordon, who did just that. I met Jordon's eyes over the man's head. I expected him to look nervous, but he was resolute. His trademark determination came to the forefront. I tightened the zip ties, and caught the deputy's eye, pointed to the cuffs. Jordon kept a firm grip on the man's arm.

"Un-cuff him, and you can be on your way," Jackson said, never relaxing his rigid stance of authority. The older sheriff no doubt knew exactly who was in charge here. It didn't stop him from trying to push a little.

"What're you going to do with him?" the older sheriff asked, as the younger deputy retrieved his cuffs.

"It's classified," Jackson answered simply, indicating for Jordon to haul the bound man into the garage.

"It don't sit right with me, leaving him here with you people like this," the sheriff said, as he handed Jackson a folder. "This is his chart from the hospital."

Jackson cocked his head to the side, silently studying the man, before answering him and taking the folder.

"This man is a threat to national security. That is all, Sheriff. I suggest you be on your way now." Jackson waved us inside. Jordon perp-walked the man into the garage and I hit the button to shut the door. Jackson waited until he heard the cruiser driving away before he pressed his comm.

"Jones, we clear?"

"Copy that, Master Sergeant," came the muffled reply. Jackson lowered the garage floor again and we marched our prize down into the depths.

Chapter 10

We went down to Sub-Level Three and into the sparring area to the side of the track. The men had rolled the mats up and pushed them aside, as the concrete floor would be easier to clean up. A lone chair sat in the middle. Most of the lights were turned off, creating strange shadows just like when I was running. This day would be ending quite differently from last night though. Instead of Jordon and me hitting the floor and ending in a kiss, there was a good chance that blood would be dropping onto the floor in moments.

Jordon and I marched the man to the chair, roughly shoving him down. I tied his legs to the chair. I motioned to Jordon, pointing to the man's head. Jordon got the idea and placed the barrel of his pistol against the man's forehead. It was the universal language for 'move and you die.' I cut the zip tie on his wrists and roughly pulled his arms behind the chair. I twisted his wrists into a stress position, the backs of his hands facing each other, before re-tying them. The man let loose a low groan. There must have been something in his chest that was hurt; pulling his arms back caused him pain.

Leaving him bound and helpless, we left the room. Jackson was standing just outside the door along with the others. I pulled my hood down and off my face as soon as I could. I hated wearing it as it made my claustrophobia rear its stupid fucking head.

"Okay, Master Sergeant, who is he and why do we have him?" I asked.

"I don't have a name for him. He was found in your aunt's yard, still alive and playing possum. The local PD had him in the hospital getting patched up before the clean-up team arrived."

The information and all of its implications hit me like a brick to the head. This man had information, information we desperately needed for a successful mission.

"Well, looks like we get to have a party," Flynn piped up. He was trying and failing to inject humor into a morbid situation.

"Are we going to torture this man?" Rook asked. I was waiting for him to voice something. The man in that room would provide me with two pieces of information; intelligence on the Vega cartel and how Rook would handle interrogations. I threw my previous half-formed plan out the window. This was almost better than anything I could have come up with for Rook. Happy day.

"Yes," I said simply. In combat, we had all seen things that happened and were against the rules. You live with it and move on. This wasn't combat though; this was going to be cold-blooded torture. Not something I was particularly a fan of, but it had its uses. "That going to be a problem?"

"No, ma'am," Rook answered in his typical style. Fine by me.

"Get in there and get started. I want reports every hour. Don't kill him." His orders given, Jackson left the room.

****

Jordon stood quietly by, taking it all in. Mic had told him someday that he would be asked to hold the bag or the bucket of ice water. Somehow he thought they had moved beyond that point. He had visions of pliers and blow torches in his head. To say he wasn't scared would be a lie. He wasn't going to let it stop him; this needed to be done. They were running out of time to hit the cartel. It was imperative they hit first, and hit hard. There would be no second round with them. If so much as one family member survived, this would never be over. Jordon thought back to when Mic was on that operating table, seeing her burning with fever and in agony. He saw Phillips's body, lying headless in a pool of blood. He felt the rip and burn of the bullet tearing through his own shoulder.

His course set; he pulled his tactical hood back over his face and was the first one through the door and into the room.

****

"Strip him," I said. I watched Jordon and Pierce advance on the man, knives in hand. They cut his clothes from his body, leaving his stained and tattered briefs on. That was a vison none of us wanted to see. I lowered the temperature on the thermostat, making the already cold room even more frigid.

The man seated before me was covered in bruises and blood and we hadn't even touched him yet. There was fresh blood seeping from a bandaged wound on his chest, cuts on his arms, and heavy thick bruises on his ribs. One leg was bandaged from ankle to knee, explaining the limp. He was giving us a lot to work with here.

"Do you speak English?" I asked him. I kept my voice calm and even; there was no point in yelling. The only sounds in the room were the heavy breathing of the man on the chair and the whisper of cloth as the men shifted around.

"*Si.*" Of course, he spoke English, but answered me in Spanish.

"Tell me your name." It was very deliberately not a question.

"Armando," he said, offering no last name.

"Tell me your last name." I walked closer to him, tapping my knife on my belt, letting him hear the metal sound. His breathing picked up and sweat beaded on his forehead.

"Fuentes. Armando Fuentes." Bingo. Using hand signals to Jones, I mined a phone call. I needed him to call the DoD and run the name. Jones left the room at a jog.

"Do you know who I am, *Señor Fuentes*?" I didn't bother to disguise my voice, though I made sure my hood was secure over my face. Looking at the men around me, their faces were also covered other than their eyes.

I ripped the hood from his face, letting him see who surrounded him. Recognition dawned in his eyes. Along with knowledge.

Seeing his face for the first time, I memorized his features: a nose that had been broken several times, a wide mouth, and flat lips. His dark bloodshot eyes burned with hate and fear. His dirty hair was overly long and matted to his head with sweat.

Jones came back into the room, his face tight with anger. Stopping close to me he leaned down and whispered in my ear.

"They took the call, but hung up as soon as I told them his name and asked them to run it. We're on our own here, Mic." I patted Jones's shoulder in thanks and took a careful step toward Armando.

"I will only ask one more time. Do you know who I am?" I showed him the knife in my hand, letting the light hit the blade and reflect onto him.

"Si. You are *El Acero*, Steel," he said in his pain-filled voice.

"Smart man. Now, we could go around in circles here, but I'm thinking you already know what I need to know. Will you tell me or do things have to become... unpleasant?" I motioned to Jones, who walked to the table they had set up. On it were two Bunsen burners and a variety of knives and some tools you'd find in any garage: pliers, wrenches, hammers of various weights and sizes. An ax.

Jones lit the burners, their dancing flames casting shadows on us all. The darkness of the large room was broken only by the sputtering, flickering lights. The wafting scent of the butane mingled with the stench of sweat and blood.

"I am a soldier of the Vega cartel, you do not scare me." His bravado was expected; they all said that. Even when they were pissing themselves they said it.

"Get the water," I ordered.

Pierce left the room and came back a minute later with a five gallon bucket of ice water. Walking directly to Armando, he poured half of it over his head. He didn't make a sound beyond a sharp gasp. He just sat there, dripping and shivering. His skin was pebbled with goose bumps and blood oozed out from under his bandages, which gave me an idea. I took a pair of latex gloves off the table and pulled them on with a snap. He jumped at the sound.

"Those bandages don't look so good, Señor Vega." I started with the one on his chest, jerking it off and taking chest hair with it. He flinched, but didn't react otherwise. Under the bandage was a neat bullet hole, tightly closed with evenly-spaced stitches. No wonder we left him there, he took a solid hit to the chest. How he was even walking around I wasn't sure. Must have been one of those miracle wounds. They look bad, but miss everything vital. Good for us, bad news for him.

I knelt at his feet and started on the one on his leg, ripping and tearing the tape off as harshly as I could. He groaned when I probed the wound with my gloved fingers. He had taken several more rounds in his leg. He was either the luckiest or un-luckiest bastard I'd ever seen. Two more bullet wounds went through his calf.

"Piss poor shooting, boys, but your poor aim is working out in our favor," I said to the men around me.

"That wasn't us. We don't aim for the legs," Jones said, even though I already knew that.

"So, Señor Vega, did your own men shoot you? Was it on purpose?" I asked. "Give me a knife, a small one." Jordon handed me a small hunting knife, hilt first.

"Crossfire," Armando gasped as I began cutting his stitches out. The wound immediately popped open and wept blood.

"How unfortunate." The stitches gave easily under the sharp knife. I finished with his leg and moved to his chest. I caught the edge of the wound, taking a bit of skin with the black thread. He grunted, but didn't scream.

"These wounds look nasty, I think we should wash them out." Keeping my gloves on, I retrieved a can of salt from the table. Showing him what it was, I let the knowledge of what was coming register in his brain. "This might sting a bit." Without preamble, I poured salt into the wound on his chest. He jerked and thrashed around, scraping the chair across the concrete floor.

"Hold him." Rook was the first there, pushing down on Armando's shoulders. I pressed the heel of my hand on the wound, viciously grinding in the salt. This time he howled and screamed. Snot and tears were running down his face, and he was breathing so fast I was worried he might hyperventilate.

Backing away from him, I gave him a few moments to come around; the pain had sent him to the brink of unconsciousness. I stripped my gloves off and threw them on the table. Jordon met my eyes and I was pleased to find no judgement there.

Rook stepped forward, slipping on gloves as he went. He swiftly assessed Armando's vitals.

"His heart rate is very high." He slipped a blood pressure cuff around the prisoner's arm, quickly pumping it and getting the results. "Blood pressure is elevated, but not dangerously so. His heart is stressed, but not in danger of giving out. Yet. As long as his bleeding doesn't increase too much more, he shouldn't die on us." He stepped away, flipping through the hospital chart.

Armando's breathing slowly calmed and he appeared to be dozing off. Pain and the stress of shock was damn exhausting. I'd give him a few minutes then we'd wake him up.

"Put his hood back on," I ordered. Jones stepped forward and took the black canvas bag from me, slipping it back over Armando's head with practiced ease.

Motioning for the others to follow, I left the room. Propping against the cold wall in the hallway, the men fanned out around me.

"Give him about ten minutes, then toss the rest of that water onto him," I instructed Pierce who was still holding the bucket of ice water.

"What do you hope to gain from this, Mic?" Jones asked.

"I would think it would be fairly obvious." I might have the hand for it, but I had never enjoyed torture. It made me sick and disheartened. Even though it gave me a hollow feeling in the pit of my stomach, I did the necessary deed. Usually we got information through some scare tactics and small pain without having to resort to jumper cables or metal spikes. There was one time that I had to pull a guy's fingernails off, two nails in and he sang like a canary.

"Maybe, but explain it anyway," Jordon joined in.

"We need a way into that village. We need to know when and where Adolfo Vega and Mercedes will be. I need to save my aunt and, in the process, us." I hated explaining myself to anyone; but in this instance, I suppose it was necessary. They needed a little reassurance.

"Works for me," Jones said, pulling his tactical hood back on his face.

"You don't have to do it all, we can take turns or something," Jordon said so quietly, I almost didn't hear him.

"No. I won't ask you to do torture while I stand back and watch. That's not fucking happening. End of discussion," I snapped at him. He visibly jerked back at the force in my words, his cheeks flushing in anger. I purposefully turned my back on him.

Just what the hell did he take me for?

"Time is up," Pierce said, going back into the room.

I followed him in and watched as he threw the water on Armando with as much force as he could muster. Armando jerked awake, gasping and thrashing against his bonds. The water had washed some of the salt from his wound; fresh blood ran down his chest and mixed with the water. Pinkish water puddled on the floor under him, reflecting the flames of the Bunsen burners. It was both beautiful and terrifying.

"How you doing over there, Señor Vega?" It was incredibly ironic. He was bleeding, dripping wet, and freezing cold. Add in the pain from his wounds and he was having just a dandy time. I didn't give a fuck; every wound was deserved and every pain-filled moment was justice. I kept seeing that old man brutally executed in front of his wife, his blood and grey matter spattering her distraught face. I felt no guilt. I would later, but right now, in this very moment, I felt justified in each wound and agonizing act I would inflict.

"I have nothing to say to you, *pinche puta*." His hood was soaked and stuck fast to his face, suctioning with each open-mouthed desperate gasp.

"Ok then, let's move on." I went back to the table, beyond your standard torture implements there was a selection of plastic bottles. Each contained a different acidic or corrosive liquid.

"Over here, Señor Fuentes, I have a variety of liquids to choose from; rubbing alcohol, acetone, paint thinner, bleach, and even ammonia. You can easily buy most of these at any retailer in the country, but when applied correctly... or should I say... incorrectly, they cause severe pain or even blindness."

Grabbing a bottle and a small knife, I slowly advanced on Armando. I could feel the others watching me, waiting to see what I was going to do. The weighted silence was broken only by the sound of my boots on the wet floor and Armando's heavy breaths. The tension in the room was palpable.

I placed the bottle on the floor behind his chair and using the small knife, cut the ties to his hood. Before lifting it, I motioned the others to move out of his line of sight. I wanted the first thing he saw to be the darkness and flickering flames of the burners. This wasn't just about inflicting pain, this was about getting into his head and injecting fear deep into his psyche. Fear is the world's greatest motivator.

I snatched the hood off in a sudden, fast motion and I dropped it on the floor with a wet *plop*. Picking up the bottle and keeping the knife in my other hand, I stepped around in front of him.

"Here, take a whiff; tell me what you think." I uncapped the bottle and placed it under his nose. The strong fumes made him jerk his head back and away.

"This stuff is pretty effective; removes nail polish, and when put on an open wound, you'd think the fires of hell reside within you." I let the idea sink into his brain—the knowledge that I was about to pour acetone into his body. His breathing picked up again and I could see his pulse racing through the skin of his neck.

"Tell me where exactly to find Adolfo Vega and that bitch Mercedes and I will put this away. Answer my questions and I won't dump this entire bottle on your leg." I watched his eyes; he wasn't going to give an inch. His words confirmed it.

"Fuck you." He spat at my feet, bloody spit hitting my boot. Well then, guess that was answer enough.

"Boys, hold him." Rook again stepped forward along with Jordon; I spared them a glance. Rook looked the same as ever, solid and unfazed, which made me think maybe he'd been in a room like this before. I would have to remember to ask him. Jordon was as blank as I'd ever seen him. I didn't need to worry about Jones, Flynn, or Pierce, we'd done this dance before.

I knelt next to Armando's leg. "Last chance," I said, looking up at him. He closed his eyes and leaned his head back as far as he was able.

Using one hand, I pulled open the wound that was closest to his knee and deftly poured the acetone inside. His muscles stood out under his skin, veins popping in his neck; he shrieked and wailed. He thrashed violently, jerking his leg, trying to escape the liquid. He shredded his throat with the volume he was producing. My head and ears pounded with the sound. His skin began to split open where the zip ties held him to the chair and still he screamed. The bullet wound rapidly swelled and turned a fiery shade of red, blood and acetone mixing together to run down his leg and onto my hands.

Shit, I forgot my gloves…

"Another?" I asked him. He was panting now, completely gone with the pain and shock. I glanced at my bloody hands, noticing that the fine lines within my palms were filled with his blood; the creases were stained brown and red. The sight bothered me, but I pushed it aside. Now was not the time.

"*Si…estoy loco…*," he gasped out, turning his head and spitting again.

"I'm not much on Spanish, but I think he just said yes," Flynn said.

"I have to agree with you there." I sloshed the bottle a bit; there was just enough left for another dose.

The lower wound was ragged and torn, not a neat hole like the other one. Using two fingers to spread it open further, I looked up and saw Jordon staring at me. The look on his face was not in my favor. I didn't have the time or energy to deal with his moral compass.

Not hesitating, I poured the last of the acetone into the wound. Armando's body tensed like a live current was running through it. He screamed and thrashed like a fish on a hook. His head was thrown back and his entire body was quivering and shaking with the shock of it. He was completely washed out, even his lips were white. I saw his expression change and quickly got out of the way.

"Watch it!" I shouted to the others, as Armando leaned to the side and vomited bile. Gagging and choking, he kept at it, until gratefully, he passed out.

"Give him a few minutes; if he doesn't talk when he comes to, someone will need to help me take his teeth." Anger brought on by regret tightened my voice.

I left the room; Armando wasn't the only one who needed a minute. No matter how warranted I felt my action were, I was still torturing someone. I paced back and forth in the empty hallway, forcing myself to focus on the old man who was executed, seeing Aunt Beatrice in his place. Or Jordon. Or any of the men. Myself. I would do whatever it took to save Aunt Beatrice. I would gladly throw my soul down upon the pyre of evil if it meant that she lived.

The door opened and Flynn waved me back inside.

Armando was mostly awake, his chin resting on his chest. Spit and drool hung out of his mouth, leaving a slimy trail down his chest. His leg muscles were twitching with painful spasms of palsy, blood freely flowing from the wounds.

I tapped Rook on the shoulder. "Hold his head back." I selected a hammer and small chisel from the tools on the table. I had seen this done, but had never actually had to do it myself. Often the threat of having your teeth knocked out with a hammer and chisel would get more results than actually doing it. I was afraid this man was finally going to make me do it.

"Ready, *Senor Fuentes*?" I showed him what I was holding: a small sharp chisel for woodworking and a five pound ball-peen hammer.

"Wait," he begged.

Internally, I sagged with relief. "I'm waiting. But my patience is wearing thin." I forced annoyance to sharpen my tone.

"My name... is not Vega." He licked his cracked lips, pausing between words.

"Come again?" Flynn said, disbelieving.

"My name is…Armando Villalobos. I am an... informant." My fingers loosened their grip and I nearly dropped the hammer in my shock. Of all the things I expected to come out of his mouth, this was not it.

"Explain. Fucking right now!" I stopped myself from smashing his face with the hammer, sure that he was lying to me. There was no way this motherfucker was the plant. If he was, it meant I just tortured and abused a protected individual of the United States and Mexican governments.

Fuck me. I wonder if they will execute me or just ship me off to rot in prison?

"When I was a young man, I joined the Vega cartel; the money was good. I had a wife and a child. A year ago, I saw a man from a rival cartel get his legs hacked off with a dull ax. After that, I couldn't live with my choices anymore. God would damn me to burn in hell for what I had done." He stopped and took a few deep breaths. It was a good story; if he was just delaying, he was doing a damn fine job. The silence in the room was absolute.

"I turned myself into the police. I prayed that my family would survive. I knew I would be killed in prison. Before I could be sent to my death, an American man came to see me in my cell. He explained how I could help the Americans and the Mexican police. I would stay in the cartel and report back to you Americans." Turning my back to him, I dropped the hammer and chisel onto the table. I felt like being sick myself.

What have I done? What if he's lying?

"Stop there. I'm going to verify your story. Pray to God I don't find out you're lying to me. If you are, I'll use this chisel and hammer on your fucking toes one at a time and work my way up from there. Got me?" I said, leaning close to his face, making sure he saw the truth of my threat in my eyes. I didn't think it was possible for his skin to bleach of the tiny bit of color he had remaining; I was wrong.

"All of you, out." Once in the hallway, I jerked my hood down off my face. I felt as if I was suffocating under it; my breath was coming fast and loud. I turned to Jones. "I need you to do whatever magic you do; verify his story. Page Jackson, I need him down here." He rushed off.

"Wait!" I shouted. "Put Doctor Hamilton on stand-by. If this guy is telling the truth, I need the doc to un-do the damage I just did." Jones nodded his understanding and hit the button on the elevator.

"Mic, there is no way you could have known," Pierce said, clasping my shoulder. He had a way of seeing to the root of a person.

"I'm aware of that." I shook his hand off. I stood with my back to the wall, *thunking* my helmet off the cement. Beating my head against the wall wasn't going to really help; I would just get a headache and be more pissed off.

Pierce leaned closer to my face. He grabbed my helmet with his hands "Mic, stop. Don't do this to yourself. We were in there with you; we're just as responsible for this as you are."

When I shook him off and went back to pacing, he stepped back to stand with Jordon and the others. Giving me space, they talked amongst themselves. My world narrowed down to the heavy sound of my boots on the floor and the ratcheting guilt of my thoughts.

"There will be no repercussions for your actions today, Staff Sergeant," Jackson said, startling me out of my pity party. "It didn't take Jones long; one call over the secure line to the DoD. Everything Señor Villalobos said is true."

"Fuck!" I shouted. My stomach turned; I had just tortured one of our own. I felt horrible, deep rooted anger. Why couldn't those DoD bastards just fucking help us for once? Jones called them before we starting working Armando over, but *no*, they wouldn't give us the time of day. Now, I'd tortured this man... for no reason.

"Calm your shit, Mic," Jackson ordered as he walked back toward the elevator. "Go in there and cut him loose. Doc Hamilton is on his way."

I met Jordon's eyes. What I saw there reflected what I felt inside, anger and confusion, misplaced blame and regret. It appeared we were on the same page. This is one of the things I liked best about Jordon, his face was an open book for me. He was closed off and stoic with the others, but when he looked at me, everything that was Jordon shined through.

As I pulled my hood back up over my face, I shoved the whispered thoughts of suffocation aside. I led my men back into the room and prepared to do what I had to.

****

Beatrice turned the TV on low, the talking heads on the news breaking the unending silence. It had been well over an hour, with no sound from anyone. The place felt like a tomb. When the others were around, the noise and constant bickering alleviated the suffocating closeness. Left alone in her room, she was at odds. One part of her wanted nothing to do with whatever was happening, but another part of her was innately curious.

A firm knock on her door broke her from her circling thoughts.

"Who is it?" Why she worried about who was at the door, she wasn't sure. There wasn't a safer place in the world.

"It's me." The deep voice had her blushing like a schoolgirl and fumbling at the door knob.

Opening the door, she was greeted by an impressive sight. Jackson in street clothes was intimidating; Jackson in his uniform had her breath catching and her heart racing. The camo pants and shirt clung to his large frame, highlighting just how massive and strong he was. You knew he was in command without even needing to see his displayed rank. His bearing screamed authority.

"So it is." Her heart might be racing, but her head was still in the game.

"May I come in?" He took his hat off and held it in front of him.

"Would I be a lady if I let a man into my room?" She asked cheekily.

"Are you a lady?" He asked softly.

"Not today." Opening the door wide, she stepped aside. Jackson brushed her arm as he walked past, making her skin break out in goosebumps.

Chapter 11

Armando sat and waited for her return, not that he had any other choice. His arms were numb; no doubt when they untied him he would be helpless for a while. He prayed they brought a doctor who had powerful pain killers. The pain in his leg was finally calming; he was bleeding the rest of the acetone out of his wounds. His chest was tight and sore. Assessing the rest of his body, he could not find one place that didn't scream or wither in agony.

The door opened and she stood in the open doorway, staring at him. He could only see her eyes, a damn shame such beautiful eyes were wasted on this vicious woman. He almost pitied Adolfo Vega. When this woman came for him, she would make him beg for death.

"Would you care to meet me, Señor Fuentes?" she asked, staring him directly in the eyes. Her voice was soft and even.

Not waiting for his reply, she released the strap on her helmet and dropped it at his feet with a heavy thud. One of the men near the door hit the light switch, flooding the room with near-blinding florescent light. He blinked against the glare, trying to clear the spots from his vision.

Her hair was blonde and still curly, even smashed flat and stuck to her head with sweat. There was a red mark across her forehead from her helmet. The rest of her face was still covered by the black half mask.

With bloodstained hands, she pulled the hood down, letting it hang limply around her neck. Fear knotted his stomach and turned his bowels to water. She had showed him her face and she had still called him Vega. His blood coated her skin and her eyes burned and flashed with anger. He had faced the cartel and seen some of the most fearsome men in the world, but this small female scared him more than all of them combined.

"You don't believe me. Just get on with it." Armando resigned himself to the inevitable: his teeth knocked out and his feet dismembered. Where she would go from there was no mystery. The tools on that table of death told their own story.

"Cut him loose, Corporal Jordon," she ordered. The big man with green eyes approached him with a knife. Armando tried not to quiver in fear or shame himself further. If he must die, he would attempt to do it with dignity. Confusion racked him as first his hands, then his legs, were freed.

"*Que?*" He gasped as feeling began to come back to his arms and hands. Stabbing pains marched up and down his limbs. He did not attempt to stand; he knew doing so was pointless.

"Your story checked out. A doctor is on his way. We're taking you to medical. Help him up, boys." She snapped her fingers and left the room. Two giants took each of his arms and stood him up. Immediately his legs crumpled under him. With a grunt, they hefted him higher and carried him from the room.

****

Jordon helped carry Armando to the elevator. Rook was on the other side, both of them getting soaked with water and blood. The man was shivering uncontrollably and slipping deeper into shock.

"Mic. How long until Doc Hamilton gets here?" Jordon asked, as they approached her waiting outside the medical center doors.

"Jackson called over to the compound. We have the jet, so he can't fly in. He's got a driver. Should be here in around two hours." She led the way into the center, slapping switches and blinding them all with the fluorescents. "Put him here." She walked around to the machines next to the gurney. Slipping on a pair of latex gloves, she got out an IV kit. "We'll stabilize him and get him prepped for the doc."

He and Rook lifted him and gently laid him on the gurney. Jordon stepped back out of the way. Mic and Rook seemed to have it well in hand.

"Let me do this, Mic," Rook said as he donned his own gloves. "I've got more advanced medical training than you. It's why I'm here, remember?"

"By all means." Mic stepped back to give the big man space. Rook rifled through one of those carts all hospitals seemed to have and selected a few vials. Rook was as competent as he was silent, filling syringes as Mic looked on.

Rook spoke softly to Armando. "Hold still, this might hurt. You're very dehydrated, which makes finding a vein harder." He held the man's arm against his body as he wrapped a tourniquet around his bicep. Feeling around the crook of his elbow, Rook found a vein, and got the IV started.

"You're good at that," Mic replied, as she handed him things as he asked for them. He pushed syringes into the IV port, one after the other. Armando's eyes flickered and he fell asleep.

Working together efficiently, they bandaged Armando's wounds and gave him a good wash down. Rook and Mic didn't seem to need to talk or the help of anyone else in the room.

"You two have this in hand. I'm out." Flynn backed out the door. Pierce saluted and followed. Jones had disappeared at some point while no one was paying attention.

Jordon was frustrated and pissed off. Rook had been here only two days and was already working closely with Mic as if they had been doing it for years. It had taken him months to get to that level of comfort with her. Jealousy twisted in his gut and he left without a word. If he had dared to open his mouth, whatever came out would have gotten him knocked flat, he was sure.

He allowed himself the small childish pleasure of slamming the door behind him. The metal clang echoed up and down the concrete hallway. The sound formless and untouchable; like his desire for Mic, loud and fierce, but unattainable.

****

"What was that about?" Rook didn't bother to look up from Armando's leg. He skillfully wrapped gauze around the wounds. He would leave the stitching for the doctor.

"Nothing I'm going to discuss. He seems stable. Stay here until Doc Hamilton arrives; then you're relieved. The doc will treat him and transfer him back to the compound. Then one of Jackson's flunkies in the NSA can pick him up and take him to a safe house until they can get his family out of Mexico. He was tortured, so he'll get a new life and new identity in America out of the experience."

I had to stop myself from screaming at Rook; he was not responsible for my mood. Fact is, I was. I surveyed the damage on Armando. For the most part, it was nothing that wouldn't heal; the wounds would close and scar. The cuts from the zip ties would scab over and grow shiny, new pink skin.

The damage this man suffered mentally at my hands would not, however, heal so easily. Would he have nightmares? Would he ever sleep again? The Vega family was responsible for a great portion of this man's suffering, but I had my own burden of the weight to carry.

"Copy that." Rook finished with the dressings, stripped off his gloves, and washed his hands in the nearby sink.

Ready to leave, I paused for a moment. We were alone and it gave me an opportunity.

"You've participated in torture before, haven't you?"

Waiting for his reaction, I was mildly surprised when I didn't get one. He looked at me; his face showed nothing, gave me nothing to go on, as he walked closer to me. "Do you mean, have I seen a man get his teeth knocked out? Or have sparking jumper cables applied to his testicles? Or heard a man pray for death to find him? Or better yet, been the one to hold the hammer or cables? Yes. I have."

I used my silence to hide my shock. His file showed nothing remotely close to any of those things.

Was the file even real?

"Get some rest, Staff Sergeant" He opened the door and pointedly waited for me to leave. "You look tired."

"This conversation isn't over, Rook," I barked over my shoulder as I strode out the door.

He smiled for the first time, showing two missing teeth. The empty gap was just about the size of the chisel I had nearly used on Armando. I opened my mouth to speak, but he shut the door in my face before I managed to form a sentence.

What the fuck?

Chapter 12

Jordon fell into bed, flopping backwards with his arms spread out. He had stripped to just his boxers. The cold air felt good on his overly-hot skin. He didn't know which way was up anymore. Mic had an aunt; they go save her, and she turns out to be as big of an ass-kicker as Mic. If that wasn't drama enough, he then willingly participated in the torture of another human being.

Phillips's death had fucked with them all. They were off their game, cut adrift. The guilt was eating them alive. He knew from talking to Flynn and Pierce that they blamed themselves for not getting to that field faster. He blamed himself for not aiming better. If he'd shot that bastard in the face instead of the arm, Phillips would still be alive.

Switching gears, he flashed back to last night when he'd had Mic under him, his hands on her silky skin, and her hot, wet lips pressed against his own. Just the memory had the power to get him hard all over again.

Grabbing his head, he groaned at the images his mind was replaying: her soft hair curled around his fingers, and her body arched up into his; pressed tight against him. She'd clung and grasped him, pulling him closer.

Lying there, he was practically panting like an untried boy. Whenever he was alone like this, she haunted him.

A knock at the door had him cursing. Looking down at his mostly naked body and tented boxers, he wasn't going to answer. Whoever was there could fuck off. He draped an arm across his eyes and tried to think of something else, anything other than Mic.

The sound of the door opening had him sitting up. "What the fuck?" He shouted before looking to see who was there.

"Having all the fun without me, boy-o?" Mic asked, standing framed in the doorway like a dream come to life. She looked the same, but something about her seemed different. More determined, if that was even possible.

"What are you doing here?" He asked, dragging a blanket over his lower half.

"I would think that's fairly obvious." Stepping all the way into the room, she shut the door, and with a loud click, locked it behind her.

"Not to me." He froze, afraid to move as she walked closer yet, stripping her shirt off as she did. A pink lacy bra cupped her full breasts, showing off the beauty that until now, he had only imagined. Her tattoos swept along her arms and shoulders, adding grace and near heart-stopping beauty. Turning her back, she showed him her wings; chain mail and rivets flowed down each side of her spine until they dipped into her pants.

"Bea. What are you doing?" She unclasped her bra before turning around and throwing it at him. He caught it purely by reflex, the material warm and shockingly soft.

"I'm done, Chris. I'm done telling myself no." She toed off her boots, her breasts bobbing as she bent over. He was frozen, unable to move. He was scared about doing this and terrified that he would fuck it up.

"Are you sure?" He forced himself to ask, even as he reached for her and drew her down on top of him. He delved his hands into her hair, loving how the curls wrapped around his fingers and clung. Burying his face in her neck he breathed deep, dragging her scent into his lungs in an attempt to keep her there. Without preamble, she slid her hand into his boxers, squeezing him tight.

"What do you think?" He gasped and took her mouth. She tasted sweet and fresh. Reaching down between their bodies, he unbuttoned her pants. Flipping her onto her back, he slid his hands down her soft legs, whisking her pants off. Sitting back on his heels, he stared at the feast before him; every inch of her skin begged for his lips... his touch.

"I think..." He spoke between kisses, making his way up her legs. Her skin was so warm and lush beneath his lips. She tasted so fucking good; he couldn't get enough, would never get enough. "You taste fucking amazing... I'm going to kiss..." He got to her lacy pink panties and allowed himself to enjoy the view for a brief moment. As pretty as they were, he wanted what was under them. "All of you. Until you beg me to stop. Then...I'm going to kiss you some more."

With a swift jerk he ripped off her panties. Wasting no time, he shoved her thighs wide and buried his face between them. Reaching his hands up, he palmed her breasts, squeezing and pulling in time with his mouth. Her moans shattered him; her begging nearly destroyed him. Her thighs squeezed his head tight, pressing him closer; her heels clasped together tight behind his back.

Jordon hummed against her and slipped two fingers inside her, curling the tips slightly. Pushing his fingers in and out of her, her muscles gripped his fingers tight. She arched off the bed and came against his mouth, screaming. He drew out her orgasm while she begged him to stop. Her legs were shaking against the sides of his face;

her hips were jerking back and forth, trying to get closer and move away at the same time. With one last lick, he let her come down.

He propped himself on one arm, licking his fingers and enjoying the sight of her, loving her face as he sucked his fingers clean. He wanted her to know he loved her taste, that he would be eating her often. She was flushed and a little sweaty. Her breasts rose and fell with her rapid breaths.

Moving over her, he brushed her hair off her face. No words were necessary in this moment as he kissed her tenderly. The force and duration of her orgasm had her relaxed around him. Her skin felt so right, so good against his own. Her breasts were smashed against his chest; her arms pulled him closer, urging him to fill her. With a smooth motion he did just that, sliding deep inside and fitting him perfectly.

This woman was made for him…

Jordon jerked awake, breathing hard. He looked around frantically, searching for Mic. She was gone. It had seemed so real. He could feel her skin, smell her on his hands and face.

What the fuck was happening to him?

****

I stripped and stepped into the shower. Leaning my head forward, I watched the blood turn the water pink as it swirled down the drain. I stood that way until the water turned cold. Washing quickly, I dried off and didn't even bother to dress. I curled up in bed, wrapping the quilt tight around me.

I let my thoughts drift and swirl as I tried to fall asleep. Almost instantly, my thoughts turned to Chris. I relived the kiss in the gym, every second… every press of his hands on my body. I let myself dream of what could be and what I really wanted, not just what I was forced to settle for.

Shoving useless thoughts aside, I rolled over and instead considered the Vega cartel. They held immense sway over their local village and the people there. The lives of all those innocent people hung in the balance, swinging like a pendulum. I feared that a misstep on my part would cause that pendulum to swing wide, crashing into the village and dragging those people to their deaths.

Chapter 13

Adolfo Vega stood in front of the large bay window in his study. Smoking a cigar, he waited for his lieutenant's report. The situation in the States worried him. He had given his word to Mercedes that Diego would be avenged. If it wasn't for the blood debt to a family member, Adolfo would not even bother. Getting involved in any feud was incredibly bad for business—but one with the Americans? They would be lucky to escape with their lives. A knock interrupted his thoughts.

"Enter." The man who came in was as sharp mentally as he looked physically. In a custom tailored three piece suit, Julio Vega was a cousin from his father's side. Behind that smooth veneer lurked a psychopathic murderer. Having a man like Julio on the payroll was advantageous, but he had to be handled correctly. Adolfo kept him on a tight leash; but just like an attack dog, he must be cut loose occasionally or he would lose his ability.

"What news do you have for me, Julio?" Turning from the expansive view, he ground his cigar out in a lead crystal ash tray. The sun shone through the crystal, throwing glimmering rainbows across the maple desk. "I hope you are here to tell me that Beatrice Michaels has taken her last breath."

"No, sir. Our team was eliminated. All dead." Julio's calm voice cut through Adolfo's own cool exterior. His temper rose, hot anger bubbling to the surface. Adolfo picked up his Zippo. It was a souvenir from his boyhood mentor. Flicking it open and closed, over and over... he began to pace.

"How?" Adolfo had his suspicions, but he needed to hear it from Julio. Stopping in front of the man, he flicked open the Zippo with this thumb and spun the flint in a smooth motion. Adolfo stared at the mesmerizing flames dancing in front of his eyes. He forced himself to look away and instead held the flame close to Julio's perfectly trimmed goatee.

"They beat us there. My men were waiting, but that bitch and her fucking mongrels were ready for us. Killed everyone and got the woman out." Julio moved back slightly, he didn't want his goatee to get singed. The smell of burning hair filled his nose, despite his efforts.

"We need to send another message. Get me on a plane to Ohio." Adolfo walked away. If he was going to Ohio to have some fun, he needed to get his kit ready. "Help me take down Steel, Julio, and you can have the bitch to do with as you please."

Julio's excited grin looked out of place; the manic within him was peeking out, eager at the prospect of coming out to play. "Are you sure you want to risk yourself by going personally?"

"Yes, this is something that I need to do myself. The message I intend to deliver is one I excel at sending." Adolfo left the study, heading to his garage and the toys there.

****

I had just finished my run and was stretching on the mat covering the bare concrete where hours ago, had been slick with blood. Dr. Hamilton had reported to me earlier that Armando was recovering quickly and other than a few scars, he would have no lasting damage from the torture.

I spread my legs wide and bent to one side; grasping my foot, I put my forehead to my knee. Switching to the other side, I repeated the motion. I was tense and worried, so I thought yoga might help. I moved onto my hands and knees and began *cat* and *cow*. Arching my back, then bowing it out, I let my body go and breathed deeply.

I was in *down dog* when I heard footsteps behind me. I looked between my legs and saw Jordon. He had stopped walking and was just standing there, not even trying to hide that he was staring at my ass.

"Can I help you with something, Corporal?" I snapped at him as I stood.

"*Uh*... yeah...sorry," he stuttered. Jones and Jackson want you... in the war room. The others are already there waiting."Grabbing at towel from the rack, I wiped my face and draped it around my neck. "Close your fucking mouth, Jordon. You look ridiculous with your tongue hanging out." I added a little strut to my walk as I passed him. If he wanted to stare, I'd give him something to stare at.

I didn't wait for him as I hit the button for the elevator. He ran in just as the doors were closing. We didn't speak on the short ride up, but I could feel him staring at me. I decided then and there, that when this mission was over, when my aunt was safe... I'd deal with Jordon once and for all.

Entering the war room, silence greeted me. The kind you get when you interrupt a conversation other people are having about you. I could feel them all thinking 'oh shit, did she hear us?'

"Spill it. What the fuck is going on?" The tension was so thick I could taste it.

"Sit down, Mic," Jackson said. Dread lined his voice like lead lines a coffin. "We're just waiting for your aunt,"

Aunt Beatrice came in just then, sitting next to me without having to be told. She raised an eyebrow at Jackson and when he ignored her, her foot began to tap beneath the table.

What the hell?

I needed to have a conversation with her and figure out just what the fuck was going on between her and my Master Sergeant.

"Jones, bring it up," Jackson ordered.

The computer tech swiveled around in his chair and tapped a few keys. The monitor came to life above us. At first it was just black and grey blobs; every few seconds it cycled and zoomed a little closer.

"What am I looking at?" I asked.

Aunt Beatrice's gasp beside me jerked my eyes back to the monitor. "That's my house. What are those men doing to my house?"

She clutched my hand as we watched the feed slow down, capturing every horrifying detail. Masked men smashed the windows apart and threw Molotov cocktails inside. One man stood apart from the others, smoking a cigar and watching the curtains catch fire. He slowly walked closer, playing with something in his hand. It was too dark to make out exactly what it was.

The masked men streamed past the lone figure, urging him to follow with hand gestures. He ignored them, and stood there watching the flames consume Aunt Beatrice's house, the same house she raised me in; the same house she had shared with my uncle.

She dissolved into tears, sobs wracking her body. I wanted to join her. Jackson stepped forward and drew her to her feet. He wrapped his big arms around her and held her close, cradling the back of her head with his giant hand. She just sobbed harder and clung to him.

I pushed the development of my aunt and Jackson to the side. I'd worry about her heart later. Right now, I needed to worry about her life. "Jones. Tell me."

"I'm running facial recognition now, but I can pretty much tell you that man is Adolfo Vega. He came personally to burn your aunt's house down." Jones's fingers were flashing across the keys: windows were popping up and closing faster than I could keep track of. "Looks like he's a pyromaniac. Fucker has been a fire bug for a long time. This cartel has a lot of arsons linked to them."

He flipped through pictures of burned homes, warehouses, and worst of all... people. Photographs filled the screen of people spread-eagle on the ground; their arms and legs were tied with ropes, and staked into the dusty earth. They were set on fire while they were still alive. Charred bodies forever screamed in pain, their blackened skin stretched and cracked open. Bones showed in places, and the clothing that remained was melted into their skin.

"It's going to be a pleasure to kill this motherfucker," Rook said, startling us all.

"How much longer do we have to wait, Jackson? How much more does this bastard have to do before we can cut his fucking head from his damn shoulders?" I advanced on him, anger rising and wiping away my reason.

"Bea Michaels, you stop right there." Aunt Beatrice placed a hand on my chest, stopping me from wringing Jackson's neck. "This man has his orders, same as you. I'm in agreement, screw the orders... but you can't do that."

"With all due respect, ma'am, no. We're going, with or without government sanction." Jordon had spoken my mind. I nodded to him, checking the faces of the others. They were grim, but determined. Jones stood, as did Rook and Pierce. We formed a wall of righteous fucking indignation.

"Master Sergeant, no more fucking around. We need to go," Pierce spoke up.

"What they said. Sorry boss." Flynn chimed in as well. They were a solid presence at my back. Rook didn't speak, just stood with us.

"Go. Get whatever information you need from Armando. GO!" Jackson shouted, pushing us from the room and into action.

Aunt Beatrice grabbed my arm, stopping me as I tried to follow the men out.

"You come back to me. You hear me, young lady? I expect to see you in the same condition as when you left." I hugged her, squeezing her hard and breathing in the scent of her perfume.

"I will. You want to tell me what's going on here?" I tilted my head at Jackson. She blushed from her neck up. She smoothed my hair, trying in vain to put it in some semblance of order. "Yes... well dear... I may be old, but I'm not dead yet."

She kissed my cheek and pushed me away. I shook my head at her as Jackson stood behind her, putting his big hand on her shoulder. She patted his hand and stared at me, waiting for me to say something. I couldn't think of anything to say that wouldn't make me a judgmental asshole, so I said nothing.

"I'll contact the Mexican police and make sure you have secure transport from the airport," he assured me as I clasped his hand and turned to my aunt.

"I'll see you soon. Jackson will keep you updated." I hugged her one last time and hurried out. The others would be waiting for me, anxious for orders... for a plan. But first, I needed as much information as Armando could give me.

Chapter 14

Back in the medical center, I sat next to Armando's bed. He was sleeping, but I wasn't about to wait. I shook his shoulder, deliberately choosing the one with the bullet wound.

Groaning, he came awake, but stiffened when he saw me. He was scared and tried not to show it. I guess I deserved that; I was the one who tortured him and I had just woke him using pain. "Sorry. Listen, we are leaving. I need everything you can give me and I need it right fucking now."

Jones came forward, preparing to write everything down and record it for good measure.

"What do you need, specifically?" Armando rasped. I held his cup of water for him, even bending the straw so he could reach it.

"I need in. What sort of security surrounds the village?"

"There are roadblocks on each of the two main roads going into the town. Men patrol the poppy fields and the area outside the village." He finished speaking and shifted around, trying to get more comfortable.

"Where does he sleep?" I didn't think I needed to say who I was talking about.

"He has a large house in the center of town. It was the mayor's... before Adolfo killed him."

"What else?" I was rushing him along. I didn't have time to play twenty fucking questions. The need to finish this once and for all was driving me forward.

"His house is very secure," Armando explained. "Guards and motion detectors, the works. It will be very difficult to get to him in his house."

"Then where?" I wasn't risking our lives more than necessary. The fucker was sure to have a weakness, it was just a matter of finding it.

"When he patrols the village and fields. He personally checks them daily. If one of your men is a sniper, it would be easy."

I looked at Jones; he nodded. A plan was beginning to form.

"What time does he do these patrols?" I wanted to be settled in place with plenty of fucking time to take care of this bastard and get out.

"Just after lunch. Unless it's raining, he's in the village first, then the fields."

"Thanks for your help. One question before we go. Why the fuck did you let me torture you? Why didn't you just tell us from the beginning who you were?" This question had been floating around in the back of my head.

"Would you have believed me?" He asked calmly.

"Probably not, but I would have checked it out before working you over." It was the truth and I saw the moment he realized that. "It's a good thing you're not in the cartel anymore; they've ruined your faith in humanity."

"True enough, *chica*. It never occurred to me to give you the benefit of the doubt. I am used to men who torture for entertainment alone."

"Get better; we'll talk soon." I patted him on the shoulder, the good one this time. "Let's go boys. We have work to do."

****

We quickly boarded the jet and flew to the compound, it was faster than driving and time was not on our side. It was a risk, but a necessary one. Most of our gear was there. Sure, we had things we could use at the Wonka House, but one thing we were superstitious about was our weapons.

"Get your shit; you have until this plane is re-fueled. Jones, I need maps of the area and best point of entry." The men hustled off the plane and into the hangar. I followed, but veered left. There was something I needed to get out of my cabin.

Unlocking the door, I went right to my bookcase, reached up, and grabbed the machete. Sliding it into its sheath, I threaded it onto my belt and tied it to my thigh. I would get rid of this machete when the cartel was dead and buried. Briefly, I considered taking Phillips's Sig, but decided to leave it where it was.

Jogging back to the hangar, I opened my locker and stripped down, I had no modesty in front of my men; the Army had taken care of that. Years of no privacy made it a non-issue anymore. Quickly changing into desert camo. I strapped on my vest and weapons.

"Desert gear, boys, and no shiny shit." The sun would easily catch and reflect off of anything. We would get into place at night, and stay in cover throughout the day. We needed to blend in with the landscape around us.

Things were moving quickly, adrenaline was streaking through my veins, damping my palms. I relished the feeling. I grabbed my M-4 and attached the grenade launcher. If I had the opportunity, I was going to use it.

"Jones, you're on today. Vega is your target; we're your backup." He nodded from his locker where he was quickly assembling his rifle. His tan ghillie suit was already laid out on the bench behind him.

Jordon was waiting next to the plane, his M-4 slung across his chest. Pierce, Flynn, and Rook joined him, tightening straps as they left the hangar.

"Time to go, boys," I said, leading the way up the steps and onto the plane, pulling on my gloves as I went. The comforting weight of my rifle bumped against my chest as I walked.

"Flynn, stay back here in the cabin. We have a lot to go over before we get there." I nodded to our captain as I passed him. Taking my seat, I watched the others settle in.

"Copy that," Flynn said, as he took his seat next to Pierce.

I watched out my window as we took off and gained altitude. The sun was setting behind the mountains. We would land in Mexico in the middle of the night. Lucky for us, there was an airport not far from the town that was big enough so we wouldn't attract too much attention.

****

Beatrice worked in the kitchen, cutting vegetables for soup. It would hold well or she could freeze it she needed to. When the team got back she wanted them to have a hot meal. She shuddered at the thought of the plastic packaged MREs they took with them. Her niece and those boys would be in for a treat when they got home. She didn't allow the thought of any of them not returning to cross her mind. The radio was on low; *Bittersweet Symphony* had her softly singing along as she worked.

She turned toward the sound of the door slowly opening. Her

nerves were jittery and a little on edge. Jackson was standing in the doorway, watching her at the counter. She set her knife down next to the potatoes she was nearly finished cubing and began to walk toward him.

"No, Beatrice, don't stop on my account." His gruff voice raised her awareness. The room felt smaller when he was in it, closer and more intimate.

"Are you hungry, Fisher?" She resumed what she was doing, pushing aside the potatoes and pulling a bag of carrots toward her.

"Look at me. I'm six-foot-six and I weigh somewhere in the neighborhood of two hundred and seventy pounds; I'm always hungry." And look at him she did. He was in excellent shape for an older man. There was nothing soft or lazy about him. His eyes were golden brown like French toast. She forced her mind back to the knife in her hand.

"I have looked at you, Fisher. I hope vegetable beef soup is okay?" Her knife thunked through the carrots, sending some rolling off the cutting board and onto the floor.

"What do you see when you look at me?" He was being bold, coming around to her side of the counter, and invading her personal space. Reaching around her body, he took the celery and began pulling stalks from the bunch before cleaning them and selecting another knife. Skillfully, he chopped it into evenly-sized pieces.

"I haven't decided yet. You gave me a lot to think about last night." She tried to ignore him, but he made it impossible. He scooted closer to her until he was brushing against her arm, impeding her movements. Just like last night…

"May I come in?" He took his hat off and held it in front of him.

"Would I be a lady if I let a man into my room?" She asked cheekily.

"Are you a lady?" He asked softly.

"Not today." Opening the door wide, she stepped aside. Jackson brushed her arm as he walked past, making her skin break out in goosebumps.

"Why are you here, Fisher?" she asked him as he looked around her room. What he was looking at, she didn't know. It was a basic room like the others; she didn't have any personal effects to make it interesting.

"Beatrice, there is something special about you," he blurted, turning to face her. The intensity of his expression caused Beatrice to catch her breath. "I see where Mic gets her attitude and strength."

"Thank you, Fisher."

He closed his eyes as she said his name. "I love how you say my name. I didn't think I would ever enjoy hearing it again."

He stepped closer to her, stopping just inches away. He raised a big hand, reaching for her face. His hand was so big, it covered her cheek from her temple to her jaw. He slid his thumb along the seam of her lips, brushing against her quickly.

"Fisher?" She said his name as a question. Her heart was racing and her breath felt stuck in her chest.

"I came here for two reasons. I wanted to tell you something and ask you a question." He retreated a few steps, swallowing hard.

"Just ask; I don't bite." She fiddled with her sweater, suddenly nervous. Why was she nervous? She hardly knew him; he shouldn't have the ability to tongue-tie her like this.

"First, let me say that I see where Mic gets both her beauty and her brass balls. I think if I made you leave now, I'd have a mutiny on my hands. You've won the men over with your cooking and your mothering. It's something we have all lacked for a long time." He cleared his throat, rubbing his hand over the top of his bald and shiny head.

"What did you want to ask me?" Her apprehension was reaching a new high. If he didn't spit it out soon, she'd just throw him out and deal with it later.

"You're a fine woman, both in mind and beauty. I don't want you to leave either. I try to be honorable... but I'm getting old and don't have the patience to screw around. Can I..." He paused, looking panicked.

"Fisher, please, just ask." She laughed, trying to ease the tension gripping them both.

"Can I... c-court you? I'd like to get to know you better." He rushed, stuttering over the words. His dark face was lined with worry.

"You look like you're about to be sick." She smacked a hand over her mouth, not believing what just popped out.

"I feel like it, yes. I haven't asked a girl out in twenty-five years." He kept crossing and uncrossing his arms.

"This is a surprise. I didn't think you were allowed to have a partner, family, or anything of the sort."

"Generally, no. But...since you're staying and you're not a solider under my command, I don't see it being an issue."

"Unless I say no." She smiled inside, enjoying drawing this out. He may not have not asked a girl out in twenty-five years, but she hadn't been asked out in nearly that long either. She wanted to enjoy this.

"Are you?" He gulped audibly. His face was a little pale even. "Saying no?"

"No," she said simply.

"Okay then, I understand." His face turned to stone and he moved to leave. Laughing she grabbed his arm, her hand looking so small against him.

"Fisher, wait. I wasn't saying no. I was saying no, I'm not going to say no. Yes, you silly man. You can court me. Or ask me out or whatever. We're too old to be boyfriend and girlfriend. How about we start at friends, then go from there?" She stared up at him, smiling at the relief on his face.

"Oh. Well then. I'm going to kiss you now, if that's okay?" He didn't wait for her response, just drew her close and pressed his lips to hers.

"Beatrice?" His voice drew her back to the present. He chuckled and took the knife from her, setting it down softly. His hands dwarfed her; it had been so long since a man made her feel so small and feminine. "Talk to me." He made it an order.

"My husband passed away when Bea was in high school. Since then I have focused all of my attention on her, leaving no room for myself. Dating has never occurred to me and now here I am, facing you, a man who is so different from anyone I've ever known." She put her forehead against his chest, breathing in the spicy scent of his cologne and a hint of cigar smoke. The softness of his shirt caressed her face. "I don't know what to do with you. Or about you."

"Whatever you want. Something, nothing, it doesn't matter. As long as you let me be around you and talk to you, I'm happy." She risked a look at him. He was smiling down at her, his teeth very white and bright against his dark skin. She clasped his cheeks in her hands and pulled him down as she went up on her tip toes. He tasted different than last night—fresh and minty instead of like scotch and cigar.

"I have to go check in with Mic and the others." He drew a small phone from his pocket, slipping it into her apron pocket when she didn't immediately take it. "Press and hold number one and it will call me. Or use the intercom on the wall over there. I'll be in the war room. Let me know when dinner is ready, baby." He kissed her forehead and left the room. She watched him go, appreciating the view. At the same time, her confusion reached a new high.

"What am I going to do with that man?" She whispered to herself, going back to the carrots.

****

Sitting in the war room, Jackson dialed a number burned into his memory. He needed to update his handler.

"Hello?" He always answered on the first ring. His voice was thick with sleep, not that Jackson gave a shit.

"I have an update." Jackson outlined what was happening. He had waited until Mic and the team were on their way before making this call so it would be too late to stop them.

"This complicates things. I have some calls to make." He hung up on Jackson, sounding pissed off.

"Goodbye to you too, fucker," Jackson said to the empty room. Propping his feet on the table, he leaned back and stared at the ceiling. Mic would have Jones call soon, he was sure of it. His thoughts drifted back to the kitchen and the woman in it. He couldn't let her go now, no matter what happened in Mexico; Beatrice was here to stay. He knew he'd have to deal with Mic gently; she might not take his dating her aunt lightly.

For the first time since before Abu Ghraib, the prison in Afghanistan, Jackson let himself think of the future. Maybe there was some happiness in store for him after all.

Chapter 15

I spread maps and aerial photographs out on the table in front of us. The landscape was not conducive to cover. Cacti and small bushes were the dominate plants, with very few trees.

"Jones, you gonna be able to work with this?" I asked, pointing to the desert surrounding the poppy fields. The fields were breathtakingly beautiful if you ignored the fact that they produced opium, which was the main ingredient in some of the world's most devastatingly addictive drugs.

"Mic, don't insult me."

"Okay then, I take that as a yes. Where do you want to be?" I wasn't a sniper, so in a situation like this, it was best to just let him pick his spot.

"Here." On the satellite photos, he pointed to a tiny ridge, more of a slope really, just above the fields. I'll be able to see both points of entry and there isn't much to block my line of sight."

"Where do you want the rest of us?" Pierce asked.

I pointed to the dirt track that was their excuse for a road.

"Armando says that Adolfo drives an armored Land Rover. We can't just hit his vehicle. When they stop and he gets out, he'll be vulnerable for a moment. That's your cue, Jones." He nodded his understanding. "I want the rest of us evenly spaced along the ridge with Jones and across the road on the opposite ridge. In the extremely unlikely event that Jones misses, I want us ready and able to provide cover for him and to complete the mission."

"It's a solid plan. Who's going to be where?" Rook broke in.

"Jones, who's your spotter?"

"Jordon? You game?" the sniper asked.

"Yeah. I got you, man." It was the first words Jordon had spoken around me all day.

I nodded in agreement. "Fine. I'll be on the flank with Pierce and Rook. Flynn, I want you with Jones and Jordon." I looked at their faces. They were focused and solid. This was Steel, right here. Making plans on the fly and executing them flawlessly.

"Pierce, if we get set up in time, I want you to lay some charges, mines if you have them. Cover our asses in case they double back."

"Already on it, Mic." He was digging through his duffle, muttering to himself.

"We need a back-up plan. What if it all goes south and they escape?" Rook had a good point.

"In the event they escape, then we pursue. I'm not going back home until this fucker is planted. Got me?"

"Fucking A," Flynn said. Jordon and Rook were silent.

"I get to blow stuff up; it's been way too long." Pierce was talking to the mine he held in his hands. He was like a junkie who'd gone too long without a fix.

"Do you need some alone time, dude?" Flynn asked, nudging a

hunched over Pierce.

"Fuck you; you get the same way when you haven't flown anything for a while, flyboy." Pierce put the mine away and punched Flynn in the arm.

Flynn's face turned bright red as his temper rose. "Fuck you, man, don't freaking call me flyboy, dammit!"

"Knock it off; this isn't the time for you two to fuck around," Rook barked at them. His display of temper was surprising, reminding me we were taking him on a mission when he'd had less training with us than Jordon had gotten before Colombia. There was something about the man which had me thinking he was more than capable of handling just about any situation.

"Rook. Can it. It's what they do." I went back to the maps. The terrain sucked; we would have to drive in, cross country. Leave our vehicles in the desert and hike to the fields. We would be cutting it close; I wanted us in position well before dawn.

"When do we land?" We'd been in the air for maybe an hour.

"About six hours," Flynn answered. "With our tailwind and this fast fucking jet, we'll make decent time."

"That's going to be damn close. We've done all we can for now. Everyone try and rest. Eat something. We've got a hell of a day ahead of us."

****

Flynn's voice came over the intercom, startling me awake. "We're on approach."

I sat up and rubbed the sleep from my eyes, shocked I had been able to sleep at all. Grabbing a kit I had on board, I went into the bathroom and enjoyed the use of a flush toilet. Peeing outside was so much easier for a guy. I opened the small canvas bag and laid out my supplies on the tiny shelf.

It would be too hot for the tactical hoods in Mexico and we always took care to conceal our identities as best we could. Dipping my fingers into my pots of paint, I smeared diagonal streaks from my temple to my chin, layering the colors and blending them together. There was a ritual in this, same as warriors of old painting their bodies before battle, we readied ourselves for the conflict ahead. I blended the black, shades of brown, and green together, concealing my features.

I slipped an elastic headband on to hold my hair back from my face. Even with the helmet, it had a tendency to fall into my eyes. I kept blending and mixing, spreading the paint over my neck, even my ears. Slipping my ear-piece in, I left the bathroom. The men were already well on their way. Rook held a small mirror up as he painted his face. He was whispering something under his breath; it sounded like a chant of some sort.

"You okay, Rook?" He looked at me, but never stopped the whispering-chant thing he was doing. I let him be; we all prepared for battle differently. Jordon was watching me as I paced, his eyes following my movements. Pierce was going over the maps again, still muttering to himself. Jones had painted his face and was watching Jordon watching me. He snapped his fingers in front of Jordon's face, getting his attention.

"You ready for this?" Jones asked him.

"Copy that. I'm good. I've done this before, man," Jordon said, as he sat next to Jones. They bent their heads together and whispered back and forth.

Flynn came back into the cabin, a bounce in his step. "Landing in a minute. Buckle up, boys and girls." He plopped down in a seat, fastened his seatbelt and stared out the window.

"Thought you'd be in the cockpit, Flynn; it's not like you to let someone else land a plane you're on," I pointed out.

"The captain has grown on me. He's not going to crash." Flynn went back to whistling and watching the ground get bigger.

"There should a Range Rover waiting for us, Mic," Jones said as we touched down. The Mexican government knows we're here and what we're going to be doing. We won't see them; they are letting us do the dirty work."

"That's kind of normal for us, Jones. Is there a problem I need to know about?" I asked. We didn't have time for drama. It would be light in just over an hour. We wouldn't have much leeway in the timetable to get into position.

"Nothing, it's fine. They could take care of this easy enough on their own, it's not as if they have a reputation to protect. He started gathering his gear as the jet came to a stop.

"Copy that." There was no response that would help, we weren't there for the Mexican government; and in fact, our own government didn't want us there. "This is about us, protecting my aunt and taking these fuckers out. Politics doesn't play into it this time."

"Affirmative." Jones stood and lowered the steps. We exited out into the chilly early morning air. Mexico was a desert, but it got cold when the sun went down.

"Captain, stay out of sight," I said as we walked past him and down the steps. "The jet is cleared to wait here until sundown. If we aren't back by then, leave without us."

He lit a cigar and waved us off. "Good luck. I'll see you tonight. Try not to get shot." He chuckled at my glare. "Again."

I flipped him the bird as I followed Jordon down the steps. Flynn was circling the waiting vehicle, checking it over thoroughly. It didn't look big enough to hold us all.

The Rover was sitting next to the runway as promised. Flynn took the driver's seat and the rest of us piled in behind. Jones was up front with Flynn, programming the GPS. We were cramped, shoved in against each other with no room to move.

"How long until we get there, Jones?" I shoved at Pierce; his pistol was digging into my thigh where he was smashed against me.

"Not long, fifteen minutes; less if Flynn can get this bucket moving."

"Stop fucking shoving me, Mic; I have no place to go," Pierce snapped from where he was pressed against the door.

"Mic, why don't you sit on Jordon's lap, so it'll free up some space." I wiggled forward enough to smack Flynn on the back of the head. It was really the only way to deal with him.

"This ride is terrible. Who asked for a Rover?" Rook complained from the back. His legs were too long; he was shifting around, but it was useless. "If I wanted to be in a slow vehicle with no space, too many people, and a shitty-ass ride, I'd be in Iraq in a Humvee." Rook kept up a steady stream of bitching.

"So he does talk; if only to cry like a little bitch," Flynn piped up.

"When we stop this fucking thing, flyboy, you better run." Rook growled at Jordon who had inadvertently kicked him as he shifted around.

"Shut the fuck up, all of you." I tucked my elbows in as tight as I could and just endured. My claustrophobia was making itself known, the hot air and tight space pressing in on me. "Someone roll down a window," I asked as calmly as I could manage. Jones hit the button for his window; cool night air slapped me in the face, gelling my sweat in place. I shivered and breathed a little easier.

The tires left the bumpy paved road and kicked up dust on an even shittier and bumpier dirt road. Rocks pinged on the undercarriage as we turned and left the road entirely. We were tossed from side to side as Flynn navigated wash outs and avoided tall cactus plants that seemed to jump out of nowhere. He was cursing steadily under his breath, but was doing a damn fine job of getting us through it.

"Nearly there," Jones said, looking up from the GPS. Conveniently there was a rare tree in the perfect position to hide the Rover. Then again, Jones was navigating, so maybe it wasn't so much convenience as a deliberate choice.

Flynn pulled as close to the tree as he could without actually parking in it. Pierce opened his door and literally fell out, hitting the dirt with an audible "oomph." He narrowly missed landing ass-first on a cactus. There was a big bright moon overhead, lending up plenty of light to move around with. We had our night vision goggles, but didn't need them. The shadows were still treacherous though; holes and loose rocks were everywhere. This was not the time to fall and break an ankle.

"Watch your fucking feet and stay together," I ordered.

"Stop fucking around; we have to move," Rook said. He'd stepped into my leadership role without even a millisecond of hesitation.

He was no Corporal. *No fucking way.*

"Jones, lead on; Jordon take point with him. Flynn and Pierce in the middle, Rook and I will bring up the rear. Jones, give me the sat phone; I'm going to check in with Jackson." We started at a good pace, with Jones's long legs eating up ground, he would get us to the fields in plenty of time.

I let Rook get some distance in front of me before dialing the secure line at the Wonka House. It hardly finished ringing before Jackson's gruff voice answered.

"Checking in. We're on foot, should arrive at the target by dawn." I fell back even more. I was not about to trust Rook at my back when I didn't know who he really was or what the fuck he was doing here. My suspicions of him were growing with every step we took.

"Copy that, Mic." Jackson's voice was crackling and sounded far away.

"You have some explaining to do, Master Sergeant." When he didn't respond, I continued. "There is something off about Rook. Explain now, before he has an accident." I was bluffing and Jackson would know that, but it got my point across.

"He's a plant. From my contact in the DoD. I had no choice. That's all I can tell you for now. When you get home, I'll tell you the rest." The click of the phone hanging up in my ear sounded very final. Someone higher up was playing a dangerous game with me, and with the lives of my men. In the abstract I knew that Jackson must have a boss, but I had never heard of him until now.

"Fuck," I said, with feeling, stowing the sat phone in a pocket on my vest. I jogged and caught up with Rook.

"So, Corporal, what flavor are you?" His head whipped around at my words, the stoic mask finally slipping, showing the man underneath. Fierce intelligence burned in his eyes, easily seen even in the moonlight.

"I'm not a Corporal. It's classified." His voice was just above a whisper.

"You're fucking kidding me right now, right? I eat classified little boys like you for breakfast. Spit it out, Rook, if that's even your name," I whisper-shouted back. I could see Pierce's silhouette ahead, too far ahead. We were spreading out too thin.

"My name is actually the only thing you know that is correct. I am Matthew Riley; it was my cousin that betrayed you." He didn't look at me, just kept trudging ahead.

"Your rank, soldier," I commanded. My patience was low on a good day. I had a long list of shitty fucking days leading up to this moment.

"Sergeant First Class Matthew Riley." he barked and it was my turn to be surprised. He outranked me. Jackson had put a man into my unit who outranked me. It didn't matter as much as it would if we were regular enlisted, but we still operated using the rank and file of the Army.

"Fucking hell," Grabbing his arm and jerking him to a stop, I got as close to his face as possible given our height difference. "Listen here. I don't care right now, but as soon as we get back; you, me, and Jackson are going to have a long fucking talk. Got it? While we are out here, I'm in command. Copy me, you lying fucker?" I snarled in his face. Shoving away from him, I hiked ahead.

"Copy that, Sergeant," I heard from behind me. The sarcasm was thick enough to be edible.

Catching up to Pierce and Flynn, I fell in next to them. Anger had me tightening my fists and cursing under my breath.

"Everything ok, Mic?" Pierce was brave enough to ask.

"Just fine and fucking dandy." I needed to calm down. We were about to lie in wait and end these Vega fuckers. I needed to be focused on that, not whatever was going on with Rook.

"Well, sounds like something has your panties in a wad," Flynn spouted at me. "Pull that shit out of your ass; we have work to do."

"True enough, Flynn." I'm not sure who was more surprised, Flynn or Pierce.

"This is a first. It has to be. I don't remember this ever happening to me! A woman said I was right!" Flynn was getting louder with each word, his excitement taking over his sense.

"Shut the fuck up, man, or today will be your last," Pierce quietly told him.

The fields were in sight. The dawn was just starting to brighten the horizon. Pinks and yellows swirled together, getting brighter with every passing minute.

"Get into position and hurry the fuck up," I said into the radio. We fanned out. Pierce was belly-crawling next to the road, laying his charges and mines. Jones and Jordon went up the small rise, disappearing into the dry grass and low bushes. If I hadn't watched them get into place, I would never have seen them. Excellent.

Taking cover just under the edge of a bush, I lay down on my belly in the dirt, propping my rifle in front of me. Scanning the fields through my scope, there was no movement. It was early, so we had a wait ahead of us. A breeze was blowing the poppies back and forth, making them dance gently. Strange how something so beautiful could turn into something so deadly.

"In position, over." One-by-one the men checked in. Pierce, Flynn and I were on the opposite side of the road from Rook, Jones, and Jordon. Each of us could see the other, but we were too far apart to communicate very well. The sun rose fully, bathing us in its growing heat. I hoped this fucker would take an early lunch; I did not want to be sitting here in the heat all fucking day.

"Radio silence until target arrives. Over." Silence settled down upon us like a blanket. Jones was in his element, dug in and waiting. I hated the waiting, the sitting still, the controlled breathing. I preferred acting on my plan, executing it flawlessly. It just so happened that this time around, sitting and waiting was the best plan.

****

Jordon settled in with the spotter's scope, tucked in close to Jones's side. This wasn't his favorite thing to do, but it was one he was decent at: tracking wind changes and elevation, and helping to execute that perfect shot. Ideally the shot would enter through the base of the throat or heart, causing instant death severing the brain stem or stopping the heart. There would be no twitching, screaming, gurgling or death rattles. Just the thud of a bullet and down into the fucking dirt he would go.

"You good?" Jones whispered. He was like a rock, not moving a millimeter. He was glued to his rifle, eyes looking for his target.

"I'm peachy keen," Jordon muttered back, when in reality his nuts itched and he needed to piss. Neither need would be met for a long while. How did Jones do this shit all the time? The man must not have a bladder.

****

Rook was to the left of Jordon and Jones. He should have been focused on the target and completing this mission. Instead, he was worried about Mic. How she had figured it out, he wasn't entirely sure. When he'd first got off that jet and saw her a few days ago, he knew right away she was in command. She wore the heavy mantel of leadership well; it suited her and fit her small frame.

Maybe she recognized in others what she saw most in herself. His tone of voice or something. Who knew? Now that she knew he wasn't what he had said he was, the only truth in his presence here was that he wanted to be a member of Steel. He had just come from something so black and so classified that the only possible place to move him was into another special operations group.

His taking command was never an option. Even if it had been offered, he wanted no part of it. He came here wanting to stay in the service that he loved and to keep his sanity. He could no longer be in deep special operations, planted inside various terrorist cells around the world. When he heard of this opportunity to join the envied Steel Corps, he did everything he could to be on that jet.

Now he was here, they were on mission, and Mic was pissed the fuck off. She had every right to be. When they got back, indeed they would be having a conversation. He just hoped he came out at the end of it still a member of Steel.

Chapter 16

Even before the sun broke fully over the horizon, villagers had quickly moved into the fields, working through them, row by row, harvesting the flowers. It was brutal backbreaking work. No machines to aid them and no shade. They sang in time with each other, keeping a steady rhythm as they worked.

A white spot floated in front of my eyes. I blinked, clearing the dust from them. Sunlight was reflecting off of an approaching vehicle. Our target was moving in.

"Target approaching. Over," I whispered.

"Copy," Jones replied. The vehicles slowed as they neared the fields. In the lead was a large Dodge truck, *sicarios* riding in the truck bed, actively scanning the area surrounding the fields for threats. In the middle was the Land Rover, completely blacked out other than the windshield. Another Dodge truck made up the rear guard.

"Jones, you worry about Vega. If Mercedes is in there, I'll take her out. The rest of you, pick off as many guards as you can. We've got them in a cross-fire." Their little convoy was smack in the middle of the road; we had elevated positions on either side of them. This was going to be a turkey shoot.

"Copy." Each of them radioed in. The vehicles stopped; the guards hopping down first. They created a loose perimeter around the Rover. I waited, breathless. One of the *sicarios* opened the rear door.

Out stepped Adolfo Vega; bells rang in my head, angels sang. Our target was falling right into my hands. A man in a sharp three piece suit followed him out. Grey and double breasted, the suit was obviously tailored to fit his trim form. Putting my eye to my scope, I surveyed him carefully. There was nothing in the file about this fucking guy.

"Target acquired," Jones whispered over the radio. "Permission to fire." The guards were spreading out, lulled into a sense of security. I wanted as many of them as far away from Adolfo as possible.

"Hold," I answered him. I flicked my safety off as Adolfo moved into the field closest to Jones. He was talking to workers and inspecting the flowers. The Suit was still beside the Rover, waiting impatiently it seemed, his hands twitching where they rested next to his thighs. The guards were spread out, a handful at each end of the road and only a few in the field with Adolfo. It wasn't going to get better than this.

"Watch the villagers. I don't want a single fucking civilian casualty. Fire when ready." The shot rang out almost before I was done speaking. I watched the bullet hit Adolfo in the base of his neck, blood spurting out behind him in an arc. He was dead before he hit the dusty ground, body limp in a growing pool of blood sinking into the dust.

Guards scrambled for cover or fell where they stood. Taking them completely by surprise we quickly thinned their numbers. The *sicarios* recovered at an impressive rate, rapidly returning fire. We made short work of them, firing nearly continuously. Our near perfect accuracy coupled with effective cover made it impossible for them to put up a viable defense. The smart villagers dove onto the ground and covered their heads. The stupid ones ran in panic, only to be cut down by the hot bullets of the *sicarios*. They didn't bother to try and avoid them; they were indiscriminately firing.

The Suit flung himself into the driver's seat of the Rover, starting it up and spinning a cloud of dust in his wake as he raced down the narrow dirt road.

"Pierce! Now!" I commanded. Mines exploded on either side of the road, rocking the vehicle, but not stopping it. Shrapnel pinged against the sides, denting it and cracking the windshield, but the heavy armor protected the engine block and the tires. Three were flat and throwing shredded rubber off with each rotation; revealing the steel bands inside that kept the wheels turning. Still, he didn't slow, moving forward at an impressive pace. The antenna on the roof of the Rover got my attention. He was already too far away for us to do much about it.

"We need to move. Right fucking now. He has a radio in that Rover." Urgency thickened my voice and had my heart slamming against my ribs. These fields were only about a mile outside of the village. We needed to be long gone before they had a chance to recover and pursue us.

"Pierce, got enough left to take out those trucks?" Rook's voice came over the radio. Most of the villagers were lying in shock, too scared to move. The guards who remained alive were too badly wounded to do anything.

"Of course I do; cover me." Pierce shimmied down the hill, stopping at the nearest truck first. He crawled under it for no more than a second or two before sliding back out and repeating the action on the other truck.

"Let's move." I signaled the men to come to me. Jordon ran to my position, leaping over bodies as he went.

"Get those villagers clear, dammit!" I was frantic, not wanting any deaths of the villagers on our hands.

Pierce began yelling and gesturing wildly at them, finally getting a few to get up and run back down the road to the village. The ones running started an exodus, then they all ran. Some stopped to drag the wounded, but most were panicked and fleeing for their lives. We probably looked like police or a rival cartel to them; they wanted nothing to do with us.

"Blow it, Pierce! Fuck, we have to go!" I shouted. A dust cloud was coming closer to us. The villagers were fleeing off of the road, hiding where they could in the brush. Pierce was running up the small hill toward us, clutching an RPG launcher to his chest. Leave it to Pierce to find more explosives in the midst of blowing shit up. I swear he was better than a bomb dog.

The first truck blew, with the other following it mere seconds later; the ground shook with the force of the explosions, fire and molten metal raining down on the fields and road. Thick black smoke choked the air with the smell of burnt rubber and gasoline. The smoke cleared for a second and I could see the road, two giant holes where the trucks had been effectively destroyed it. What was left of the road was blocked with pieces of engines and unidentifiable hunks of smoldering metal. The *sicarios* would have to drive through the fields to give chase, destroying what was left of their precious poppies.

As we ran, I counted heads quickly, confirming everyone was present. We moved as one with Rook on point, and Jordon and I in the rear, covering our asses. The dust cloud was getting closer, close enough that I could make out the vehicles in the lead; more trucks, built to go off road and through this sandy, shitty terrain.

"Move your asses!" I shouted, pushing them forward. Our Rover was in sight. Flynn broke ahead, diving in behind the wheel. I could hear the engines growing louder as they got closer. I covered Pierce as he ran toward me; firing rapidly, my finger squeezed the trigger as fast as it could. I clicked empty; popping the spent mag out, I slammed a full one in with a hard smack of my palm. Pierce reached me. Dropping to one knee, he took aim and fired his only rocket with a *whoosh*.

We both watched in fascination as it spiraled through the air, leaving the tell-tale smoke trail in its wake. The rocket hit the lead vehicle square on, turning it into a fire-ball and throwing both frag and bodies into the air. The shock wave hit our faces and threw dust into the air in a thick cloud. The other vehicles stopped their advance and quickly reversed out of range.

"Was that your only rocket?" Jordon asked from where he had stopped to cover us. He shouldered his rifle and fired, hitting two more *sicarios* through the windshield of the closest truck. The truck swerved out of control and ran nose first down into a washout, throwing the men in the back clear. Most didn't get up and the two who did Jones and I made quick work of.

"Yeah," Pierce answered. "I didn't see any more and I wasn't going to waste time looking." He dropped the launcher and ran for the Rover. Men were pouring out of the stopped rear vehicles now, giving chase on foot. I spun and popped off a few rounds, hitting one man who fell to the ground screaming, holding onto his leg. *Dammit, rushed the shot.* I reloaded again as I ran, dropping the empty mag onto the ground and quickly slamming in a full one.

Following Jordon and Pierce, I jumped in just as Flynn stood on the gas. I landed in the back seat, knocking into Jordon, causing him to grunt in pain as his rifle barrel got jammed into his leg.

"Good thing you put the safety on, huh?" I laughed, righting myself in my seat. I turned as best I could and watched out the back as the *sicarios* ran after us. Flynn cut the wheel sharply, the tires spinning into the soft dirt of the road. It wasn't long until I couldn't see them anymore. The dust we were kicking up would give away our location easily enough.

"Flynn, get us the fuck out of here before they catch up, dammit," I felt exposed and vulnerable out here in the daylight.

"You want me to pull over so you can drive this fucking brick, Mic?" Flynn shot back at me over his shoulder.

"Watch the fucking road, dammit!" We bounced in and out of ruts and over rocks. If the suspension in this thing had been any good before, it was fucked now.

"Yes, ma'am. As soon as you shut up your back-seat fucking driving. I'm the wheel-man here!" Flynn kept smarting off. Whipping the wheel back and forth and throwing us against each other.

"Fine, have it your way. Could you pretty fucking please, get us the fuck out of here?" I calmly asked, giving him my best smile.

"Sure, no problem, Staff Sergeant. There's no excuse for bad manners you know." Flynn finally put his attention back on the road. The blacktop was in sight; the trip back to the paved road had seemed to go by so much more quickly. Why is that? Why did return trips always feel faster?

"For fucks sake," Jones muttered from the front. Our tires hit the pavement with a screech and Flynn stomped on the gas. I think everyone gave an audible sigh of relief at the smoother ride.

"Nice shot, Jones." I gave him a high five and just like that, the tension fell away. We were alive, no one was wounded, and our mission was a success. Mostly. "Who was the fucker in the suit?"

"I don't know, but as soon as I'm back on the jet, I'm going to find out," he growled. I think the only thing that pissed him off more than a missed shot was a hole in his intelligence.

"He looked important. Maybe Adolfo's number two. This may not be over, guys. We didn't get Mercedes either." I would personally gut that bitch at my first opportunity.

"We'll get her, don't worry," Jordon said, trying to reassure me.

"They're going to be pissed. Not only did we eighty-six their leader, but we destroyed a fair portion of their poppy fields," Pierce added.

"I know, I know." My adrenaline high was quickly fading. Cartels could be wounded, but they were very difficult to kill. There were more sick fucks willing to do their job, than there were good guys willing to do ours. Humanity really was a cesspool of shit sometimes, with greed overtaking any vestige of common human decency left.

"Fuck me, I need a beer." Today was done; tomorrow we would fight again. Tonight, I would celebrate this small victory. "Who wants to go to Finnegan's?"

Chapter 17

I was on the jet, headset strapped on while I debriefed Jackson. I had kicked Jones out of his chair and was calmly spinning back and forth while I talked. Wheeled chairs were fun no matter how old you got.

"We missed the guy in the suit, whoever that was. Jones is gathering what information is available now. Mercedes didn't show at all. We need to plan a second assault to take those two out."

"Copy that. My phone has been ringing with the aftermath. Apparently one of the villagers talked to a newspaper. Now the media is on this, trying to find out who the vigilantes were that took out half of the Vega cartel. You're being heralded as heroes by most of the populace, it's just that the government has to make a show of trying to catch you. Even though they know exactly who you are."

"How's my aunt?" For a moment I thought I had lost the call, the silence was so thick.

"She's good." There was a slight catch in his voice.

"Oh really? Well, we'll pick up that topic of conversation when we get back. We're going to the compound; all of us need a beer. We'll be back at the Wonka House in the morning."

"I love how you ask permission, Michaels," He said dryly.

"I love how you give it, Master Sergeant. Mic, out." Hitting a button, I ended the call. Looking around at the men, I saw exhausted and dirty faces. We all needed showers and sleep. Even as I watched, Flynn and Pierce nodded off. The mark of a true soldier was the ability to sleep anywhere. Compared to some of the places we had slept in, these were five-star accommodations.

"Can I have my seat back now, Mic, or are you going to find the fucker in the suit?" Jones whisper-shouted at me.

"Sure, sure. Here ya go." I stood and sank gratefully into my own seat, trying to ignore the sand that was all over me and the acrid smell of our unwashed bodies. The paint on my face was itchy and tight-feeling. I wiggled my jaw around, cracking the paint on my cheeks.

"What the hell are you doing, Mic?" Jordon's voice startled me.

"The paint itches," I said, as he rose and took the seat next to me.

"Then go wash it off." All he left out was the 'duh.'

"I would, Jordon, but I need my face wash." I looked at him; his own paint was starting to flake and crack.

"I see, girl problems. Today was pretty intense. I always imagined my first trip to Mexico would be different. Less violent." He shrugged.

"You're fucking kidding me, right?"

"No, I always wanted to do the tourist thing in Cancun. You know, lots of drinking and pretty *senoritas*." He grinned at me, turning the charm dial all the way up. Lucky for him, charm had never worked on me. Until him.

"Uh huh. Well then. Maybe you'll get your chance one day. For now, you have to settle for Finnegan's. Get some sleep, Jordon." I was small enough and the seat was big enough that I could turn away from him and onto my side. I closed my eyes and tried to sleep. Mostly though, I thought about Willie. I thought back to the note I left for him the last time I saw him.

Willie,

Thank you for being here, always. I'm sure we will see each other again, but tonight was the last time for us. I'm a coward for leaving you this note. For that I'm sorry, but I can't let you grow to care about me, to miss me or mourn me.

Goodbye.

Bea

I could see it in my mind like I had just written it. In the wake of Phillips's death, none of us had felt like going out and with nothing to celebrate we had stayed in. I wasn't sure how Willie would react to seeing me again. I knew that he would try to charm me into his bed; it was guaranteed. Willie's charm wouldn't work any better than Jordon's had.

No matter how much I tried to deny it to myself, Jordon played a big part in this. I couldn't be with Willie, not now. I had shared two kisses with Jordon and he had ruined me for other men. Dammit.

Jordon's breathing got heavy and regular as he fell asleep. The cabin was quiet, only punctuated by a few snores and the occasional mumble from Flynn. He wouldn't shut up, even in his sleep.

****

Mercedes stood at her bannister and watched the sun set, a crystal champagne flute clutched in her perfectly manicured hand. Tapping her nails against the crystal, her mind strayed to the events of the day.

Her useless cousin was dead. Just like her husband and her father-in-law before him. Julio was in charge now, but his interests were not parallel to hers. Julio was not constrained by family obligation like Adolfo had been. Julio was a pit viper who was only looking for his next meal. Mercedes just needed to ensure that he began searching in the direction she wanted him to go in.

Avenging Diego had gone beyond a widow's grief; it was now a matter of pride and reputation. She could not allow Steel to live; she must complete her husband's mission. Reputation was everything in her world. It was unusual for a woman to be involved in her husband's work, but Diego had treated her differently. He recognized her strengths and valued her opinions. They had been the King and Queen of their cartel. She truly mourned him and she would honor his memory by using every tool at her disposal to find and destroy Steel.

Her power was limited by her sex, but she had always found manipulating men easy. Just smile pretty and make your body available and they will do whatever you want. The thought of giving herself to Julio was repugnant. His tastes ran to the exotic and depraved. She would not survive a night with him; few girls did. Offering someone up in her place would have to work. The question was: who?

The answer was so obvious... the woman who led those men. A small and strikingly beautiful woman, who was both strong and fierce. She would not break easily under Julio's care. His chief complaint had always been that the girls gave up too easily; they quit fighting and accepted their fate. Maybe when Julio had that bitch in his clutches she would stand back and watch.

The thought brought a genuine and nasty smile to her lips. Toasting herself, Mercedes drained her champagne in one long swallow. Leaving the glass on the bannister for the maids, she went in search of Julio, long dark hair brushing her slender silk-clad hips as she walked.

****

I woke to the dinging of the *fasten seat belt* sign. We were preparing to land. The others were all stretching and groaning awake. My neck was stiff from sleeping in a somewhat unnatural position.

"Fuck me, I'm stiff as hell from sleeping in this chair," Pierce complained.

"Easy, dude, there's a lady present," Flynn said. I expected him to point to me. "Jordon here doesn't want to see your morning wood."

"Fuck off, Flynn," Pierce and Jordon snapped in unison.

"See, you're already a cute couple, finishing each other's sentences and shit." The pain-in-the-ass kept up a steady dialogue of bullshit as we landed.

As we stood to grab our weapons and packs, I'd had enough. "For once, can you just shut the fuck up, Flynn? Save it for later. We're all tired and dirty and hungry. Unless you want me to kick your ass down the steps, shut your fucking trap."

Pushing past him, I hurried down the stairs and out into the cold morning. My breath puffed out in white clouds as I walked to my cabin. I didn't wait for the others or take time to talk to them. I needed a shower and some food. Coffee needed to be in there somewhere too.

I thumbed my nose at the rules and took my rifle into my cabin with me. I would clean and oil it after I scraped off the Mexican desert I had brought home. Toeing off my boots, I left them on the porch, sand falling out of them in a small shower. If it wasn't so cold, I'd take my clothes off out here as well.

As it was, the best I could do was to leave them in a pile at the door. I almost made it to the bathroom before there was a knock on the door. Standing there in my panties, bra, and Mexican dirt, I debated ignoring it. With my luck, it would be something important.

Donning a robe as I opened the door, I saw Jordon standing there, looking just as cold, dirty, and tired as I was.

"This better be important, Jordon. I need coffee and a shower." My mood was already in the toilet and was deteriorating rapidly.

"Nice robe," he stuttered out.

"For fucks sake. Did you come here to admire my choice of loungewear or do you have something constructive to say?" I tapped my fingers on the doorjamb impatiently.

"What time are we leaving for Finnegan's?" He was struggling to maintain eye contact. I looked down and saw that most of my cleavage and part of my blue sports bra were showing. The bra was old and unsexy, but boobs were boobs in a man's eye, I guess. Snapping my fingers in front of his face, I brought his attention back to the conversation.

"Sorry." He actually blushed. If I wasn't so pissed off right now, it would be comical.

"Whatever. Six, we're leaving at six." I turned my back and shut the door in his face. Leaning against the door, I stayed there until I heard his footsteps go down the porch steps.

"Why is nothing ever simple around here, *huh*?" I muttered to myself before getting into the steaming hot shower.

****

Outside his cabin there was a new car parked beside to his Judge. Jordon forgot about Mic for a moment as he circled it. The matte gunmetal grey monster had gleaming chrome details. It was sex-on-wheels, a 1969 BOSS 429 Mustang, mean and bad-ass looking in a way that only cars from that period could look. It had to be Rook's car and it suited him—dark and sleek and fast. The sight of it irked

Jordon... Mic would like this car.

Jordon stomped back into his cabin, impatiently waiting for his turn in the shower. Jones was already out and Rook was in there now.

"What's with you?" Jones asked from where he was rapidly flipping through channels on the TV.

"Nothing." Jordon's skin itched from sand being in places sand had no business in. Why were there so many fuck-ups in deserts, *huh*? Just once he'd like to chase a bad guy around a nice temperate forest or something.

"Doesn't look like nothing." Jones air quoted the word.

"None of your business. Is that better?" He was pacing, anxious to get clean and blow off some steam in town.

"Fine... fine. Don't get all butt-hurt. Just trying to help, man." His teammate went back to the TV and promptly pretended Jordon wasn't even there.

Rook came out, rubbing a towel over his dripping hair.

"Finally." Jordon brushed past him in the hallway.

"Sorry, dude, the hot water ran out just as I was getting out of the shower." Rook had the gall to smirk at him.

"Of fucking course it did." Jordon slammed the bathroom door behind him. Wasn't the first cold shower he'd had and he was sure it wouldn't be his last.

Chapter 18

I had a moment of *deja-vu* as we walked into Finnegan's. The same people were in the same places; the same shitty music was playing. A few new pictures were added to the rows on the mantel, but the wood of the bar gleamed softly under the same lights. *I* felt different. Looking at the faces of my men, I could see they were different as well.

"Hello, Bea." Willie's voice stopped me in my tracks. He looked the same as ever—thick flannel shirt rolled up past his elbows, scars shiny in the low lighting. His amber eyes were burning with longing.

"Willie." I was cool; I had to be. Jordon was tense beside me. This could go very bad, very quickly. Tension charged the air, I felt stuck between two rams about to butt heads. Little did these boys realize, I was no lamb to be fought over.

"Who's that?" He asked, gesturing at Rook. "Where's Phillips?" My silence was answer enough.

"Rook. He's the new guy." I realized in that second, with everything else that had happened, I hadn't done the much needed 'come to Jesus' talk with Rook. Now was as good a time as any.

"We're going to take the big table in the back. Bring us two rounds each, please. Rook, what do you drink?" Willie knew what the rest of us liked.

"Coke is fine. I don't drink."

"What? What do you mean, you don't drink?" Flynn asked.

"I don't drink. I don't need to explain it more than that," Rook shrugged and left it at that.

"Alright then. The waitress will be right over." Willie walked away, in as much of a huff as was possible for him.

"Come on guys, we have something to talk about." I led the way to the back of the bar, past the pool tables. There was a room off to the left with a large family-style table in the center and not much else. At one point, Willie planned to hold small events here, but it never really panned out for him. "Sit down, everyone, Rook has some explaining to do." Anger tightened his jaw at my words. I sat... and waited.

"What exactly is this about, Mic?" Pierce asked, though if anyone had an idea what was coming, it would be him.

"I'll let Corporal Riley start. Or should I say Sergeant First Class Riley?" My anger had faded. He owed us an explanation, though, and I was going to get it if I had to beat it out of him.

"What the fuck, Rook? You've been lying to us?" Flynn was instantly furious. His temper continued to simmer just under the surface. He'd always been a bit of a hot-head, but it was so much worse since Phillips's death.

The waitress came in carrying a large tray laden with our drinks and a bowl of pretzels. The sudden silence had her rushing to serve us our drinks and get the hell out of the room.

"Ya'll just let me know when you want another round, kay?" She scurried out before we had a chance to respond.

"Nice Mic, thanks for this, Rook snarled at me, his anger turning him ugly. "I really appreciate it,"

"It's time, Rook. Either you're Steel or you're not." I took a long swallow of my Guinness, the creamy beer sliding coolly down my throat. "I thought about doing this in private, with just you, myself, and Jackson; instead, we're doing it this way. The time for secrets is past."

"Fine." He rubbed his hands up and down the condensation on his glass, not really looking at us as he began to speak.

"Mic knows a little. I was in a different operations group. One even more secret than this one. Yes, such a thing exists. Close your fucking mouth, Flynn." Rook spat out. "I needed to get out; I couldn't do it anymore. Being under deep cover for long periods of time was getting to be too much for me. But I can't just go back to civilian life. My boss is also Jackson's boss. He ordered Jackson to put me in this unit. That's all he did, though. He told me if I didn't hack it with you guys or pass your tests, I was out. He wouldn't undermine your unit to that degree." He sipped his soda, not making eye contact with anyone.

"So, are you in command now?" Pierce calmly asked.

"No, never. My rank really is corporal now. I took one a hell of a demotion to be here." He glared at me. "Satisfied, Mic?"

"Yes. For now." I raised my glass. "To Rook; welcome to Steel." I held up my glass until one-by-one, the others joined in. Flynn was the last; he was reluctant, but he did it. Rook was one of us now. "Drink up boys, we've earned it."

****

Julio Vega observed the glorious play land before him. Adolfo was gone; he was the leader now, *el jefe*. He carefully draped his suit jacket over the back of the simple chair, the only furnishing in the room other than the stainless steel table in front of him. Rolling up his sleeves, he donned latex gloves, loving the snap against his wrists and the powdery slickness on his palms.

His victim was tied to the table. Her arms were over her head, bent at the elbow and tied to the table legs. Her small bare feet with their red painted toes were tied to the stirrups they rested in. Shiny white synthetic fiber rope was wrapped around her narrow, delicate ankles holding her fast to the stirrups. She was blindfolded and naked. Her white skin was so fair it looked porcelain. She was pebbled with goosebumps and shaking with fear and cold.

Adolfo had allowed him to indulge in his pleasures, but only with permission. With Adolfo gone, there was no one to stop or slow his play time. He traced a gloved finger over the girl's stomach. She whimpered and shivered in response, thrashing her head from side to side. She was not gagged yet, but he would do it if she began to annoy him with her begging and crying. Tears dripped from her closed eyes, running down into her hair. He liked it when they screamed, when they sighed and trembled. With each breathless sound, he felt his power grow. In these moments, he was their god... giver of both life and death.

He pulled a small metal cart closer, the wheels screeching slightly. He must remember to oil them; such imperfections were not to be tolerated. The cart was full of all of his favorite toys: steel clamps in various sizes, needles and thread, a speculum, electrodes on sticky pads, and even a few surgical-grade knives. He selected a pair of shears; they gleamed sharply in the low light.

Standing at her head, he began to cut. Clumps of hair fell to the floor in a golden cloud. He could get Mexican girls much easier than these Russian and Ukrainian girls. A *papa* once offered his daughter to him for a mere fifty pesos. He'd killed the man for his impudence. He didn't like Mexican girls with their dark brown or dyed blonde hair. Natural and pure blondes with perfect white skin was all he ever wanted. It's what he had to have; nothing else would satisfy him.

Perfection... he thought as he cut away her hair, piece by tiny piece. He would gather it and laboriously braid it into a long rope before adding it to his box of trophies, his collection of beauties. Whenever he was in the mood, he would open the ash-pine box and take out the braids, running the long strands through his hands, reliving every glorious moment spent with his girls.

She was crying heavily now, sobbing hard enough that she was hiccupping; snot and tears soaked her red blotchy face. Her hair was becoming damp, which just would not do. Placing the shears next to her head, he slapped her hard... again and again until the crying stopped and his palm stung and burned. Her face was bruised and bloody, but that was okay. Her face didn't matter.

Snip... snip... he continued while she slept.

****

Leaning back in my chair, I watched Flynn and Rook playing pool. Flynn was as trashed as I'd ever seen him. Rook was running the table, sinking ball after ball, barely pausing between each shot. Flynn was doing his best to keep up a running commentary.

"Rook, you bastard. Give a guy a chance here. If there was a girl around, you'd be cock blocking me." Flynn slurred his words and swayed around a bit on his bar stool.

I leaned closer to Pierce, who was sitting next to me. "Get his beer from him; I'm cutting him off." He groaned, but got up to do what I asked.

Pierce slung his arm over his buddy's shoulder, making the drunken idiot stumble into him.

"Hey man... how's it hangin'? Have I ever told you how much I love you, Pierce? You're the best friend...," Flynn started laughing and snorting to something only he understood. "It hurts... oh my god, it fucking hurts to laugh." He stumbled away from Pierce, veering to the side and promptly falling onto Jordon's lap. Wrapping both arms around Jordon's neck, Flynn leaned back and kicked up his feet like a burlesque dancer giving a lap dance.

I was laughing so hard, I had tears running down my cheeks and I couldn't breathe. Rook stopped what he was doing and stood there staring, as if he was witnessing a car wreck or something.

"Flynn, get your fucking fairy twat waffle ass the fuck off me right now," Jordon snapped, his face bright red with embarrassment and anger. He tried to move, but Flynn clung like a burr. He grabbed Flynn's arms, trying to shove him off, but Flynn just moved with him, flowing like water. Trying to stand, Jordon only made it worse. Flynn straddled him on the chair, clinging tight to his neck; he wrapped both legs around Jordon's waist, nearly hooking his feet together behind the chair.

"Yeehaw! This is a fun ride, lover boy. Does Mic get to ride like this?" Rook was around the pool table before anyone else could react. He grabbed Flynn by the collar and hauled him off of Jordon.

Flynn was twisting around, trying to knock Rook off. Jones was trying to hide under his Stetson, pulling it low over his face.

Jordon was standing red-faced, fists clenched at his sides. "Hold him still, Rook, I'm going to beat the mother fucker to death," he shouted as he began to advance on Flynn, bloodlust mingling with the anger in his eyes.

"Get him the fuck out of here, Pierce," I ordered. Willie came into the room, not what I fucking needed right now. "Willie, its fine. We got this."

"Okay, Mic. He needs to go, though," I've never heard Willie use that tone before... with anyone. He turned his back and left. I had to force myself to keep my mouth shut and not follow him and bitch at him.

He's hurting and it's my fault...

Guilt ate at my insides, souring the beer sitting in the pit of my belly.

Pierce took a still laughing Flynn from Rook and dragged, pushed, and pulled him stumbling from the room.

"Well, that was fun," Rook said flatly.

"Fun? Lap dances from strippers are fun. Lap dances from Flynn? Not fucking fun. Rook," Jordon complained, his face still red with fury and humiliation.

"True enough. Fun would be me smoking your little car in a race," Rook shot back.

"Wait? What?" Jordon's confusion made him forget his anger for a minute.

"Let's race, lover boy." The challenge was thrown down as effectively as slapping Jordon with a glove.

"Fine." Jordon led the way out the door. Jones and I were left in the room and he emerged from under his hat long enough to give me a stare that spoke volumes.

"Yeah, we better follow them." I threw a couple of twenties on the table and raced out after Rook and Jordon. The sound of engines roaring to life assaulted my ears as soon as I flew through the door.

"Jones, if they wreck..." Jumping into the Jeep, I followed the taillights. There was a straight stretch up ahead they would no doubt take full advantage of. I shifted as fast as I could and sped after them.

"They won't wreck. They love their cars too much."

"Jones, people don't usually wreck on purpose..."

"Too true. Fucking drive faster then," Jones urged me. I didn't need prompting much. I hit another gear and stepped on the gas.

****

Jordon shifted and pressed on the gas; the engine growled in response, lurching the car ahead. He hated to admit it, but maybe this was just what he needed. Feeling the power under his hands and the vibrating roar of the engine liberated him in a way he couldn't describe. He was being torn apart wanting Mic and not being able to have her.

Rook had a damn fine piece of machinery, but then again... so did he. The Mustang was stopped up ahead. Pulling up beside it, he got out, tucking his hands into his jacket pockets. He approached Rook where he was standing near the hood of his car.

"So, what are the terms?"

"What do you want them to be, lover boy?" Rook had the nerve to smile at him.

"Call me that again, ass-wipe, and after I'm done smoking your fucking car, I'll beat you unconscious," he threatened.

"I'd love to see that. Might even sell tickets." Rook had the balls to smile at him, showing two missing teeth.

"Found your sense of humor, did you, fucker?" Jordon advanced a few steps. He was spoiling for a fight and Rook was looking like a great place to start. Lashing out might be stupid, but it sure felt good to let go of his tightly leashed emotions.

"Always had it. It only comes out on special occasions. Like races."

"Then nut up or shut up, ass-hat. Let's keep it simple; first to the speed limit sign down there wins. Loser has to wash and wax the winner's car."

"Fair enough. I'm adding an oil change in there, boy-o. I use Royal Purple." Rook held his broad hand out for a shake.

He took Rook's hand, there was no stupid squeezing or grinding of knuckles, just an honest handshake.

"I'll be waiting for you at the finish; don't crash." Jordon turned on his heel, noticing Mic and Jones standing next to her Jeep, knee-deep in weeds. He looked away and got into his car, unreasonable rage clenching his jaw and spiking adrenaline through his already heated blood.

****

We quickly came up on them. They had stopped at the beginning of a long straight stretch. They were standing near their hoods, talking and gesturing with their hands. I pulled off to the side into the weeds.

They shook hands just as I was getting out with Jones. Jordon quickly glanced over his shoulder at me, but didn't say anything; just got into his car and started it up. Rook either didn't notice us or didn't care that we were there. I wondered what the start signal would be. No one was waving a flag or anything. I didn't have time to figure it out because with a cloud of burning rubber, they were off; tires screeched and gears slammed. They were even at first, but one more gear change had Rook pulling ahead. The noise was deafening; the ground vibrated with the power unleashed from the engines. Time slowed down; the race lasting mere seconds, but felt much longer.

"Rook has it," Jones muttered from next to me. He was correct, Rook slowed once he got to the speed limit sign. Jordon was behind him by only a fraction of a second. It was damn close.

"Let's go. I've seen enough." I got into the Jeep and turned around in the middle of the road. I didn't want to see anymore. I drove us in silence back to the compound.

Chapter 19

I stood at my window, watching the night. There wasn't much to see. No lighting bugs, no animals, not even snow. Just the cold and wind moving the naked branches of the trees around. I clutched a cup of coffee in my hands. I'd made it more to warm up my hands than anything else.

My thoughts wandered around from Jordon to Aunt Beatrice and Jackson, to Willie, to Vega, and back to Jordon. Always back to Jordon. The man pulled at me, drew me in, and sucked me into a rabbit warren of impossible dreams.

A knock on the door startled me out of my reverie. Opening it wide, I wasn't surprised to find Jordon standing there.

"I need to talk to you." He stepped inside, brushing past me and not waiting for an invitation.

"Just come on in, Jordon; make yourself at home in my personal space. No problem, manners aren't necessary."

"Gee thanks, Bea, for the hospitality." He stood in front of me, arms crossed over his broad chest, green eyes burning with emotions that I didn't care to examine.

"For someone who wants to talk to me so bad, you sure aren't saying much." I don't know if it was my feelings about him or my attraction, but he brought out my snarky bitch in full force.

"Fucking hell, you're a real bitch, you know that?"

"Of course I do. I make sure I excel at everything. As entertaining as this verbal sparring is, cut to the chase or get the fuck out." I turned from him and went back to staring out the window. What I saw there defied explanation.

"Jordon, come here. Tell me you see this too and I'm not having some crazy-ass PTSD episode."

Standing behind me, he looked out toward the training yard. The view that had been boring before was a hell of a lot more interesting now.

"Is that...?" Jordon covered his face with his hands, trying to unsee that awful thing out there.

"Yes. I do believe that's Flynn. Naked." I stepped around a sick-looking Jordon and walked out onto my porch. I could hear the fucking idiot singing 'Girls Just Wanna Have Fun' at the top of his lungs.

Pierce was chasing after him, being outpaced by a drunk and naked man. Flynn was running in circles, waving what looked like Jones's Stetson over his head. It was like a car wreck and I was rubbernecking in horror. Flynn's upper body was tanned a dark brown, but from the waist down to about knee height, he was snow white. His pale white legs flashed in the moonlight. It was hilarious and sickening at the same time. Each time he faced me, I closed my eyes. A naked, running, bouncing Flynn was not something I wanted stored in my memory banks.

"Pierce! Tackle him, goddammit!" I shouted, stepping down off my porch into the yard. Flynn saw me and shouted "Horray!" He then ran toward me, dropping the hat which Pierce scooped up on the fly.

"Oh no, Mic, he spotted you," Jordon said from beside me, quickly moving out of the way.

"Oh fuck." I sidestepped a slowing and now stumbling Flynn; no fucking way was I going to let him tackle me. He tripped over his feet and somehow rolled, landing on his back in the cold wet grass. He was breathing hard and laughing his ass off.

Pierce arrived just in time. He tossed the hat like he was throwing the golden ring. It landed with perfect accuracy on Flynn's privates, not quite in time though, I got an eye full of Flynn's surprising package before putting all of my attention on Pierce.

"What in the ever loving fuck-all is going on here?" I nearly screamed.

"I would think it's fucking obvious Mic!" Pierce shouted back, losing his normally controlled composure.

"The fun never stops around here, does it?" Rook said, appearing out of nowhere.

"For fuck's sake, someone get him up," I ordered.

"I'm not touching naked Flynn." Jordon held up his hands and stepped backwards. "He's your best friend, Pierce, you do it."

"Fuck you, man, I can't carry him alone," Pierce shouted again. His face was beet red and he was drenched in sweat. I wondered how long Flynn had been out here leading Pierce on a merry chase. "I am not fucking doing a fire-man's carry with him when he's naked." Flynn chose this opportune moment to pass out, his snores shaking his whole body. I nudged him with my boot; he didn't stir.

"Well he can't stay here; he'll freeze to death," I said. Flynn was already turning a light shade of blue.

"Oh for fuck's sake. You guys are a bunch of pussies. Grab his fucking feet, Pierce." Rook stepped in and took Flynn under his arms.

"Make sure that fucking hat stays where you put it. That is nothing I want to see again." Rook began walking backwards, grunting when he had to lift Flynn a little higher. Flynn's ass was dragging on the grass.

"Hope they don't snag him on any rocks...," Jordon said. "Can we go back inside now and finish what we started?"

"And what exactly did we start, Chris?" My use of his first name tightened his jaw. He found his balls and took me by the upper arm, moving to drag me back into my cabin. I jerked my arm from his grasp. I would not be pulled around like an errant fucking child. "Watch it, Jordon. Do that again and I'll feed you your fucking fingers." I stomped past him, slamming the door against the wall on my way in.

He threw the door closed behind me. His eyes were blazing as he threw off his jacket and toed off his boots, not missing a step or stumbling at all. How he did that without falling over, I wasn't sure. I jerked my eyes from his stocking feet; a casual looking Jordon was too much.

"What the fuck, Jordon?" I was in full retreat mode. Any time he gets that look in his eyes he kisses me, gropes me, or both. And I like it. Too fucking much.

"What does it look like? For such a smart woman, you sure are stupid sometimes." He continued to advance, slipping off his shirt as he did. I forced my eyes to his face. I refused to play into his hands.

"This isn't happening." His hard chest hit my palms just as my back hit the wall. His skin was warm and taut and lightly-fuzzed with hair.

"Don't you see, Bea?" He asked, burying his hands in my hair, using it as a handle to pull me tight against him. "It already is..." My breath caught in my throat, trapped by my beating heart. "I'm not talking to you anymore. I'm done talking. It's your turn to spill some truth." I met his gaze, the green irises were almost swallowed by his black pupils. He was begging me with his eyes to stop this torture, to end our mutual suffering.

"Tell me, Bea, tell me it's not just me dying here. That you feel as drawn to me as I am to you. Tell me you look for me every time you walk into a room, tell me that the thought of me makes your heart beat faster. Fucking tell me that you can't fight this anymore..."

His lips descended to mine. I stopped him by freeing a hand and putting my fingers against his mouth. "No, Chris."

He closed his eyes and sighed. He rested his forehead against mine, staying close to me even as I tried to push him away.

"Why? I know you want me," he whispered against my face, his breath tickling my cheek and sending shivers down my spine.

"Of course I do. It's just not possible for us, Chris. It wouldn't be just one time and it can't be more than that." I pushed against his chest, trying to get some space for myself.

"Bea, no. Dammit, no! I'm not letting you go." He kissed me then and I didn't stop him. He tasted as fresh and delicious as he always did. He was so warm and smelled so good; spice and sweat... he smelled like a man and I ate it up. His big hands cradled my face as he kissed me gently, brushing his lips back and forth across mine.

I kept my palms against his chest, allowing myself a moment to feel him... to feel his skin. I traced his tattoos along his shoulders, letting him take my mouth fully. He was waging a war, using my body against me. I pulled back, getting some air, forcing some space between our lips.

"Chris, you have to go. Right now. You need to go. I won't be alone with you again." I started pushing at him, shoving him as hard as I could. I wouldn't look at him; I couldn't, because if I looked into his eyes again, I would fall... and keep falling.

He finally stopped pushing back and I pointed him toward the door. He gathered his boots and shirt, slipping them on as quickly and smoothly as he had slipped them off.

"One day, Bea Michaels, you *will* stop running. One day you'll realize just what it is you're pushing away. When that day comes, I'll be here... or I might not be." He turned his back and softly shut the door behind him.

"Maybe so, but that day is not today," I said aloud as the door closed. Picking up the small remote, I switched on Sinatra and took off my clothes, getting ready for some much needed sleep. It was then that I noticed Jordon's jacket draped on the couch. Picking it up, I pressed it to my face, deeply inhaling the scent of him. I hung it in my small closet, tucking it behind a dress I never wore.

****

Jordon tossed and turned, trying in vain to sleep. Mic had him in knots, squirming and tied to her with no hope of release. He couldn't concentrate on the mission; he was worried he wasn't going to be able to do his job. Giving up on sleep, he padded down the hall and got a bottle of water from the fridge. He considered a beer, but thought better of it. He went out into the living room. Sitting on the couch, he kicked back and propped his feet on the table.

Stacking his hands behind his head, he stared at the ceiling. He counted the tiles there and tried to just let his mind wander and find some peace.

"You won't find any answers there." Rook's voice startled him.

Sitting up suddenly, Jordon dropped his feet to the floor. "What do you mean?" he asked, as his teammate sat beside him.

Leaning forward, bracing his elbows on his knees, Rook clasped his hands and stared at him. "There are no answers for you on the ceiling, my friend. Women are a paradox. Don't bother trying to figure them out and you will be much happier." Rook's face as blank as ever. This guy gave Jones a pretty good run for his money in the stoic department.

"Who said anything about a woman?" Jordon was on the defensive.

"You didn't have to. You've been in combat enough, that I know you aren't losing sleep over the op today. There's nothing else going on; so it's a woman and Mic is the only one around."

"Your powers of deduction are astounding," He kicked the coffee table with the heel of his foot, shoving it a few inches across the room with a screech.

"I know. Forget her, kid; just for now. Let's get through this mission and when it's over, if you still want to get her in the sack, we'll figure something out. Does she like you too, or is this one of those pathetic one-sided things?"

"She likes him too." Jones joined in, sitting in the available chair, and rubbing his hands over his face. "I've known Mic for years and I've never seen her like this, not even over Willie." He got up again and grabbed a couple waters, passing them around.

"Yeah, she wants me too. She won't give us a chance because she's worried about losing the team's respect." Jordon put his head in his hands. He couldn't believe he was having this conversation with Rook and Jones of all fucking people.

It was always the quiet ones…

"Trust me, we're sick of seeing you two mooning over each other. Since day one, you've both been making eyes back and forth. Rook is right; when this mission is over, we're solving this," Jones added before retreating back to his room.

"Jones is correct you know," Rook said, also standing. "Is this little talk about your feelings over or should I revoke your man card now?"

"It's over, fucker." Jordon threw his empty water bottle at Rook, who, true to form, caught it almost without looking. "I just wish I knew what to do."

"It's simple, just pin her against the wall and show her how you feel," Rook said with a shrug. "It's always worked for me."

"Do you really think that will work?" Jordon asked, hope seeping into his voice.

"No, I think she'll eat your ass alive, but you'll die happy." Rook slapped him on the shoulder and went down the hall to his room.

"Thanks, I feel so much better now," Jordon muttered to himself.

Oddly, he did a little bit. Maybe pinning her against the wall and having at each other really was the best solution. They needed to finish taking care of the rest of the Vega cartel first.

Chapter 20

Mercedes glided into the parlor, her ever present champagne flute clutched in her hand. She had just finished dinner; the grilled snapper was delicious, as was every meal their five-star chef served. Julio was seated in his favorite gilded chair, going over papers of some kind. The sight of him made her skin try to crawl off of her body. It was a shame that such fantastic good looks were wasted on the twisted evil excuse for a man.

"*Buenas noches,* Mercedes," Julio said, without looking up. His voice was smooth and cultured with almost no trace of accent. He'd been raised in the United States, even though his mother was Mexican. He had the icy blue eyes of his American father.

"Good evening to yourself, Julio," she replied coolly. Seating herself across from him, she crossed one long leg over the other, the sheen of her silk stockings reflecting the low light.

"Good of you to grace me with your presence." He rose and walked over to the bar, refilling his glass of cognac.

"You didn't give me much choice in the matter, Julio. I trust your evening was enjoyable?" She sipped her champagne, trying to hide her revulsion.

"Very much so. She performed perfectly." Her stomach rolled at the thought of that table of his.

"What is your plan now that Adolfo is gone? How do you plan to avenge Diego?" Pushing him was not always the best idea, but she wanted answers. Steel needed to pay and she needed Julio and the cartel to help her avenge her husband.

"Don't worry your head about that, my dear; you will get your revenge. Steel is powerful; one cannot just waltz up to their gates. It must be done with finesse and careful planning." Julio drained his cognac and waved his now empty glass at her. She rose gracefully to refill it, turning her back to him to hide her shaking hands.

"Diego would be very pleased that you are taking care of me, Julio." She poured the cognac, almost spilling it across the shiny maple bar.

"I'm sure he would be. I can see that I scare you my dear, let me assure you, you have nothing to fear from me. You are Mexican and I find Mexican girls distasteful. However, that *puta* that leads Steel..." he paused to savor the thought, licking his lips. "I must have her. That will be my gift to you; first I will break her, and then I will consume her." She handed him his glass, shuddering when his hand brushed hers. His touch was like that of a snake; such a foul creature should feel slimy and disgusting, but instead he felt cool and smooth.

"How do you plan on doing that Julio?" She pushed her fear of him aside. "She isn't going to deliver herself to you."

"Oh, but she is, my dear... she is." The devil himself stared out of Julio's eyes, smiling with pure, unaltered evil.

****

I waited in the hangar for the men. We needed to get back to the Wonka House and I needed to check on my aunt and Jackson.

"Morning, Mic." Pierce walked in, carrying a cup of coffee in each hand. Sitting next to me on the bench, he handed me one.

"Thanks. Morning yourself. Where's Flynn?" I asked as I took a drink. Damn good stuff.

"He should be staggering in here soon. He was awake when I left."

"What the hell was that all about last night, anyway?" Flynn getting wasted was nothing new. Flynn streaking was.

"I'm not sure. I don't think he even remembers doing it. Mark down another escapade for Flynn. He's done shit like this off and on since we were kids," Pierce said in a very rare reference to their childhood together.

Jones and Rook strolled in, clutching their own cups of coffee and hiding their eyes from the glare of the bright morning sun behind sunglasses. They were twins in mannerisms despite being opposites in looks.

"I see you have your hat back, Jones. I didn't think you'd want it after where it was last night." I said, laughing. He didn't look amused, taking a seat in the corner and pulling the hat low on his forehead.

"He sprayed it with disinfectant last night and again this morning," Rook added, leaning against the lockers, crossing his arms over his chest.

"Fuck off, man. There was no need for that. I was drunk, not diseased," Flynn growled from the doorway, wincing when the door slammed behind him.

"Loud noises hurt your head there, Flynn?" I shouted loud enough to hurt my own ears. Pale and sweating, he clutched his head in both hands. "Good thing we have a pilot since you're in no shape to drive a scooter, let alone fly a plane."

"It's a jet." He sat down heavily next to Pierce, still holding his head in his shaking hands.

"Fuck off. Where's Jordon?"

"I'm right here, Mic." He'd come in behind Flynn and I hadn't even noticed.

"Everyone have your shit? We're rolling out in five." I grabbed my bag and left the hangar. The stairs on the jet were down and waiting for us. I climbed aboard and waited while the others filed in behind me.

"I do love this jet…" Rook's voice trailed off as he went to the back, sitting down and kicking back.

"Jones, sit with me. We need to talk." I waited while he stowed his rifle and settled in. "What do you have on the Suit?" Urgency sharpened my voice.

"Not much, unfortunately. Armando saw him a few times, but never got close to him. All I could find out was his first name is Julio, and that he was Adolfo's second-in-command. There is no one in any database by that name and description."

"Well, fuck," I said, with feeling. "What about Mercedes?"

"Her, we know more about. She comes from a wealthy Mexican family. Her father was involved in the Vega cartel; her cousin of course was Adolfo. Her marriage by all reports was a political alliance, but some also say that it was a love match."

"Great, we've got a woman scorned on our hands. What else?" I was desperate for information. It was already personal, now it was more so.

"What the hell do you expect, Mic? This is a cartel, they don't exactly advertise their information. We're lucky to know as much as we do. No one likes to talk about them; to talk is to be killed, and for your whole family to be killed." Jones was obviously frustrated at the lack of information.

"Let's give what we have to Jackson and go from there. Maybe he has some more information for us." As soon as we got back we needed to come up with a plan. We didn't have the luxury of waiting around; they would be coming for us. We needed to be in their backyard before they had a chance to recover from the blow we dealt yesterday.

****

Jackson looked at the satellite images in front of him; his stomach dropped to his feet. There would be no keeping this from Mic or keeping her the fuck out of it. As soon as she saw this, she'd be on a plane, heading back to Mexico.

The intercom beeped; he answered it with the press of a button. "Yes?"

"Food is ready, Fisher." Beatrice's voice soothed his old battered soul.

"I'll be there in a moment."

"Make sure that you are, eggs get cold quickly." Beatrice's subtlety was better than Mic's, but not by much.

Closing the folder, Jackson left it on the table and went down to the kitchen for dinner. He didn't want to keep Beatrice waiting. Tonight might be his last calm evening for a while.

Pushing the kitchen door open, he was greeted by the scent of grilling steak and a beautiful voice singing a haunting melody he'd never heard. Beatrice was swaying slightly to the music as she turned the steaks on the built-in grill.

Her hips rocked back and forth to the music, mesmerizing him. There was true beauty; not just in her looks, but in the curves and motions of her body. Her movements were sexy and tantalizing. He swallowed hard, trying to get the thick lump brought on by the sight before him to go down.

"Beatrice...," he managed to force out. He hadn't been so affected by a woman in his memory, not even when he was a young man.

"Fisher! Don't sneak up on me like that; you startled me." She waved the spatula at him, as if she was chastising a child.

"Force of habit." He reached around her and flicked the burners off, killing the flame and probably ruining the steaks.

"What are you doing?" Her brow furrowed in confusion.

"You were dancing alone. No one as stunning as you should ever dance alone." He turned the volume up and swept her in against his body. "What's this song? I've never heard it before."

Resting one hand on her waist, he clasped her hand with the other and held it against his chest. Her scent filled his nose as he buried his face in her neck and hair. She smelled of cloves, lemon, and woman. His mouth watered, begging him to take a taste.

"It's by Adele. The song is called *When We Were Young*." She looked up at him, her deep brown eyes shining with surprise and wonder. It was a look he didn't feel he had earned yet; but if she was willing to give it, he was willing to take it. He moved them around the kitchen and when the song ended, he started it again.

"You do something to me, Beatrice, something I can't describe or explain. Whatever it is, don't stop. I've only known you for a few days and I know it's insane, but... I don't want to go back to the empty life I had before I met you. I'm alive around you."

"You're insane; there is no doubt about that, Fisher. Anyone who has to deal with Bea on a daily basis is bound to be nuts." She raised her face to his, her eyes shining with laughter and the beginnings of something more.

He took her invitation and kissed her deeply, groaning at her taste.

"Maybe so...," he said, speaking against her mouth. "...but that's okay. It makes me crazy enough to do this." Grasping her waist with both hands, he lifted her up and onto the counter behind her; quickly stepping between her legs, he didn't give her a moment to react. Cradling her face between his hands, he kissed her again and again until they were both gasping for air. Hearts racing against each other, chests heaving and hands sweating; he stared into her eyes, seeing a future there. A future filled with happiness and family. Pulling her even closer, he bent her backward over his arm and kissed her some more and gratefully he let his mind shut off. His heart stuttered with hope... hope that what he'd seen in her eyes would become his reality.

Chapter 21

The elevator closed behind me. The men had all gone to change and eat. I went directly to the war room. I wanted to use the computer there and review the fire fight data from yesterday. I needed to get a better look at that Julio fucker. You can tell a lot about a man by how he reacts to a fight. Be it guns or fists, the adrenaline rush freezes some and throws others into action. I needed to study my target and find an opening. There was one... of that I was sure.

The soft carpet of the war room cushioned my feet as I let the door shut behind me. The monitors were dark, the computers cold. I switched one on and waited for it to start up. There was an orange folder on the table. It was not like Jackson to leave Top Secret folders lying around. Opening it, the name stamped on the top made me flip through it. Photos spilled across the table in a glossy wash of death.

People from the village, butchered and burned. Women and children along with men, young and old. No one was spared this cruelty. They were lined up in neat little bloody rows. Each one was the same, dismembered and then the pieces burned; a name was carved into their foreheads.

My name.

There were at least thirty photos spread across the table. A single note accompanied the pictures, scrawled in elegant script on expensive stationary:

> **This will continue every day, until either Bea Michaels delivers herself into my care or I run out of villagers. Tomorrow starts another day. She has until dawn to get here.**
>
> **-Julio**

I left the room at a run, rifle bumping against my leg and my pack slung over my shoulder. The others were still either at dinner or changing. I only had a few minutes to get out of here before they could stop me. Pulling out my phone as I hit the elevator, I accessed the security for the garage. They would know where I was going and I knew they would follow. I exited the elevator and raised the control panel near the door. Activating the lock-down was easy, changing the security codes wasn't. The door locked with a magnetic *click* and the elevator descended. The door to the elevator would open, but pushing the buttons would get them exactly nowhere. Jones would have to hack into his own system and change the security protocols.

Tossing my pack onto the passenger seat, I jumped into the SUV and peeled out of the garage, leaving a trail of rubber and smoke behind me. I put the accelerator to the floor and headed to the airfield, hoping the fucking jet was still there getting re-fueled for its trip back to the compound.

I nearly put the SUV onto two wheels turning onto the airfield. The jet was still in sight, thank fucking Christ. The fuel truck was pulling away from it and the steps ascended as I watched. I nearly dropped the tranny by throwing the SUV into park before stopping all the way. I ran for the jet, screaming and waving my arms.

The steps lowered back down and the captain peered out at me. His look of confusion only increased as I got closer and he saw that I was alone. "What's going on? I had orders to go back to the compound."

"Orders changed. We're going to Mexico. Right fucking now." I climbed aboard, grateful beyond measure that I still had my rifle and gear with me.

"Copy that. You're the boss." He headed into the cabin as I raised the stairs. I loved that he didn't question me or hesitate.

I stowed my gear and sat in my favorite chair. I found the silence deafening. Usually the guys were around me, bullshitting and screwing off. Once we were in the air, I needed to get to work. I had to pull up everything I could on Villahermosa. Going in alone was damn dangerous, but the faces in those photographs were haunting me; those innocent people, dead... because of me. I fingered the handle on the machete still strapped to my thigh. I had nearly forgotten it was there. I would bloody its blade again, and soon. I couldn't let anyone else be slaughtered. Even if it meant my own life.

****

Jordon paced with the others in the war room; the photos and note on the table were all the evidence they needed to know where Mic had gone.

"Jones, get the fucking shit changed; we don't have time to dick around," Jackson growled from where he was wearing a hole in the carpet. Beatrice was sitting at the table, tears tracking down her face and falling softly onto her folded hands. Her lips were moving in a silent prayer.

"Master Sergeant, the jet just took off," Jones calmly reported, his fingers flying across the keys.

"Fuck!" Jackson shouted, making Beatrice jump. She stood and took him by the arm.

"We'll be in the hall," she said, dragging the much larger man behind her like an errant toddler.

The door shut behind them. Flynn ran over and pressed his ear to the door. Pierce smacked him on the back of the head.

"Get the fuck away from there, you nosy bastard." Pierce grabbed hold of Flynn, trying to drag him back.

The door opened suddenly, knocking them both onto their asses. Jackson's head popped in quickly. "The adults are talking, children, be patient. Jones, track the jet."

"On it," Jones answered at the door shut again. The man was as focused as Jordon had ever seen him. Sweat was sliding down his temples, but his eyes never left the screen.

"What the fuck was she thinking?" Jordon was furious that she would do something so fucking stupid. Giving herself up to that monster, with no back-up and no plan. "When I get my hands on her, I'm going to beat some fucking sense into her." Jordon repeatedly ran his hands over his head and down his face. His beard was thick now and it itched like a motherfucker.

"Obviously, she's a fucking dumbass and we're going to have to go back to motherfucking Mexico to bring her stupid fucking twat home." Rook's colorful language had them all staring.

"Well, Rook, don't hold back, brother. Let her have it." Pierce stopped his pacing long enough to say.

"I'm going to tell her you called her a stupid fucking twat," Flynn added from where he was standing over Jones's shoulder, trying and failing to make sense of the lines of numbers scrolling down the monitors.

"So fucking what? I'll tell her to her fucking face after I save her stupid ass." Rook was nearly foaming at the mouth. "Jones, hurry the fuck up, man."

"Listen here, ass wipes, this isn't easy. It's a process and if you don't stop your bitching and fucking off, it's going to take me even longer. She knew I would get through, it just takes a little time. So unless you think you can sit here in this chair and get us the fuck out, shut your fucking traps." Jones lifted one hand and gave them all the finger over his shoulder.

Jordon sat at the table and laid his head on his arms. His gut was a twisted mess of anxiety and fear; adrenaline was pumping through his veins, making his heart race a marathon in his chest. If he didn't get there in time, if he couldn't save her... he didn't allow himself to follow that train of thought any further. They *would* get there, they *would* save her, and he *would* make sure she knew what she meant to him. In that order.

****

Beatrice hauled Jackson behind her down the hallway until they got to the medical center. She wanted a little privacy for this conversation. Pushing the door open, she ignored his stuttering questions. She shoved him down onto a bed and stood in front of him. It was the only way to get him near to eye level.

"Listen to me, Fisher Jackson," she began, stepping between his legs and taking his face into her hands. "You listen well, my Fisher king. You will go and you will find my niece; you will bring her back to me." She kissed him softly and quickly. "Now go, go be with your men and find her. I will be here, waiting for you to return."

He grabbed her face and pulled her into him, kissing her like he was breathing her, holding her tight against him. He slid a hand down to her lower back and buried the other in her hair, pulling her impossibly closer.

"Beatrice...," he gasped against her lips before kissing her again, his tongue sliding against her own. His taste was intoxicating and exotic.

She pulled back, breaking his hold on her. "Fisher, stop." Once again she cradled his face in her hands. "When you get back, we'll finish what you just started."

"Damn right, we will, woman," he growled.

"You're letting me distract you. Why?" She looked deep into his chocolate colored eyes, searching for an answer.

His giant shoulder rose and fell with a deep sigh. "It's my fault she's gone. I left the folder out on the table. I was so focused on seeing you, that I left it there."

"Did you know she would find it? Did you leave it there on purpose?" Beatrice asked calmly.

"No, of course not."

"Then shut up and go do your job." She kissed him one last time and stepped back out of his reach.

"Roger that, ma'am." He tugged her by the hand and towed her back to the war room.

****

The door crashed open against the wall, startling them all. Jordon's head flew up in surprise. Jackson was standing there, holding hands with Beatrice who had a very self-satisfied smirk on her face.

"Jones. Update." Jackson ordered.

"Almost there," Jones snapped in return, his patience nearly gone.

"The rest of you clowns, get your shit together. We're going to get her." They jumped into action, tightening rifle slings and double-checking gear.

"Got it!" Jones shouted in victory, throwing his hands into the air. He stood so quickly the chair flew out from behind him and crashed to the floor.

They hurried past Jackson on the way to the elevator. "Go on up,

I'll be right there."

Jordon glanced behind him and saw Jackson reaching out for Beatrice's face. He shuffled into the elevator with the others. There wasn't much room for Jackson anyway.

"Question. Since Mic took the jet, how are we getting to Mexico? I don't think they'll let us fly in coach," Flynn piped up in his usual smart-ass manner.

"Don't worry your pretty little face, flyboy. I got you a toy," Jones replied.

"You think my face is pretty? Aww, Jones, I didn't know you noticed." Flynn winked at him.

"Flynn, do you ever shut your fucking mouth?" Rook fast losing patience.

Jordon had enough of their crap. "All of you, cut the shit. We need to get Mic; that's all we need to focus on right now. I get you're stressed as fuck, but just shut it!" He was the first off the elevator and into the waiting Suburban. The elevator went back down as soon as the last man got off.

Pierce slid into the back beside him. "You're right man, but that's how they let off steam. We're all scared for her; we're all worried and anxious to kick some ass."

"I know, I just need to do this. If she dies while we're here dicking around, I'm going to lose my fucking mind."

Jackson took the driver's seat and the others piled into the Suburban around him. "Jordon, you have met Mic, right? No fucking way is she going to let that bastard have the upper hand. I'm not sure she's capable of dying."

"Let's go get our girl, boys." Jackson was chewing on an unlit cigar as he pulled out of the garage, driving one-handed. They were soon flying down the road, racing forward in the hope that they could reach

Mexico in time.

Chapter 22

I stepped off the plane and ran to the waiting Jeep. The advantage of being at the controls was that I could get the ride I wanted. I tossed my pack in and secured my rifle. It was an older model, but a Jeep was a Jeep. I didn't have much time; dawn was an hour away. I prepared to retrace my steps from yesterday, only this time I would drive right into the village square.

I headed out into the desert, the cool evening about to give way to the warmth and heat of the day. My headlights bounced along the tire tracks from yesterday. I followed them at a steady pace, my nerves and adrenaline ratcheting up with every mile I drew closer to the village.

I quickly came upon the wrecked vehicles from the fire fight, their blackened remains pushed off of the road. Everywhere I looked, I saw flattened and useless poppies. That sight gave me great pleasure. Turning onto the road between the fields, I dodged the holes left from Pierce's bombs and headed straight for the faint light on the horizon. The lights of the village drew me in as a light rain began to fall. I switched on the wipers and sped up.

I was rushing forward, more than likely to my death, but I hurried all the same. The way I saw it, as long as I got the chance to take Julio with me, I didn't mind dying too much. I was a soldier, a warrior, and I was bred to sacrifice my life for others.

****

Julio sipped strong coffee from a delicate cup as he watched the rain begin to fall, impatiently waiting for his prize to arrive. He'd brushed and steamed his best suit before donning it. Slicking his already perfect hair back from his forehead, he spotted the approaching headlights. There wasn't much traffic out here so she was easy enough to spot.

Looking at his Rolex, he noted that she was a tiny bit early. Dawn wasn't for another fifteen minutes. Punctual... he liked that in a woman.

Sending those photos was the best idea he'd had in a very long time. Everyone had a price, be it money or motivation. Getting that bitch here was just a matter of the correct amount of motivation. She was a soldier, a leader; it was in her nature to sacrifice herself for the greater good. Killing the villagers was no issue for him; he viewed them as cattle anyway. They had their uses, but at the end of the day they were easily slaughtered to suit his needs.

There was only one vehicle approaching and he was positive that she was stupid enough to come alone as he had instructed. No doubt her team would follow, no matter what her orders were. He would have men ready to do deal with them; a few well-placed snipers should do the trick in delaying them. He planned to be otherwise... occupied.

Finishing his coffee, he let a smile stretch his face; anticipation gripped him, hardening his cock to the point he needed to adjust his pants. He couldn't wait to show the *puta* what he did to little blondes like her.

****

I slowed as I drove into the dark town; the rain had picked up and was puddling all over, creating thick mud which I was careful to stay out of. Trying to escape with a stuck vehicle would not be a good start to the day. I was halfway through the village square when my escort arrived. Two trucks, similar to the ones from the other day, pulled up alongside me. Men in rain slickers kept AKs trained on me as I more or less ignored them.

They didn't really worry me overly much, since their boss wanted me alive. They were just here to intimidate me, which of course wasn't working. The fucktard in the back of the truck closest to me waved at me to pull over. I gave him the finger and kept driving.

I may have been surrendering myself, but I was going to do it on my terms, and that meant having this Jeep as close to the house as possible. Preferably within running distance. As I neared the brightly lit house, I pulled my pack closer to me. Digging around, I found what I was looking for and stashed it under the dash. They would no doubt take my pack and weapons, but when I got out of there, I wasn't going to be weaponless if I could help it.

The guy in the truck kept waving his gun at me and shouting something in Spanish; I kept on ignoring him. I risked a glance and it looked like he was about to blow a blood vessel in his overly large forehead. The temptation to pull my M-9 and shoot him was strong, but now was not the time. Instead I followed the truck into the short circular driveway, making sure that the Jeep wasn't blocked in and the front end was pointed directly out. Moving quickly, I took the spare key off the ring and stashed it under the seat. I was betting my life on the fact that they wouldn't bother to search the Jeep. It was a risk I had to take. But, I didn't come here without back-up. I tapped on my phone, activating the GPS. Waiting until now would give Jones my exact location. I sent a text to Jones, knowing that he would trace it and ping it back to my location. As long as the phone was on, he could track it. Switching it onto silent, I shoved it under the seat with the spare key and back-up pistol I'd stashed.

My door was jerked open and I allowed myself to be pulled out by the arm. A *sicario* was screaming in my face, spit landing on my cheek with each word. I wiped it off and flung it in his general direction. He raised his hand to slap me, but was stopped by a hand on his arm.

"No. Girl is for Julio. No marks," the man said, flinging sir-spits-a-lot away. He turned to me and efficiently stripped me of my rifle and side-arm. He reached for my belt, but I slapped his hands away.

"Must have machete. Take off or I cut off." He pulled a long knife from his belt and pointed at my waist.

"Fine, you fucker." Jerking the ties off my thigh, I slipped off my leather belt and pulled the sheath from it. I dropped the sheath carelessly at his feet and rethreaded the belt onto my pants. "I'll be taking my weapons and that machete back, just so ya know."

"Come. Now." His broken English was easy enough to understand even with his thick accent. The others stood around my Jeep, rapid fire Spanish pouring from their mouths. When I didn't immediately obey, the man grabbed me by my upper arm and dragged me.

"Let the fuck go." I planted my feet and pivoted my weight, throwing him off balance and making him lose his grip on my arm. "I'll walk on my own. Keep your fucking hands off me." I snapped. He nodded his understanding.

He spared me a last glance before leading the way into the mansion. The sound of my boots striking against marble echoed back to me. It was eerily similar to the mansion in Colombia.

Maybe cartel drug lords all had the same decorator?

Thick carpeted hallways led off to wings on my right and left; directly ahead was a grand staircase, sweeping upward in a curve of white and black marble. It wasn't the architecture that caught my eye, but the man standing at the base of the stairs. Though to call him a man was to insult true men everywhere. This fucker was a monster in a suit.

"Ah, Miss Michaels, you've made it. Welcome!" He clapped his soft manicured hands and walked toward me, one meticulously graceful step at a time. He was impeccably groomed from his Italian kid-skin shoes, to his grey Armani suit with fine black pinstripes. His appearance might have been G.Q, but the madness in his eyes was obvious even from this distance.

This fucker is looney tunes...

"My name is Mic, but you can call me Staff Sergeant Michaels." He was within arms-reach and before I had a second to react his thug behind me grabbed my arms and twisted them up and back.

"Now, now, Luis, don't hurt her. She is, after all, a guest in my home." He swept his hand wide, encompassing the gilded space around us.

"I'm no guest. Cut the crap, fuck-face. What do you want from me?"

Anger tightened his face for a brief second before he schooled his features back into a polite mask.

So... he gets pissed when I'm rude. Well he's just going to love me...

"Rudeness is unbecoming in a woman so beautiful." He reached a hand past my face and stroked my hair. A near blissful look appeared across his features.

"Touch me again; I dare you." I growled in his face. He was really starting to piss me off. "Get your dancing monkey off me, right now." I jerked on my arms suddenly with no regard for my joints. The *sicario* lost his balance and stumbled into me slightly, but didn't release my arms.

"Oh I think not, my dear Staff Sergeant. Your reputation precedes you, I'm afraid. You won't be released, now or ever, in fact. It's going to be a joy to break someone so strong..." He circled me slowly, trailing his hand down my arm, fingering my tattoos, "...someone so brave and selfless... you're going to be my finest work yet," he finished, as he faced me once more.

My stomach balled up in fear. His eyes were filled with something I could not name. I'd never seen such lust and hate mingled together into one look before. He wanted me... his tented pants were proof of that, but this wasn't about sex. This was about power...

"Good luck with that. Many a man has tried, and yet... here I am. Bring it." I ducked my chin and spat on his fine Italian shoes. I saw the back-hand coming, but had no way to dodge it. The *crack* of his palm against my cheek was nearly as shocking as the pain of it. I saw him move again and tried to dodge the next hit, but couldn't, and ended up taking most of the vicious hit on my temple. My face was numb from the blows and my head was swimming.

Guy hits like a fucking mule...

The third hit was a closed fist; the last thing I felt before my world went dark the impact on my chin, the painful shockwaves clacking my teeth together, and I bit my tongue, filling my mouth with warm, salty blood.

****

Jackson led the way onto the tarmac of the small airport, the SUV Mic has taken still sitting where she had left it. Waiting for them was a twin of their jet, only it was white and slightly smaller; it was hard to get an exact replica when theirs was a custom job.

"Jones, you never fail to amaze. Where the fuck did you get this?" Jackson fought to get his bulk up the narrow staircase. Damn things were made for tiny little businessmen and their girlfriends, not soldiers.

"Well, Master Sergeant... do you really want to know?" Jones looked sheepish, rubbing his hand along the band of his Stetson.

"Was it illegal?" Jackson didn't care much for legalities, but he still needed to answer for any blatant law breaking.

"No," Jones replied, taking a seat next to Rook. The interior was smaller and much narrower than their jet. There were no bank of computers nor cozy little tables, just six chairs and what looked like a pull-out couch.

"Okay then, that's enough for me. Flynn, get this can in the air; she's got enough of a head start on us as it is."

"Buckle up, kiddies, we're taking off." Flynn came over the intercom. Why he used it when he could just turn around was anyone's guess.

Seat belts clicked and Jackson was grateful that the seats weren't as narrow as the stairs. He didn't fly often; at least not in a plane, but this wasn't too bad. "Jones, get on that tablet of yours and pull me up some intelligence,"

"Yes, Master Sergeant." Jones's finesse with technology never got old. It made life for them a lot easier. Seeing him in combat gear while handling the delicate electronics was always interesting.

"Master Sergeant, are you going to stay on the plane or are you coming in with us?" Rook had the balls to ask.

"Son, I have my rifle, my sidearm, and three knives. Do you think I brought them because they look pretty?"

"No, Master Sergeant." Rook looked at his boots.

"This is Mic; she's one of our own. She may be a fucking dumbass for going it alone, but I for one, am not willing to stand over her coffin. Got me, soldier?" Jackson swallowed the egg-sized lump in his throat. Showing emotion was out of the question, but Mic was like a daughter to him and he refused to stand back while the others went in and saved her.

"Copy that, Master Sergeant." They each replied in turn.

"Flynn, what's our ETA?" Jackson barked over his shoulder.

"Right around six hours, sir."

"Make it less if you can. Jones, I want transport on the ground when we get there; a chopper if possible. If the Mexican government won't provide one, you get me a private contractor. Got me?" Jackson's skin was itching with impatience. A man who would willingly slaughter dozens of innocent people just to make a point and send a message was not someone Mic needed to be spending any length of time with.

"Jones, where's our jet?" Anxiety was balling his stomach into knots.

"She's about an hour ahead of us; once she lands she's got a bit of a drive. I'm assuming she obtained a vehicle somehow. She'll make it there before dawn, but only just in time." Jones kept tapping away on the tablet, cursing under his breath occasionally.

"She'll be alone for five hours. That's a long fucking time. God dammit, Mic, what were you thinking?" Jackson rubbed both hands back and forth over his head. "Everyone try to relax; maybe get some rest. We've got a long day ahead of us."

Jackson pulled out his Sig Sauer that Mic had gotten him for Christmas last year; the gold leaf inside the engravings was still as shiny and gorgeous as the day she gave it to him. He'd never fired it outside of the range; it was intended as more of a show piece. He would use it for its intended deadly purpose tonight if he got the chance.

The others kicked back as best they could. Jackson wouldn't be able to sleep until Mic was home safe. Losing her wasn't an option. Phillips's death had nearly broken them; if Mic were to die it would be the end of Steel.

His thoughts turned to Beatrice as he holstered his pistol. She was an amazing woman and there was nothing he wanted more than to get to know her better... in every way. He couldn't allow himself the option or even the thought of such happiness with her if he didn't bring her niece home in one piece.

"Sir! Master Sergeant!" Jones's voice startled him awake. He hadn't intended to fall asleep, but like most soldiers, he could sleep anywhere, anytime when on a mission. It was sleeping at home in a bed that was the trouble.

"What is it, Jones?"

"I've got her. She texted me and activated the GPS in her phone." His voice was laced with excitement. He flipped the table around so Jackson could see the text.

Hurry up, Eagle. I'm waiting.

"That's our girl!" Jackson rose and took the seat next to Jones. "Can you pull up satellite on this thing?" he asked, pointing at the tablet.

"No. Sorry, boss. I can pin point where she is on Google Earth, but that's it."

"It'll have to do. Pull it up. Fuck, I wish we had a big monitor. This screen is too small for us all to crowd around."

"Just tell me who to shoot; that's all I need to know," Pierce said.

"I'm sure it'll be easy enough to figure out. It's usually the guys with guns shooting at you." Flynn joked from the cockpit.

Pierce laughed. "Always have to be the smart ass, *huh*, Flynn?" The little bit of levity was welcome.

"Let's just focus on getting there in one piece and getting her the fuck out, then I'm going to kill her myself," Jackson growled.

"Copy that, Master Sergeant," Pierce said, echoed by the others. Rook was the only one who remained silent, focused on the passing clouds outside his window, seemingly lost in thought.

Chapter 23

I woke by degrees, quickly recognizing the pain in my head. Moving too fast would be a very bad idea. I was lying on my side, cold seeping into my skin from the floor; at least I thought it was the floor. I tried to open my eyes, but only saw blackness. There wasn't a blindfold or hood on me that I could feel.

Fuck... fuckity... fuck... I'm in the dark...

My breathing picked up as my claustrophobia rose to the surface. Panic gripped me in a vicious, choking hold. I tried to swallow it down... calm my breathing. I needed to focus on something else, like getting out of the dark.

I tried to pull my arms forward, but they were tied behind me. Wiggling them back and forth got no response. I couldn't feel my fingers; I was tied too tightly. Bad for me, but damn effective.

Fine, moving on...

Trying to move my legs got the same result, my ankles were tied together; any movement sent shooting pains rising from my feet, flashing up my legs to my hips.

I've been out for a while...

Panic was a living thing inside of me; it threatened to choke the life from my body. I'd been tied up before, and beaten, but this was a new level for me, left alone in the dark... with no escape.

This wasn't the movies, you couldn't break free from ties this tight. There was a madman after me and he had me exactly where he wanted me. I had to calm down; I was covered in sweat and my breathing was bordering on hyperventilation. The only sound were my gasping inhales and exhales. Saliva pooled in my mouth as bile rose from my twisted gut. I swallowed it down. I might be tied like an animal and about to die, but I would die with some fucking dignity.

I closed my eyes tightly and let my mind take me somewhere else. The brain is a powerful thing, I could go anywhere just by concentrating hard enough.

I felt the seat of my Jeep under me. I heard the loud rumble of the powerful engine; I felt the bumps and jerks as I climbed the mountain. The familiar track was my second home, my place of peace. Music poured from the speakers playing my favorite song, 'I Will Not Bow'. I turned my head and met the startling green eyes I never expected to see. The eyes that belonged to my secret favorite person, though I suspected it wasn't much of a secret anymore.

Laughter brightened his face, making his eyes sparkle and dance. His smile hit me like a punch to the gut; warmth spread throughout my whole body while his smile shined upon me. His hand reached toward me. His palm nearly covered the entire side of my face and a warm glow seeped into my cheek from where his skin touched my own. The thick callouses on his hand were rough against my face. I loved the roughness because it meant that he used his hands a lot. The callouses were formed over years of gripping weapons and climbing ropes. I saw myself reflected in his eyes and it was a beautiful sight indeed...

I was wrenched from my dream suddenly. Frigid water soaked my clothes and froze my already cold skin. I blinked against the water, trying to clear it from my eyes. The room was no longer as dark; there was a silhouette, backlit by a dim light behind him. The angel of death stood before me, darkness seeping from his body, forming his grotesque wings. Fear froze me more solid than the cold ever could.

Blinking some more, I could see the outline of the doorway that he was standing in. I shook my head, trying to clear the last of the dream from my vision and seat myself back into reality. He was just a man; his wings were gone, a figment of shadows and shock.

"Time to wake up, my darling. It's nearly show time for you." Julio's cultured voice washed over me, threatening to do what panic could not; bile was a sickening thickness in the back of my throat.

"Go fuck yourself, you cowardly motherfucker!" I screamed at him. Rage warmed my cold muscles. "Untie me and we'll dance, you bastard. You won't be standing so pretty when I'm done with you!"

"I abhor foul language from a woman. It's worse than rudeness. Keep screaming at me and I will cut out your tongue and feed it to you. I have an excellent recipe for tongue, my dear." He crouched next to me, reaching a long-fingered hand toward my face. I jerked backwards, but had nowhere to go. Uselessness and impotence curdled into immense frustration. I was trapped, incapacitated, and unable to defend myself.

My entire hope rested on the GPS chip in my phone and the slim fucking chance that Julio might make a mistake or give me an opening however small, that I could exploit to my full advantage.

"Fuck off, you sick bastard." Taunting him wasn't a good idea. I had no doubt he would carry out his threat.

Julio pulled a slim and wickedly sharp knife from his pants pocket. Flicking it open with a practiced motion of his thumb, he gripped my jaw; squeezing down, he tried to force my mouth open. I jerked back and forth, attempting to escape his punishing, bruising grip. He might look like a dandy, but he possessed real strength. My jaw ached with the need to open; muscles screaming, I resisted as long as I could. I yelled and swore, spit flying from my mouth.

He shoved the blade into my open mouth. "Hold still, my darling. I would hate to see you cut yourself." He put a knee into my chest, rolling me over onto my back. My tied hands protested and ached with our combined weights. The pain from that, though, was quickly outpaced by the pain in my chest as he leaned his weight down, digging his knee viciously into my ribs

I heard a rib crack; the pressure increased ten-fold and stabbing pain stole my breath. I grunted and heaved, pushing hard with my hips, but he didn't move an inch.

"Stop struggling, stop swearing, and be a good girl. Forget hope...," he spoke into my ear, forcing shivers down my neck, "...it will not save you. Nothing and no one can save you, darling. I am your god; now and forever."

The sharp metallic tang of the metal in my mouth halted my movements, the bitterness on my tongue competing with the fading hope in my heart. I tried to rally myself and find that core of strength and hardness. It escaped me, fading away with every second that ticked by.

What the fuck am I thinking? I'm Staff Sergeant Michaels, I lead the strongest band of warriors that ever existed.

I swallowed that fear, choked that shit down into the abyss of my soul.

I nodded as much as I was able to without cutting my mouth to shreds on his knife. I tried to convey with my eyes my willingness to acquiesce to his will.

For now..., I thought to myself, just for now. Endure, Mic. Endure this like you endured your bastard of a father.

He slowly slipped the knife from my mouth, lifting the edge of my lip up with the blunt side, exposing my upper teeth and gums.

"I will start here the next time you act up. I will cut your teeth from your gums. Do you understand me?" His face was inches from mine, the madness shining from his eyes. "Blink once if you understand." I blinked.

"Good!" He exclaimed, happy as a child again, slipping his knife back into his pocket and clapping his hands with glee. I spit, trying to clear the taste of metal from my mouth. "Oh dear, you must be terribly thirsty. Where are my manners? I'll be right back with a drink for you, darling. Wouldn't want you to be dehydrated and pass out, now would we? Not when we are just starting to have fun." He retreated from the room, a noticeable bounce in his step. The door shut behind him and the sound of the lock turning echoed loud in my ears.

I was in complete darkness again. The smell of the small room was dusty and slightly wet at the same time. I closed my eyes, transporting myself back to the mountain and picking up where I left off with Chris's hand against my face and his smile warming my heart.

****

Mercedes tried to halt the echo of her clacking heels as she walked down the narrow concrete hallway, but it wasn't much use. Taking her shoes off was out of the question; the floor down here was disgusting. Doors lined either side of the short hallway, and evenly spaced low-wattage bulbs hug from the ceiling every ten feet or so. There was enough light to see where you were headed, but only until you got to the next light. She switched on a heavy flashlight, trying not to look at the filthy floor that was ruining her expensive shoes.

Sobs and muffled screams grew and faded as she passed each heavy iron door. Julio kept a few women here all the time. When he tired of one, he simply killed her and ordered his thugs to bury her in the desert. There was an entire field of his victims a few miles away.

Reaching her goal, she paused in front of the last door on the left. Every door was equipped with a sliding panel that allowed someone on the outside to observe the occupant inside. Carefully sliding the panel aside, Mercedes stepped closer and shined her light through the small opening.

A woman was lying on the filthy floor, hands and feet bound, curled into as much of a ball as she could manage. She didn't get the impression that this woman was afraid, more that she was huddled from the cold. Her black pants and t-shirt were sopping wet and stuck to her skin. What must be blonde hair was stuck to her face and, was beginning to curl wildly.

The woman was breathing rapidly, rasping and obviously in great pain. Her face was swollen and bloodied, but even under the seeping blood and bruises, Mercedes could see that this was a very beautiful woman. She was striking, even in her agony.

Suddenly, the woman's eyes sprung open. The look in her grey-blue eyes had Mercedes stumbling backward. Never had never seen such rage and hate co-mingled with an iron will. Fear crawled down her back, tightening her muscles with the need to flee. Even though the woman was bound and there was an iron door between them, Mercedes feared for her life. If given the chance, this woman, this leader of *El Acero*, would kill her. Of that, Mercedes was certain.

Quickly sliding the panel closed, Mercedes hurried from the basement. With each step she took, the need to run dragged at her. She must convince Julio to kill this woman immediately. He should not take the time to play his games with her. She feared that they had made a grave mistake; this woman would be the death of them all.

Chapter 24

Jordon was the last to climb aboard the small military helicopter the Mexican government was so kind to provide. Jones had been assured that even though it was old, it would fly. Strapping himself into the last seat near the door, he tried to calm his racing pulse.

He wanted to shout at Flynn to hurry up as he ran through a pre-flight check, flipping switches and talking to the tower. Finally the rotors began to turn and they took off.

"Flynn, give me an ETA!" Jackson shouted to be heard.

"Twenty minutes, if this weather holds. Storm coming," Flynn said into his headset. Apparently Jackson forgot he had one on. Shouting was not necessary.

Jackson pulled out a map, spreading it out on his lap. "Someone get me a light here."

Jones aimed a small penlight at the map. The pre-dawn sky was dim, compounded by the dark clouds that hovered on the horizon. They were flying right toward the storm.

"Okay boys, gather round. Here's the plan. We're going to land near here." Jackson pointed to a small depression in the desert about five miles from the poppy fields. "We will have to go on foot. It was all we could do to get this chopper, so no vehicle this time. We're operating on the assumption that Mic used a vehicle to get there. If she's injured, we will use her vehicle to return here. We steal one if we need to. The goal is to get Mic; that is our number one priority. Killing that fucker that has her is the second goal. Pierce, I want you to raze that fucking place to the ground. Got me?" Jackson looked at them, huddled as close together as the confines of the chopper would allow. All of them were focused, driven with a single-minded determination; they would complete their mission or die trying. Julio and his thugs chose the wrong people to fuck with; they were Steel and they would bring fire and death in equal measure.

"We got you, Master Sergeant," they all replied.

"This mission isn't going to take much finesse. I don't care how you fucking get it done. We get our girl, kill this bastard and get the hell home. In that order. Any questions?" Jackson was fierce; this was the first time any of them had seen him in the field. As a young man, he must have been a force to be reckoned with.

"I do, Master Sergeant," Jordon said, raising his hand.

"Ask it, but put your fucking hand down. I'm your NCO, not your fucking teacher."

"Julio is mine. Any objections?" Jordon calmly said, his voice not giving away the rage boiling inside his gut.

"None. Flynn, update on the ETA." Jackson had the ability to give orders without needing for them to be actual questions.

"Ten minutes. Gear up, fuckers, we're almost there."

Jordon clutched his weapon close, fingering the trigger guard softly. He had never been so ready to kill someone before. It was a necessary part of war and being a soldier, but never a task he looked forward to. Today was different; he would bathe in Julio's blood and make him pray for death to take him with its dark grasp.

****

The cold woke me up. I was freezing, shaking, and shivering with it, my whole body trembling with the attempt to warm up. After the cold, the next thing I noticed was that I was in a different position. My arms were no longer tied behind my back, instead they were extended over my head and bent backward at an awkward angle. I jerked on them, but they were tied so tightly and in such a strange position, that I couldn't move more than my fingers.

There was enough light that, though it was rather dim, I was able to get a good look at the room around me. I *was* somewhere else. I was in what appeared to be a utility room of some sort. The room had grey stone walls, and the little bit of the floor that I could see was concrete. It eerily reminded me of the sound proof room back on our compound. There was no two-way mirror here, at least not that I could see. I didn't see furniture or tables of any kind.

How did I get here? I don't remember moving.

Confusion was thick in my mind, muddying my thoughts. The last thing I remember was a young girl bringing me a glass of water. It was slightly bitter, but I'm in fucking Mexico; the water sucks here. It must have been a drug, something to knock me out. My head ached and my mouth was dry and cottony.

As my mind slowly cleared, I became aware of my legs; they were no longer tied together at the ankles. I was able to raise my head enough to look down. The sight of my bare skin explained why I was so cold; I was naked. My feet were tied into stirrups with shiny white ropes circling my ankles, lashing them tight to the stirrup supports. My legs were splayed open; the cold air brushed against the most intimate parts of my body, making me cringe in humiliation. My feet faced the door; I was spread out and bared for all to see as soon as that fucking door opened.

I was tied naked... on my back... on a gynecologist table.

Oh fuck...

****

The chopper landed without incident kicking up dust and sand, swirling it around them. Jordon squinted, trying to keep the grit out of his eyes. The team left the chopper behind and began the five mile hike in the direction of Mic's GPS signal.

"These guys must be really fucking stupid or Mic stashed her phone somewhere," Jones said, as he led the way, tablet in hand.

Jackson and then the others shadowed him, with Jordon bringing up the rear. He began to jog, quickly passing Pierce and Flynn and coming up alongside Jackson. The rest of them followed suit, picking up on his urgency.

"Hurry the fuck up. I have a horrible fucking feeling that something really goddamn awful is about to happen to her." Jordon shoved Jones a little, getting his attention and causing him to run. They were Steel; five miles in a desert was nothing to them.

"Jordon, let Jones lead. Move your asses' boys!" Jackson barked.

They picked up the pace, quickly moving from a slow jog to a run. The warmth of the sun sapped their energy, but they did their best to ignore it. Adrenaline spiked through them all, sharpening their focus and speeding their hearts.

****

The door swung open on well-oiled silent hinges. A light flicked on directly above my eyes, blinding me for a few moments. I was still blinking the spots away when a shadow appeared over me. Julio's face came into focus, his eyes burning with a sickening combination of lust and hate.

"You are even more beautiful than I imagined..." His hand reached for my face and I tried, but was powerless to evade it. His long fingers stroked from my forehead, down to my chin, over...and over. He was petting me.

"My dear, I cannot wait to show you this new world I've brought you into. You may be scared at first, but you don't need to be. I will set you free." He stopped touching my face and stepped away. I could feel him down near my feet, but he was far enough away that I couldn't see him anymore.

A loud screech of squealing wheels assaulted my ears. Julio came back into view, pulling a small metal cart behind him. I lifted my head as far as I was able, trying to see something beyond my toes and the door.

"I apologize my darling; I really must remember to oil these wheels. Do lay back; straining your neck like that will make you very uncomfortable."

"Fuck off," I snapped at him. Panic gripped me in an iron vise. I racked my brain for some way, some method, to free myself. Short of convincing him to let me go, I was coming up empty.

I didn't see the slap coming, but it felt like my face was exploding with the force of it. The back of his hand struck out again, cracking against my other cheek and my mouth. He'd re-opened my already split lip. I could feel warm blood trickling down my chin and new bruises would soon blossom.

"What have I told you about your language? I would hate to cut out your tongue so early in our time together, but I will if you force me." He flashed a knife in front of my face, catching the light on the blade. I saw my reflection in the blade for a brief second. I looked just as terrified as I felt.

A knock on the door startled me. Julio sighed heavily and set the knife aside on the cart. While he went to answer the door I looked at the cart, knowing even as I did, that I shouldn't have. I know better than most which tools are used in torture and which ones are for show. There were no props on this cart, but real instruments of torture: scissors, various knives, a large hammer, chisels, and worse yet, a blow torch. There were also cabinets below that could hold so many other untold horrors.

Come on, boys... hurry up and get here or you will only find pieces of me...

****

They had the village in sight.

Fucking finally... Jordon thought, as he crouched beside Jones near the first house they came upon after the poppy fields.

"What do you think?" He whispered to Jones. The village looked empty; there were no people going about their day. The windows on the small shack-like houses were tightly shut; doors were closed and probably bolted. When they had passed the poppy fields, there were no people harvesting the remaining blossoms.

"I think they know something is up and they're being smart," came Jones's reply. "Watch for snipers; they might be on rooftops near the mansion, covering the village." Jones pointed forward at the small houses closest to the mansion.

"We don't have time to dick around. We need to get to her. What's the plan?" Jordon asked as Jackson crouched beside him. The others were covering their flank and rear.

"I think we need to go in quick and quiet. I'm not worried about the villagers; they won't want to get involved. He's got her in the big house just past the town square. Let's get a better look. By twos, gentlemen." Jackson signaled to Rook to pair up with him, Jordon stayed with Jones and Flynn and Pierce covered their asses.

"Watch your six, stay down and behind cover as much as possible. This fucker must know we're coming. Stay frosty," Jackson spoke into the radio.

Jordon watched Jones's back as they crept past houses, checking corners and staying in a disciplined formation. There was not a soul in sight. All this place needed was a few tumble weeds and it would be a veritable ghost town.

They were one street away from the mansion off of the village square. "Fan out, I want eyes on every angle of this place," Jackson ordered.

Jordon followed Jones around a side street to observe the front of the house. There they saw a Jeep encased in ankle-deep mud. Jordon looked at the sky where the thick clouds still swirled and boiled, but held their rain.

"She's here. The Jeep out front corresponds to the GPS," Jones said into the radio.

A shot rang out, forcing Flynn and Pierce to run forward, as bullets smacked into the ground at their feet. They reached the cover of a house near the front of the mansion.

"Where is that shit coming from, dammit?" Jackson's irate voice coming through their head-sets.

"Rooftop, twelve o'clock," Rook said. Crouching behind the corner of a building he sighted in and fired. His aim was true: the *sicario* on the rooftop took the bullet in the chest, and then another as he stood in panic. Rook fired again; the third shot knocked the guard off of the roof and down into the mud below.

Pierce broke off from Flynn, streaking across the courtyard of the house. He selected a truck parked off to the side well clear of the Jeep.

"Guard at two o'clock," Jones reported from his position at the western corner of the mansion. The guard was standing near the truck Pierce had slid under. Pierce stayed there for less than a minute before he was back out and running to a shed near the rear of the property, out of their line of sight.

Jordon fired before Jones could, dropping the guard into the dirt with a thud. A second guard popped out from behind the cover of Mic's Jeep. That guard fired wildly, panic rushing his aim. Bullets whistled through the air, forcing them all to take cover. Chunks of plaster flew off of the houses and sand sprayed into the air all around them.

"Someone take care of this fucker!" Rook shouted from where he was huddled beside Jackson. Flynn exposed himself long enough to get eyes on the guard. He fired rapidly, the bullets striking the man in the chest and neck. Blood burst into the air and he fell in a heap.

A split-second of silence was broken by the earth shattering explosion of the truck. Fire and scorched metal flew into the air. Smoke billowed out as the fire grew and burned brightly. Flames and black smoke belched out and darkened the sky. The truck crashed to the ground, throwing blackened metal in all directions.

A bullet hit the dirt in front of the shed. Jordon checked the rooftops of the houses. There was a hunched figure on the roof of the house that Jackson and Rook were taking cover near.

"Sniper on the roof-top," Jordon said into the radio. He signaled Jackson to look up. "Pierce, stay behind cover, sniper is on you."

"Copy that," was his response.

"Take care of it, Jones," Jackson ordered.

"Copy." Their marksman sighted the guard on the roof and taking only a brief second to aim, fired quickly. The sound was muffled by the suppressor on the end of the barrel. A soft *pop* was the only noise. The hunched figure fell down behind the edge of the roof.

"Well done, man," Flynn said.

Pierce ran out of the shed and re-joined Flynn on the east side of the house. Guards were running out from the village, converging on the mansion.

"Pierce and Flynn, help Rook and me make a hole. The time for subtlety is past," Jackson barked into the radio. "On me, Rook." Jackson ran across the courtyard to Flynn and Pierce's position, Rook tight at his back.

They opened fire on the guards, drawing their fire to the east. "Jordon and Jones, get into that house," Jackson ordered.

The guards were running now, trying to advance toward the team. Their rifles fired nearly non-stop until most of the enemy lay dead or dying. Their superior skills had made short work of the motivated, but poorly trained, Mexican guards.

Jordon ran forward, taking cover near the Jeep first, then advancing forward to the door. Jones was right behind him.

"Get in there! We'll be right behind you!" Rook waved them on, running to catch up. Jackson and the others were pinned down by a few remaining industrious guards who had taken cover behind the truck. Rook had advanced before the others got pinned. He was turning and firing, trying to flank the guards. Two dropped in quick succession; a third attempted a last-ditch assault on Pierce, whose well-placed bullet tore through the guard's forehead.

Jordon kicked the door right beside the lock. It didn't budge.

"Some help here?" Jones and Rook came up beside him. "Count of three. One... two…three!" They kicked together; the door cracked open, ripping splinters of wood from the frame and knocking the door onto its side with a crash that echoed loudly in the marble foyer.

They advanced through the downstairs, checking rooms as they went. There was no sign of Mic or anyone else.

"What the fuck? Jones, go upstairs. Rook, come with me; maybe there is a basement." Jordon was giving orders like he'd been born to it.

"We shouldn't split up, Jordon," Jones replied. "She's not upstairs, I can almost guarantee it. If there is a basement, that's where she is."

The floor shook and the windows shattered with the force of the blast from the shed. Jordon tucked his face into his chest as best he could while glass rained down. Deadly shards of wood flew through the air, shooting right through a chair-back beside his head. A few inches to the right and he would've needed an eye-patch.

Jordon was up and moving, dust and debris filling the air in a thick cloud. "Come on, dammit! We have to find her before he kills her!" Jordon ordered Rook and Jones. Looking over his shoulder, he saw the others coming in the door, Flynn bleeding from his eyebrow.

"Go; we'll take the upstairs, you find that basement." Jackson led the way up the marble staircase, kicking pieces of splintered wood and chunks of glass out of his way.

Jordon picked a hallway that led deeper into the house. The structure must have been very old, as it had narrow winding hallways and random staircases. None led down. Suddenly, the hallway opened up into the kitchen. There were two oak doors on either side of the fridge.

"Jones, take left; I'll take right. Rook cover us." Jordon barked out orders, not thinking about chain of command or proper procedure. His entire being was focused on finding the basement and finding Mic.

"Copy," Rook said, shouldering his rifle and providing cover while watching the door to the kitchen.

Jones stepped to the side as best he could; reaching a hand out, he turned the knob and threw open the door.

"Clear!" Rook shouted. Looking over, a well-stocked walk-in pantry greeted them.

"My turn." Jordon did the same as Jones; stood to the side, turned the knob, and eased the door open, pushing until it was flush against the wall.

"Steps," Rook confirmed. Looking inside, it was pitch black with a small amount of weak yellow light filtering up from the bottom.

"Time to walk into the abyss. She's down there, I can feel it." Jordon took the first step into the darkness, switching on the light on his MP-5 as he did so.

Chapter 25

I struggled and twisted to no avail. The explosions that rocked the house were music to my ears. Sweet release was coming, my boys were here. No one else made an entrance quite like they did.

"I see by your excitement that you still hold out hope for rescue. To do so is to waste useful energy, my darling. You're going to need your breath for screaming..." Julio raised the gleaming knife again and with a swift motion, sliced through the top of my thigh in a quick slash; burning pain shot through flesh in a fiery wash. My muscles spasmed and twitched under the assault. I did scream then; I screamed from the burning pain and from the humiliation I was suffering. I screamed at the injustice of my situation.

Warm blood slid down my thigh and pooled under my leg. I was panting and gasping for air. The pain was intense, but nothing that I couldn't live with. I'd been shot and stabbed before. This wound, while painful, was not going to kill me.

"Is that all you've got, fuck face?" Gasping from pain, I taunted him because it was in my nature; not to, would mean I had given up. I refused to give up. My rescue was here. I just needed to make it a little longer.

His face darkened with rage; veins popped to the surface of his neck as he flushed red. Without uttering a word, he viciously grabbed me by the jaw. Squeezing my face in his large hand, he held my head still as the knife in his hand descended.

"I have told you for the final time. Do. Not. Curse. At. Me." He drug the knife down my right cheek, the sharp blade laying it open nearly to the bone. If I thought the pain in my leg was bad, this was extreme. I couldn't draw a breath to scream, but I tried anyway, gurgling and gasping as blood filled my mouth. Fiery agony spread in my face. Blood washed down my neck onto my shoulder and chest. I struggled for air, trying to breathe past the pain that encompassed my face.

I tried to speak, but couldn't. The pain was pushing me over the edge and into shock. I'd held up okay until now, but I was slipping. The fight was seeping out of me with every pump of my heart that sent blood sliding out of my face and down my neck. My breaths were coming too fast. I was in danger of passing out, which would be an escape and sweet release from my reality. The thought sobered me and I forced myself to drawn a single breath deep into my stomach. The motion moved the flap of skin that used to be my cheek and sent waves of pain cascading through me.

"Breathe through the pain, my darling. You cannot give up so soon! Show me that famous attitude of yours." Julio taunted me, smearing his fingers through my blood and down my body. He placed his palm on my bare blood-coated breast, smearing the blood across the rest of my chest and down my stomach; painting me with my own blood.

I smiled at him as blood seeped out of the gash in my face, my mouth hanging lopsided in a grotesque smile.

"Why do you smile?" He asked, cocking his head to the side like a child.

"I smile...," I gasped, talking caused the blood pouring from my ruined face to slip into my mouth. "... because... your death is nearly here... I rejoice in your imminent demise." I spit blood to the side, unknowingly coating my hair in my sticky life-blood.

Julio snarled at me, grasping my thigh and digging his hand into the gash there. His handsome face was as twisted and ugly as a demon from hell itself.

I screamed... long and hard as hot pain tore through my body. I screamed and I prayed. I prayed for Steel and I prayed for Jordon...

Hurry, Jordon... please...

****

A scream tore through the hallway, raising the hair on Jordon's arms and slamming fear into him like the *thunk* of a bullet.

"Which door?" He yelled. The hallway was sparsely lit and there were doors every ten feet or so. Jones and Rook worked in tandem with him, kicking open locked doors and flinging open those that weren't locked.

"Jackson, the basement door is in the kitchen. Get down here," Jones barked into his radio.

"Copy that, we're en route," Jackson responded. Jordon tuned everything out; he was focused on the screaming that he could still hear. She was close. Kicking in another door, Jordon halted in his tracks.

There was a woman in this room; she was bloodied and nearly every inch of her naked body was bruised and cut. Her hair was shorn off in clumps, down to her scalp in places.

"Jackson, we have civilians. Over," Jordon spoke into his radio, trying to appear as non-threatening as possible. She was plainly scared and terrorized; he didn't want to make it worse.

"Copy that. Get me a count," Jackson answered.

"I have two over here," Rook spoke from behind Jordon.

"I have three," Jones answered from down the hallway.

"Five total so far, Jackson, but we don't have all the doors open yet. Over." Jordon left the girl where she was. Turning his back, he followed the sound of flesh striking flesh, the distinctive noise of someone being beaten.

Jones kicked open the second to last door; the rotting, fetid stench washing out confirmed that not all of the rooms were still occupied by the living.

One door left. Jordon didn't pause or hesitate; she was in there. She had to be.

"Jones!" Jordon kicked with all his might, fueled by fear and the knowledge that Mic was in there, being hurt. Adrenaline spiked through his blood, firing his muscles into overdrive.

The door flew open, striking the wall and bouncing back toward him. He caught it with a gloved hand and entered the room, rifle up and ready to fire. What he saw before him stopped him dead.

****

Julio drew back the thick rubber club again, striking it down across my thighs. Blood poured from the cut with every burning strike. My suffering was at a new high; it spread throughout my body, tightening my muscles before seeping away and leaving my body in a rush. A throbbing ache encompassed my entire being, giving me a second to relax by a tiny measure before he struck me again, starting the process all over.

Mentally I withdrew, sliding inside the safety of my mind where there was no pain or despair, and hope was still a living thing.

Where were they? Were they all dead? Why couldn't they find me?

I slipped in and out of consciousness and reality. I was in a black place... I was floating away. Looking down at my body, I saw myself tied to the table and Julio standing above me.

A loud crash forced me back to the present. I jerked, causing myself more agony. The door was open and like an avenging angel sent by God, Jordon stood in the doorway, rifle raised to his shoulder.

Why didn't he fire?

My relief was immense, only out-paced by my confusion. A sharp sting, barely felt, answered my question. Julio held a blade to my throat. My mind was clearing rapidly, adrenaline forcing the fog of hurt from my brain.

"Let her go. Right fucking now, or you die," Jordon growled, sighting in on Julio's head. Julio had dropped to his knees behind the table. He held the knife to my throat and used me as a shield.

"Do you trust yourself to make that shot, my friend?" Julio taunted, digging the blade into my neck slightly, drawing a few drops of blood.

"No, but I do." Jones stepped into the room, skirting Jordon. Rook closely followed. I tried to close my legs, but it was useless. There was no way for me to spare myself even a second of this humiliation. The boys were zeroed in on Julio, thankfully, and not paying too much attention to me.

One step at a time, they flanked Julio. He was cornered and unpredictable, like an animal.

With a quick flash, Julio rushed Jones who met him head on. Jones grabbed the hand with the knife and swiftly disarmed him. Julio managed to get enough space to land a solid punch to Jones's jaw, knocking him sideways into the wall. Jordon was trying to get a shot, but the space was too small, the fighting too tight.

Julio pulled another knife from his belt and stepped forward with his right foot, lunging straight for Jones, who was still recovering from the hit.

Rook pulled his knife and ran forward. Catching Julio's arm, he drove the knife deep into Julio's side, twisting the blade, making sure to shred the kidney. Rook pulled his knife free with a jerk, as blood washed out over both Julio and Rook. He plunged it home again, up and under Julio's ribcage into his back, destroying his lung.

Dark red blood poured from Julio's mouth as Rook released him. He staggered and stumbled, trying to gain purchase as he bled out and began to drown in his own blood.

"Fuck this guy." Rook kicked Julio in the back of the knee, dropping him like a stone to the unforgiving concrete floor.

He lay there on his face, gasping and bleeding, dying by inches. It was a slow justified death.

"Guys, if you're done playing with him, can you please get me the fuck off this table!" I bellowed at them, reopening the wound on my cheek, fresh blood mingling with the old that covered my face.

Jordon ran forward and cut the ropes at my ankles first. I snapped my legs closed, trying to preserve a molecule of my dignity. Jones and Rook respectfully turned their backs, pulling off their vests and weapons as they did so. Both stripped their shirts off and tossed them to Jordon before putting their armor and vests back on over their bare chests.

Jordon draped one shirt over my lap and the other over my chest; the warmth from their bodies transferred from the fabric to my skin.

"Oh, Bea; what did he do to you, baby?" Jordon lost all composure as he looked at me, trying to cradle my face in his hands. Everywhere he touched was either coated in my blood or still bleeding.

His voice was thick and his eyes shone in the low light.

"Jordon, I'll be fine. Just get me off this fucking table and get me some clothes." Talking sent shooting pains throughout my jaw and face. I could feel the cut muscles in my cheek trying to move, but it was useless. I gritted my teeth against the pain. I needed to be brave right now; not for myself, but for my men.

"This is going to hurt," Jones said from above my head, right before he cut the ropes. He gently helped Jordon move my arms down to my sides. I screamed again as needles of pain shot through my numb arms.

"Jackson, we've got her," Rook spoke into his comm. "She's in bad shape. We have to get her to a hospital."

"No hospital. You can sew me up." I groaned and cursed. I had so much more that I wanted to say, but I couldn't manage it. I reached a hand up, begging someone to help me up off my back.

"No, not yet." Rook gently pushed my arm back down. "I need to look you over. I know you want off this table and away from this freak show, but let me do an assessment first. I have a couple of questions. Were you raped?" He gave me solid eye contact. The silence in the room was thick as they waited for my answer. It was a valid question, considering that they found me nude and splayed open.

"No." The pain was getting worse by the minute. I wanted to close my eyes and escape, but I couldn't. I needed to deal with this.

"Sure?" Rook asked again. I summoned what little strength I had remaining and punched him in the shoulder.

"Fuck off, I said no."

"Okay, good. I'm going to wrap up your leg and then bandage your face. I'll do more on the jet. I'll have to suffice for a doctor, we don't have time to get Doc Hamilton. Just try and relax." He pushed the shirt covering my lap to the side enough that he could see the wound on my thigh. The tops of both my thighs were striped purple with bruises from the heavy club Julio had used on me. The cut was straight and clean, only seeping a small amount of blood. Rook spread his kit open on my stomach and pulled things out.

"This guy knew what he was doing; he didn't even come close to your femoral artery." Rook wiped blood off and sprinkled Quik Clot into the cut before wrapping it with an Israeli bandage and more gauze. It didn't hurt all that much anymore; maybe I wouldn't even need much more than a few stitches.

Jackson barreled into the room just as Rook was finishing with my leg.

"Mic, what the fuck?" Flynn gasped from beside Jackson, taking in the blood all over the floor and the dead Julio lying in a growing pool of his own blood. It looked like a slaughterhouse in here.

I rolled my eyes, giving up on speech. Rook was starting to work on my face. The deep slice went from just under my right ear, down to the corner of my mouth. I hissed and jerked back as Rook tried to clean it. I slapped at his hands, not thinking, just animal instinct trying to escape the pain.

"Stop it. This needs to happen. Jordon, hold her."

Jordon grabbed my hands and held on tight. He spoke softly, reassuring me. "Let him work, Mic. Then we can get you out of here."

"Hurry up, Rook," Jackson ordered. "We have to get moving. Pierce is on the roof, keeping an eye on things. This calm won't last" His voice was music to my ears. He finally allowed himself to look at me, taking in my wounds and bloodied body.

"God, Mic, your aunt is going to have my ass for breakfast." I never thought I'd hear fear in Jackson's voice; it was definitely a first.

I tried to laugh, but gasped in pain instead, my broken rib

reminding me it was there.

"Chest hurt?" Rook asked, as he stuck a large pad to my cheek and wrapped my head in gauze. Great, 'mummies-r-us'.

"Yeah; broke a rib...," I ground out past my clenched teeth.

"We'll deal with it later. Get her up." Rook motioned to Jordon, I clutched the shirt to my chest with my free arm.

"Clothes... weapons."

"Get her dressed. We'll meet you upstairs. Flynn, let's go." Jackson led the way; Flynn followed close behind, though he kept looking over his shoulder and staring. I felt like a car wreck.

"Jones, you too," Rook said calmly. He nodded and followed Flynn out. Jordon ripped open the cabinets of the little cart; tucked neatly inside were my clothes and shoes. The machete was also there, but no rifle. I didn't think I had the strength to carry my rifle right now anyway. Rook held my arm at my elbow and upper arm, then helped me sit up and swing my legs off the side of the table. I pulled my forearm tight against my waist. The broken rib was stabbing me and making it impossible to breathe correctly.

Jordon handed me my bra and underwear first. There was no way that bra was going on my chest right now. I threw it to the side and took the panties from him.

"Turn. Please," I begged. I'd had enough open viewing of my lady parts to last me a lifetime. They respectfully turned their backs. I dropped the shirts and forced myself to ignore my blood-coated skin as I slipped on my clothing. My leg throbbed when I stood, but it held.

My belt had disappeared, so I had no way to attach the machete to my thigh like before. I kept it in my hand.

"Okay, guys," I spoke, trying to move my mouth as little as possible. "My boots... I need help." I fucking hated that I couldn't bend over and put my shoes on. Just bending down to step into my pants had sent blood pounding through my head and cased my broken rib to stab into my side viciously.

Jordon knelt at my feet and quickly laced my boots.

"Mercedes?" I gasped the word out. *Where the fuck was she?* She'd stared at me earlier, but I hadn't seen her since.

"No show. We didn't see her." Gunfire erupted from above; the guards must have rallied and were attempting to take back the mansion.

"Hurry the fuck up! We need to leave!" Jackson's voice erupted from the radios, punctuated by more gunfire and another explosion.

"Let's go." I grabbed Jordon's arm and hustled out with them. He had one arm slung around my waist and the other held his rifle out in front of him.

We passed room after room; I saw that each had just a small mattress on the floor and a bucket. I looked back the hall to the one door was still closed, but Jordon stopped me when I moved to open it. "She's gone. Don't open it."

We were almost to the stairs now; I was slow as fuck, but it couldn't be helped.

"Where are the others?" I asked. It smelled of death, decay, and broken dreams down here.

"Flynn and Pierce got them. They're upstairs. Mexican police are on their way now," Rook explained.

"Are we waiting for the police before we leave?" Jordon asked as we reached the stairs which loomed large and dark before us. The pain was progressing to nausea, but I forced myself to swallow it down. I didn't have time for this. I could be sick later.

"Yes. They're on the way." Rook paused to press the button on his radio. "Jones, ETA on the police? Over."

"On approach. Over."

"Copy that; we're almost out of the basement. Over." Rook led the way up the stairs, which were too narrow for Jordon and me to traverse abreast.

"You go first; I've got your six," Jordon gruffly said.

I limped up the stairs, pain jarring through my battered body with each step. After about what seemed like a hundred painful steps, I finally reached the top and the bright daylight of the kitchen.

"Screw this," Jordon said, reaching to pick me up.

"We're not in Colombia, my leg works fine. No." I stepped away and followed Rook. I found myself back where I started, in the expansive marble foyer, staring up at the sweeping staircase. There were five women huddled together in the corner, holding onto each other while they shivered in fear like frightened animals. They each were bruised to the point of being unrecognizable, their hair haphazardly shorn off. From what I could see, they were all blonde, and under the bruises and blood they were stunningly beautiful.

Where did he get these girls?

I stepped toward them, holding my hands out in front of my body, letting the machete dangle from my fingers near my leg.

"Don't bother Mic, they don't speak English," Jackson said from above me. He was hurrying down the steps.

"What?" I asked in confusion.

"Best I can tell, they speak German or Russian. We'll hand them over to the Mexican police in a few minutes. What forces of the cartel are still alive, have retreated. The immediate threat is over." He slipped an arm around my waist and helped me hobble to a plush and gilded chair.

"Take a load off; you look like shit," Flynn said, from behind Jackson.

"Fuck you guys; I've had a shit day." I leaned my head back against the chair and tried to breathe past the pain; past the anger and despair coating me like a shroud.

I felt warmth press against my good leg. Looking down, I saw Jordon squatting on the floor, leaning against me, rifle at the ready. I had a feeling he wouldn't be letting me out of his sight anytime soon.

"Don't do that again, Bea," he spoke.

"Okay," I said, knocking his hat off with my hand. I rubbed my fingers through his hair; it was just long enough to brush between my fingers. The fact that he was coated in sweat and dirt and I was probably smearing blood into his hair didn't bother either of us.

"You're in so much trouble when you heal up. You have no fucking idea," Jordon said, leaning into my hand and softly groaning.

"Okay." I ran my hand down the back of his shirt and along his neck and shoulder. His skin felt amazing. I needed to reconnect with someone, to feel a touch that wasn't painful. The adrenaline that had fueled me for hours seeped away. I was crashing hard. I kept my hand where it was, tight against his skin, as I let the pain go and finally, gratefully drifted off to sleep.

Chapter 26

I slowly came awake, noticing that I was warm and somewhat uncomfortable. There were raised voices echoing around me. I was still in the chair in the foyer, but Jordon was no longer against me. He was standing beside me with his arms crossed, observing the exchange going on. Lights shone from chandeliers above us and the windows were dark. Night had fallen while I had been sleeping.

I shifted and pain racked my body, forcing a groan from my lips. Jordon looked at me, concern carved into his handsome features.

"I'm sorry. We're trying to get you out of here, but the Mexicans don't want to take those girls and Jackson says he can't either."

"The fuck they can't." I stood, shaking with pain and fatigue. I lightly touched my face, the bandage on my face was tacky with blood. I needed to get it seen to, sooner rather than later.

"What seems to be the *problemo,* boys?" I snarked off from beside Jackson. I kept my arm pressed tight to my ribs, trying to hold them snug to lessen the pain. Shock registered on their faces. I'm sure I was a sight to behold. Standing before them, covered in blood and questioning them.

"No girls. We cannot take them." The man speaking must be their commander. His broken English was no better than the thug who first took me.

"I told you; you have to take them. We can't." Jackson's face may as well have been carved from stone; he was really pissed.

I pulled Jackson's pistol from his side before he had a chance to react. "Either you take them, or I shoot you." I held the barrel against the leader's forehead, his sweat shiny against his dark skin. His men pulled their weapons and mine followed.

"No." I pulled the hammer back; it was unnecessary on a semi-automatic weapon, but it got my point across. "I just spent the better part of a day under that bastard's care. These women have been here for much longer. Either you help them, or I'll kill you and your men can pick up your humanity from your brains that are about to be splattered onto their chests. Got me, fucker?" When he didn't respond, I pressed the barrel harder into his forehead. "Listen here. We're special operations. We don't exist. We can't help them. Take them, get them medical care, and we'll arrange for transport to the U.S. Fair enough?"

"Mic...," Jackson started to say, but I cut him off.

"No! They need help. These fuckers can get them to doctors. Then you get on the phone and get them placed in safe houses. That's what's going to happen, dammit! If they experienced even half of what I did, they need extensive medical care... food, water, the works. We can do this, I know we fucking can." My speech was exhausting me, I was only just managing to stand and my hand was wavering all over the place. I was too weak to keep it pressed to this bastard's head.

"*Si*, we go." He nodded and backed away. I lowered the pistol and handed it back to Jackson.

"Now, can we get the fuck out of here?" I didn't wait for an answer. I just threw open the double doors and limped into the cool night air. It felt amazing on my face and arms, so fresh and cool. Rain was pouring down in sheets, puddling on the walk.

I stepped out into the rain, the water washing away the blood and dirt. I rubbed my hands all over my arms. If I had been alone, I would have stripped my shirt and washed my chest clean. As it was, the puddle under my feet turned brown, then a dull pink, as the refuse of my torture ran from my body.

"Mic. What the fuck are you doing?" Rook shouted, trying to pull me out of the rain.

"Why are we still here? I'm getting in that Jeep and I'm driving back to the airfield. I have to call the captain back. I told him to leave without me if I wasn't back by nightfall."

"We already did. He's on his way; that's why we're waiting. No sense in waiting there, piled into a small car while it rains like this." Rook gently pulled on my arm again, but I jerked away. Jordon stepped up beside Rook.

"No! I'm not going back in that house!" The bandage on my face was sodden and falling off, so I tore it away, throwing it into the mud. The rain stung and burned my face, but I tipped my head back anyway. I let the rain wash over me, absolving me and washing me clean.

"Come on, Mic, let's go." Jordon took my hand and led me to the Jeep. "The jet will be there by the time we get to the strip." He had my machete clutched in his other hand, no doubt knowing I would want to keep it. I took it back from him, the weight comforting me like a security blanket.

"How did you guys get here?" I asked him.

"We brought a chopper in, then hiked the rest of the way."

"Wait!" Jackson shouted from the doorway. "Take Flynn and

Rook with you. Rook can patch her up while Flynn returns for us in the Jeep. Leave the chopper where it is, if the Mexican military wants it back, they can come get the fucker." Jackson turned back to the house, leaving the door open behind him.

"Come out of the rain. I have to get my gear before we leave." Jordon tugged on my arm, trying to get me into the Jeep.

"I need some air, dammit. I'll wait out here." I jerked my arm from his grasp and walked further from the mansion. I stepped over debris from the explosions; an engine block lay about twenty yards from the remnants of a truck body. Dead corpses of the guards littered the area, along with what appeared to be hundreds of rounds of spent brass. The boys put up one hell of a fight to get me. It was amazing that none of them were wounded beyond a cut or two.

The rain began to let up slightly and the moonlight broke through the clouds, its white shine lighting the way enough that I didn't trip. As I rounded the corner of a house, I stopped in my tracks, frozen like a deer caught in headlights.

Mercedes stood in the middle of the street, dripping wet and filthy. She must have been out here the entire time.

"This is all your fault," she said slowly advancing.

"Mercedes. What are you doing here?" I needed to stall. I had the machete, but I was alone. Finding myself in the same position as earlier but with only slightly different circumstances made me reach a new level of immense frustration.

"I have to finish it... honor... demands... that I finish it. Finish this! Fault... all your fault..." She kept ranting as she drew a pistol from the small of her back. Stepping closer to me, she kept it trained on my head.

"What's my fault?"

Keep her talking... just keep her talking..., I thought to myself as I slowly stepped closer to her. I needed to get into her space so I could disarm her.

"Everything!" She screamed, becoming even more agitated. She advanced on me slowly, pointing the small Derringer at my face. Jabbing it closer with each word, she shrieked. "He's dead and *you* killed him! He's dead!" She turned her back and resumed pacing. It was then that I noticed she was barefoot; the bottoms of her feet were sliced open and bleeding. Each step left a tiny footprint in the thick mud.

"I thought Julio would take care of you. He wanted you so bad, but Adolfo said no. Then you killed Adolfo! My only family left in this god-forsaken world! You've destroyed everything!"

"You're still alive. Not everything is lost, Mercedes." I kept my arms at my sides, hoping the patchy moonlit darkness hid the machete.

"I'm a shell. In a matter of hours, you took everything away from me. You killed me and now I must kill you."

I balanced on the balls of my feet, shoving the pain of my wounds aside. Stepping backward and to the right, I drew her out into the open street; I needed more room to maneuver. She was overly skinny, but anger and insanity makes even the smallest person strong. She didn't fear death; I could see that in her madness-glazed eyes. I kept walking backwards, drawing her out.

I could see the mansion again and I hoped one of the guys would look out a window and see us.

"Mercedes, you don't want to do this. My death won't finish this. My death won't bring Diego back."

"Don't you think I know that, you bitch? This isn't about bringing him back. This is about vengeance! This is about honor! I will kill you and follow him to the afterlife." She had crazy on her side, but she lacked skill.

Striking out with the machete, I smacked the flat of the blade hard against her wrist. Her hand fell open and the pistol dropped into the mud below.

She rushed me, hands curled into claws, going for my face and eyes.

Using my forearms, I blocked her and kicked her in the chest, forcing her back. Balling up a fist, I punched her in the jaw as hard as I could, which in my weakened state, wasn't hard enough.

She shook it off and kicked out, catching me in my already injured leg. The mud was slippery beneath my feet, making my footing treacherous. If I fell, I'd be dead.

I grunted and nearly went down. She took advantage of the moment and rushed me again, slapping at my hand and wrenching the machete from my grasp. I stumbled backwards, desperate to stay out of reach of the deadly blade.

"Now, bitch, you die." She swung at me, lunging forward and chopping through the air. I ducked and bobbed; backing up with each vicious swipe, I barely managed to keep my feet. My back hit the wall of a house.

Striking downward, screaming her hatred into the night air, she aimed for my head. Blocking the blow with my forearm, I caught her arm, but she still managed to hit me with the tip of the machete. Stinging pain burst from my arm as I felt blood trickle out. It was not a deep wound, just a painful one.

Jerking hard, she freed her arm from my hold and drew back for another jab. I kicked her in the side of her knee. She shrieked in pain as the knee collapsed under her. She went down hard, mud splashing up around her. I didn't give her time to recover. Swinging my leg back like I was going to punt a football, I kicked her in the face, I tried to plant my foot inside her brain, putting the full weight of my body and heavy boot behind the blow. Her nose gave way with a crunch and blood flew out in an arch; splattering into the dirt and mud behind her.

Her fingers finally released the machete from their grasp, and I scooped it up with my good arm. The wound on my left arm stung fiercely, but the bleeding didn't seem too bad.

She tried to sit up, spitting blood to the side and gasping for air through the destroyed remnants of her face. It looked like my heavy combat boot did more than break her nose; her orbital bone was shattered and her face was lopsided and swelling rapidly.

"Kill... me," she begged, bloody bubbles bursting from her nose as she kept trying to breathe through it.

"Gladly, you fucking crazy-ass bitch." I knelt one knee in the mud beside her chest and gripped her throat with my left hand. Pushing down and squeezing tight while I angled my right elbow and arm back, I prepared to drive the machete deep into her chest.

I put my face close to her, leaning down toward her ear, her gasping breaths warm against my cheek.

"You messed with me and mine; your husband died by this blade, wielded by my hand... and now so will you," I whispered into her ear.

I lifted the machete straight up and drove it into her chest, digging under her rib cage. I angled it a little wrong and caught a rib, the cracking of her bone loud in the small space. It sounded like chicken bones snapping under a chef's hands. Her chest rose upwards, arching her narrow back off the ground. She gasped and gurgled as blood filled her lungs and throat. I wrenched on the blade; twisting it back and forth viciously, doing my best to hit her heart and shred her lungs. I wanted her to fucking die, right now.

She twitched a few times, and finally her hands went limp against the ground as bright red blood welled up around the blade and slid down her side to puddle under her. The blood looked unnaturally bright under the white light of the moon. Her head fell to the side, hiding the swelling and bruises. Blood slowly trickled out of the corner of her mouth, running down her once beautiful face. Insanity had made her ugly, but in death she had relaxed back into the cultured beauty that she had been before madness consumed and destroyed her.

Planting one foot for leverage, I gripped the handle of the machete with both hands, and jerked it free. The blade made a nasty, wet sucking noise when it pulled free from her chest cavity; it was enough to force bile into my throat... almost. I stood as blood dripped off the blade in a steady stream and gathered near my foot in a small puddle.

The rain picked back up, falling harder, washing the blood from her face and the blade.

"What the ever loving fuck happened now?" Jackson roared as he came around the corner of the house. I dropped the machete onto the ground and took a step back from the growing spread of blood.

Rook and the others appeared seconds later.

"You really need to try harder to keep your blood *inside* your body, Mic," Rook snapped at me, taking in the sight of my new wounds.

"Tell that to machete-wielding lunatics."

"Right. Well, get in the Jeep so we can get you patched up on the jet." Rook stomped off the way he came, back in the direction of the Jeep.

"At least we know she's not out here plotting revenge or something," Pierce said from where he was crouched beside Mercedes. "You really did a number on her, Mic." He found her small pistol in the mud, inspecting it for a few moments before dropping it back where he found it. "Lucky she didn't just shoot you."

"She was too busy ranting at me," I said, leaning heavily against the house behind me. "Crazy will only get you so far; she didn't know how to fight."

"True enough. Flynn go in the Jeep with Mic and Jordon. Come back for us once you drop them off," Jackson said, before walking back to the mansion with a silent Jones.

Jordon took my hand, pulling me to his side and supporting me as we hobbled my broken ass to the Jeep.

"Shotgun!" Flynn shouted, running for the Jeep. Jordon released my hand and opened the driver's door. He pushed the seat forward, ushering me into the back.

"You're fucking kidding me, right?" I kept my hand pressed to my cheek; blood was leaking out from between my fingers.

"Are you going to drive?" Flynn leaned over, brushing water off his face. Rook was calmly standing in the rain, ignoring us all.

"Fine. Fucking jerks." I climbed into the back and scooted over to the passenger side, pain wracking me from the movement.

Rook took his cue and slid in beside me. "For fucks sake, Mic. You undid all my work. Bandages are your *friend* when you are bleeding from your face, dammit woman!" He berated me while pulling out his IFAK again to put a new bandage against my face. "Flynn, I need your kit." Rook extended his hand over the seat, impatiently waiting. "Numb-nuts here used all my rolled gauze and threw it in the mud."

"Fuck off," I gasped and jerked when he put pressure on my face, not even pretending to be gentle. I tried to pull back and make him ease up, but he just pressed harder and held my head still. We hit a large rock or something, rocking us sideways. I groaned in pain, my broken rib again making its presence known.

"What happened in there?" he asked gently, his voice even and full of sympathy considering his touch was not.

"I'll tell everyone at the same time. After I've had some drugs."

Rook finished taping the ends of the gauze down and I leaned my head back, letting the rocking motion of the Jeep and the sound of rain lull me into a trance. It wasn't sleep or wakefulness, but somewhere in between; a soothing limbo where I didn't need to think or feel, I could just *be*.

****

"Mic, we're here," Jordon said, as he shook me gently awake. "Let's get you out of here so we can fix you up." He slid an arm behind my back and slowly helped me step from the Jeep. I landed ankle deep in a puddle.

"Really? I mean, really? Because I didn't have a shitty enough day, now I have wet socks. Nothing is worse than wet fucking socks." I grumbled and whined as Jordon helped me into the small hangar.

"When will the jet be here?" I asked. My answer came in the sound of an approaching plane.

"Now," Rook said, casually leaning against the wall of the hangar.

"I'm headed back. See you guys soon." Flynn hopped in the Jeep and drove away with a splash of muddy water.

Jordon kept his arm around my waist even though I was perfectly capable of standing on my own. I was debating whether I should use the ruse of my injuries to allow him to continue or if I needed to man up and step away from his comfort. Jordon decided for me by urging me to sit in the only chair.

"They're circling to land. I have the gear on board to stitch you up and manage your pain," Rook said. "If there's anything you need to explain about your injuries before the others get here, now's the time." He turned his dark head toward me, his long hair dripping water down his cheekbones and onto his still bare chest. I realized we'd left his and Jones's shirts back in that basement.

"I have a cut on my thigh, one on my elbow, and one on my face. A broken rib and some bruises. That's the extent of it," I was angry, and not in the mood to answers there fucking questions.

"It's just that I saw how you were tied up. If you were raped and don't want people to know, Jordon and I will take it to our graves. But if you need medical care, I need to know."

"Listen, Rook. I meant it when I said I was not raped. He was probably headed in that direction, but you guys got to me first." I gave him solid eye contact, hoping he would see the truth in my eyes. "Besides, rape is about power; not sex, if I was raped; which I wasn't; I wouldn't be ashamed to admit it."

"Okay, Mic, I believe you." He turned from me and watched the jet land and taxi over to the hangar, the noise deafening and not allowing for conversation.

The plane came to a stop and the engines shut off, the silence a welcome relief. The stairs came down and we walked out into the rain. My bandage was again soaked in seconds. The pain was a dull throb in the background. I was still running on an adrenaline high, but I knew once I truly felt safe and relaxed I was going to want an injection of something wonderful.

Rook headed into the jet first. I followed with Jordon close behind me. "How long do you think it will be until we take off?" Jordon asked.

"As soon as Flynn gets back with the others; so maybe a half hour or so" Rook answered.

Boarding the jet was like stepping into a luxurious paradise compared to where I'd been for the last day. It felt so much longer than a day; I was a different person from the one who had gone into that basement. Since the moment I saw those pictures, I had been running toward what I had considered might be certain death, and now…I was free. The abrupt change was messing with my head.

"Come on back, Mic." Rook motioned me to the rear of the jet where the once fully-stocked galley was now an advanced field-medic station. There was a small fold-out table, just big enough for someone to sit on and have a tiny bit of room to spare.

"Jordon, stand guard," I ordered as I tipped my head back and let Rook begin to unwind the soaked bandages from my head and face.

"For a bit, then I'll need your hands, Jordon," Rook said, to his back as he ducked out of the cabin door.

"He really did a number on you, Mic. Do you want to see before I stitch you up?" Rook had his hand on a small mirror.

"Sure, why not? May as well get used to having a fucked-up face." I took the mirror from him and surveyed the damage. While large and deep, the cut wasn't too jagged. It curved slightly on the end closest to my mouth. If closed properly it wouldn't be too bad of a scar, just a long white gash.

"A scar from battle, especially a facial scar, showcases that you've faced great hardship and overcome it with courage. It's the mark of a true warrior; wear it with pride." Rook took the mirror from me and prepped a suture kit, snapping gloves on each hand.

"Is that an Indian proverb or something?"

"We prefer Native American, if you must call us something. And sort of. It's more common sense than anything. Don't worry, Mic, it doesn't take away from your looks." Rook was filling a syringe with a local anesthetic.

Is this day every going to be over?

I held up my elbow, trying to get a look at the wound just as Jackson and Jones stepped into the jet.

"Motherfucker!" I yelled with feeling. The cut had gone right through one of my tattoos. The Archangel Michael was cut neatly in two, right across his regal face. "Mother fucking crazy-ass bitch. Look at this. She ruined my tattoo!" I held my arm up for them to see.

"Mic, really?" Jackson glared at me in disbelief. "You almost died for the second fucking time today and you're pissed about your tattoo?"

"Well, yeah. Almost dying isn't that bad. Actually dying is. I'm alive. Besides, that crazy ass never had a chance in hell of killing me. I ranted.

"Wow. I'm impressed," Flynn said from behind Jackson, trying to see around his large frame. "The captain is going to kick your ass when he sees the mess you made of his jet, Mic." Jackson and Flynn followed the muddy trail to the back of the jet.

As soon as the words finished leaving Flynn's mouth, the cockpit door popped open and the captain stuck his head out, pulling his ear buds out as he did so.

"What the fuck happened to my jet?" Fury was etched onto his face.

"It should be fairly obvious, Captain. We had a shitty-ass day. Took you long enough to come out; thanks for the concern." My pain was hitting an all-time high. I stared at my legs dangling off the edge of the small table; mud and blood mixed with water puddled under my boots.

"Tufo's new *Zombie Fallout* book is on Audible... Talbot has this plan..." Shamefaced, he ducked his head back into the cockpit.

"For fucks sake..." Jackson rubbed his hands over his face. "Mic, sit your ass down over here on the pull-out." I slid off the table and followed orders like a good little soldier.

"What the fuck, Mic? Can't you get along with anyone?" Rook said.

"No, I guess not. You lot are the only ones who can stand me." I said, laughing, but quickly wished I hadn't. The pain from my rib and collection of wounds could no longer be ignored.

"Rook will get you an IV and some pain meds. We'll knock you out and stitch you up while you're sleeping." He pushed on my shoulder gently, forcing me to sit down. Any thoughts of resistance flew out of my head as soon as my ass hit the softness of the seat. I reclined slowly, trying to spare myself as much pain as possible. The only injuries that hurt worse than ribs were ones to the back. You don't realize how much you use those muscles until it hurts to move them. I'd had a hell of a day. *God, it feels good to lay down right now...*"Sounds like an excellent idea. Where's Jordon?" I stopped Rook who had a needle at the ready. Jordon was the only one not seated around me.

"I'm here." He spoke from above me. "Everyone's on board and accounted for, Mic. Don't worry, we've got this." He was leaning over the seat back, looking down at me. Rain water dripped off his hair and ran down his cheeks; a few drops hitting my face. His green eyes shone with something I couldn't name. A flash of sharp pain hit me as Rook started the IV. Before I knew it, my eyes wouldn't stay open. They were weighted down and I didn't fight it. Jordon's concerned face was the last thing I saw before I slipped easily into a black void where there was no pain and no fear. Peace enveloped me and I welcomed it with open arms.

Chapter 27

Beatrice paced the floor of Jackson's room. He'd told her to use it if she wanted while he was away. He'd reassured her that she was perfectly safe here, that even if someone found this place, no one other than a member of Steel would be able to get inside.

Bea had been gone for over a day and Jackson nearly as long. The phone hadn't rung and the door hadn't opened. She paced and prayed. Her family was out there, fighting for what was right. She was so proud of the woman her niece had become, but that wouldn't stop Beatrice from worrying about her.

The shrill ringing of the telephone had her running to answer it, tripping and stumbling her way across the room in her haste.

"Hello!" She nearly shouted in excitement.

"Beatrice, its Jackson."

"Oh, Fisher, it's so good to hear your voice. Did you find her? Is everyone okay? When will you be back?" The questions rushed out of her mouth.

"Slow down," he said, chuckling. "Everyone is fine, more or less.

We found her. We'll be back at the Wonka House in an hour or so. I waited to call you until I knew for sure when we'd be back." He paused and his voice became grave. "Now Beatrice, I need you to listen to me."

"What is it?" Anxiety gripped her; fear washed over her body in cold shivers.

"We found Mic, but she's hurt. Not anything life-threatening, but... she was cut. Her face, Beatrice. Her face is cut open. She has a broken rib and some bruises. A few other cuts. She's going to be fine. I don't want you to worry about that."

"Oh, Fisher..." she trailed off, beginning to sob softly.

"Don't cry, baby. She's okay. This is Mic we're talking about. I don't know anyone stronger. She wouldn't want you to fuss over her. She's more pissed off that one of the cuts messed up one of her tattoos than anything else."

"Okay. I'm okay. Just bring her home, Fisher." She wiped her tears and straightened her back. Her girl was amazing and strong and beautiful. Something like a scar wasn't going to affect her too badly.

"I'll see you soon. I'd let you talk to her, but she's sleeping. We knocked her out while we stitched her up. She's been through a lot and we figured she could use some rest."

"I'll have food ready. I hope you and the boys are hungry. And by the way Fisher, your bed is very comfortable, but it would be better if you were in it with me."

He growled in response and the volume of his voice dropped. "Woman, you are going to be the death of me. You can't talk like that when I'm around my men."

Beatrice laughed in his ear and quietly hung up the phone. She grabbed her apron and tied it on as she went. She wanted to make sure they had something they loved ready for them when they got back.

These were her boys. And her girl. And her man. She wanted to spoil them all.

****

I was awake and enjoying the view. This was so similar to when we had gotten back from Colombia: me injured and watching the mountains out my window. Instead of late summer though, this time it was early winter. Heavy fog hung on the mountains and all of the leaves were gone from the trees. The sky was heavy with grey clouds that looked like they might hold snow.

The compound appeared below me as we began our descent. We would land here, then drive to the Wonka House. The jet needed to be left at the compound, since we'd be returning tomorrow. I wanted to get my iPod from my cabin before we drove back; I needed my music right now.

I touched my cheek lightly, feeling the neat, tight stitches under the bandage. At least it was just a pad taped to my face, I hadn't been a big fan of the gauze head-piece. The stitches pulled and stretched a little as I moved my jaw around. The pain was down to a dull ache, nothing I couldn't handle. My leg had needed ten stitches, but Rook said he had put over fifteen in my face. The scar would be long and narrow, but very prominent. The tape holding my rib in place itched and stretched my skin as I tried to move. As uncomfortable as it was, having it on was still better than going without.

I wasn't sure how I felt about the scar yet. I wasn't the type of girl who worried about her looks too much and I was pretty used to people staring at me. With my tattoos, how I dressed, and the company I kept, eyes following me through a room was nothing new.

The jet landed with a soft bump and a screech. The others were all standing, grabbing rifles, and getting ready to disembark. I joined them, limping only slightly.

"Come on Mic, I want to get going in ten." Jackson spoke to me over his shoulder as he descended the steps.

"I'm coming." I followed him down the stairs, grasping the railing tightly. Jordon stayed close in case I needed him.

"Whose vehicle are we taking?" Flynn asked from where he was standing just inside the hangar.

"Unlike some of you, I think ahead." Jones pointed to his left. I radioed ahead and had one of the guards bring the Suburban back over for us."

"Everyone has ten minutes to get a change of clothes, then we're leaving," Jackson said.

"Jackson, why are we still staying at the Wonka House?" Rook asked. The Vega cartel is destroyed; the threat against Beatrice is over."

"I second that," Pierce said, raising his hand and staring longingly at his cabin.

"She made us a meal or something. We'll transfer back here in the morning," Jackson said, forcing nonchalance.

"So, let me test my understanding here." Flynn said, cheekily. "We're staying at our secret hideout another night, unnecessarily, because Beatrice cooked for us?"

Jackson glared at him. "Yes. That a problem, Corporal?"

Flynn did his best to hide his grin, but it was a wasted effort. "Not at all, Master Sergeant." He let loose his laugh as he walked away to a safe distance.

I stood there watching the exchange, wanting to question Jackson about his growing relationship with my aunt. I decided to wait until I saw her; I knew she would explain it to me.

I glanced over at Jordon who was standing silently nearby. He hadn't followed Jones and Rook to the cabin they shared. Instead he was studying me.

"Can I help you with anything, Jordon?" I asked, limping closer to him.

"Not yet, Bea. But soon you will," he responded cryptically before spinning on his heel and turning away.

Shaking my head as I went, I made my way slowly to my cabin. I didn't have much with me, just the machete dangling loosely from my right hand. One of the boys had cleaned it for me while I was out. It was once again sharp, well-oiled, and free of blood.

Entering my cabin, I debated about taking off my boots. If I did, I wasn't sure that I would be able to get them back on again by myself. After a moment, I made my decision. Sinking carefully onto my loveseat, I took my boots off and then stared at the machete in my hands. The blade was nicked and gouged in places, no doubt from hitting bones or the like. It seemed macabre to keep it, but I didn't think I could part with it just yet.

I looked at my arms, what wasn't bandaged or bruised was coated in blood. I was a real fucking mess. I didn't have time to spend an hour in the shower like I wanted to, a quick wash-up would have to do.

Plugging the drain of the bathroom sink, I filled it with water as hot as I could stand. Refusing to look up into the mirror, I plunged my arms into the deep sink. The water immediately swirled with brown and pink, getting darker with each passing second.

I scrubbed soap all over my arms, up to my elbows, trying to make at least a little effort to keep my bandages dry. I scrubbed until my skin turned pink, ignoring the overly hot water. My mind drifted back to that room and the monster who had held me.

I felt the blows all over again. I felt the sickening fear, and I smelled the dankness of the basement and the stomach-churning stench of death. My hands were shaking and my breath was coming in short gasps. I licked my lips, tonguing the swollen cut on my bottom lip. I remembered the sting and burn of the slap exploding across my cheek, followed by the cracking pain of Julio's fist knocking me out.

The rope burns on my wrists felt like fire in the water. My mind replaced the feel of the hot liquid with the sensation of the ropes holding my wrists tight. My arms began to ache in memory of their painfully awkward position. I was cold and shaking; I could feel a cold draft on my privates and shame tore through me anew.

I kept scrubbing, trying to feel clean, hoping that if I washed enough I could reach the dirty feeling inside me.

"Mic!" Someone was screaming near my ear. Rough hands jerked me from the sink and pulled me away, shaking me violently. I struck out blindly, slapping and kicking at whoever was holding me. I was screaming unintelligently. My voice shredded my vocal cords; feeling like a trapped animal, I became one.

"God dammit! Mic, fucking stop it! It's me, it's Chris!"

His eyes... I knew those eyes. The bright green orbs were filled with worry and fear. His hands cupped my shoulders. I felt so tiny and fragile in his hands. I followed along the strong angle of his arms with my eyes. His tattoos swirled and rode along his biceps in thick graceful curves. My gaze reached his face, and suddenly I was coming back to myself. The familiar cheekbones and tempting lips comforted me.

"Bea, baby. Please... stay with me," Chris pleaded. I grasped his face in my wet hands which caused dirty water to run down his cheeks and neck. His skin was so warm against mine; his jaw was covered in thick whiskers that rasped against my palms. He put his hands over mine, holding me to him.

"I'm here," I whispered. I drew his face down to mine, for the first time initiating a kiss. His lips found mine and stayed there. He groaned into my mouth and held me closer. The pain in my mouth quickly brushed aside by the pleasure of his lips on mine.

He buried his hands in my hair, not caring that nearly every inch of me was filthy. He kissed me like he was breathing me; as if I was his very life. He backed me up until my legs bumped into the counter, he grunted in frustration before swiftly picking me up and setting me on the countertop. Stepping between my legs, he pressed against me. I responded by wrapping my one good leg around his hip and gripping his back tight with my hands, holding him as close as I could.

"Bea...," he whispered my name, kissing along my neck and ear. Shivers erupted through my body, warming me from the inside and chasing the last of the demons away.

"Chris... please." What I was pleading for I didn't know. I just knew I didn't want him to stop kissing me.

Sliding his hands under my shirt and over my stomach, he encountered my blood-encrusted skin. He pulled back from me, taking his clever hands with him. He was breathing hard and coated in a slick sheen of sweat.

"We can't do this right now," he sighed, putting his forehead against mine. "What you just went through... you need time."

I pushed him away from me, all at once disappointed, and slid down off the counter. I needed to pack a change of clothes; the team was waiting for us.

"Why did you come in here?" I snapped, as I walked past him into my bedroom. I jerked open my closet door and pulled random things out, throwing them in a gym bag.

"The others are waiting. You were in here a long time. I just wanted to make sure you were okay."

"You accomplished that. I'm okay. Now go." I yanked the zipper on the bag closed violently. My hands were shaking with anger and embarrassment. I was taking my emotions out on Jordon, which wasn't fair, but in that moment, I didn't fucking care. "Get out. I'll be out in a minute." I stood facing him with my arms crossed under my breasts, taking a stance of irritation that every woman through time has perfected.

"Fine, Bea, but this isn't over. Not for a second." Jordon left, slamming the door shut behind him.

I desperately wanted to shower for a week and sleep for a month, but such luxuries weren't available to me right now. Jackson and the others were waiting, and I knew that if I didn't get a move on, Jackson would come in here and drag me out. I couldn't bear to put my boots back on… ever… so I threw them in the trash and slid on a pair of flip flops. My feet would be cold, but better cold and clean than covered in blood.

Before I left, I took the time to carefully arrange the machete back in its place next to Phillips's Sig. As I stood staring at them, I tried to figure out why I was keeping them.

"Fuck it, I've had enough self-analysis for today." Swiping my iPod off the table near the door as I left, I put my ear buds in, switched on shuffle, and cranked the volume high. *Crawling* by Linkin Park filled my head, the lyrics speaking to my soul in that moment.

"About fucking time, your highness," Flynn grumbled at me from the driver's seat. Jackson was seated next to him.

I opened my mouth to respond, but Jackson cut me off. "Don't start, just get in the fucking truck." He rolled his window up, cutting off any further conversation.

I did as I was told and got in the fucking truck.

****

He sat in his quiet spot, nestled deep within some fallen leaves. Under a large tree, he was well hidden from what few prying eyes there might be. The compound was directly below him. He watched them scurry around like rats; entering and leaving their cabins, clustered together near the large black Suburban.

He pressed the binoculars tightly against his face, straining to see the one person he hated the most. One of the men came out of her cabin, slamming the door, obviously furious.

So the bitch pissed him off too…

She emerged a few minutes later. The sight of her bandaged face and limping gait gave him great joy. He wished he could shake the hand of whoever had marked the cunt up. Maybe when he got to her, he would cut the other side of her face and make her a real hideous freak. It was no more than she deserved after what she had done.

She was no hero; she was a destroyer of lives…

He couldn't wait to get started. A broad smile stretched his face; thoughts of sweet revenge warmed his heart. His hands itched with the desire to wrap them around her fucking neck. Maybe he would give her a true traitor's death. Gut her… bleed her out slowly… dance on her entrails, and slit her throat. He reached down and adjusted his pants, not at all bothered that the thought of her death excited him so much.

Chapter 28

Jordon leaned his head back, ignoring Mic and everyone else as they drove back to the Wonka House. He reflected on the past few days: finding Mic gone; tracking her down; and finding her tied to that fucking table, thinking the worst had happened. She was the strongest person he knew and he didn't begrudge her the freak-out she'd just had; she was entitled to one.

He would never forget the way she looked when he broke through the door to that room: naked and afraid, displayed like a trophy for that bastard. His beautiful girl had been tortured and nearly killed. If she had died, a large portion of himself would have died with her.

It had scared him to see her vulnerable and terrified; to find her in the grips of a waking nightmare. He didn't think she feared much of anything. She was so fierce and brave. He'd pulled her out of it, never intending for things to go the way they had. She'd kissed *him*! The other times they had kissed, he'd started things along. No matter how impossible their relationship was, it made his chest swell with happiness to know that she wanted him as badly as he wanted her.

Jordon didn't know what to do about her and his growing feelings, but he knew soon he would have to act; and settle their relationship in one way or another. She had him tied up in knots, both physically and mentally.

He spared her a glance, seeing the thick dark circles under her eyes and the anxiety written plain on her face. He wished he could rewrite that past few days for her, but he knew that even if he could, she wouldn't want him to. She was just too fucking stubborn for her own good.

Pierce elbowed him hard in the ribs, forcing him to tear his eyes away from her.

"Stop it. You two have enough problems without you being so fucking obvious about it," Pierce hissed into his ear.

"Fine," Jordon continued to watch the passing trees, lost in thought.

****

We arrived back at the Wonka House without incident. I didn't speak to the others as we descended in the elevator. The smell of our bodies in such a close space was powerful, but not in a good way.

"Jesus Christ, everyone, go to your rooms and get in the fucking showers before we eat. I don't think I can take the smell of you fuckers over dinner," Jackson grumbled as the doors slid open. Before we could all break away to our rooms, a small blue flash rushed at me and attached herself to me. I grunted in pain at the force of her hug. She was squeezing the life out of me.

"Aunt Beatrice... please... my ribs." I gasped out, trying to extract myself from her embrace.

"Oh, Bea. Your gorgeous face." Finally releasing me, she cradled my cheeks in her hands as tears softly fell down her cheeks.

"Aunt Beatrice, I'll be fine. Rook stitched me up." I grasped her wrists, pulling her hands away from me. "Please, I'm a mess. Let me get cleaned up and I'll explain everything. You're safe now, that's the important thing."

"I don't care about that. I know you and Jackson will always keep me safe. Are you okay?" She was swiping at her tears, but they just kept falling.

"Please, don't cry. I'm okay. I've had worse. I'm a soldier, a warrior; I'm not going to let something like a little scar on my face bother me." I kissed her forehead softly, not wanting to sully her with my nastiness, even if my hands were clean.

"I made your favorite." She sniffed and produced a tissue from somewhere, wiping her eyes and nose. "I made everyone's favorites. Go get cleaned up and come eat. A warm meal will do you all good." She took Jackson by the arm and unceremoniously pulled him down the hallway in the direction of his room.

"Well, ain't that something?" Flynn said, looking at me.

"What?" I snapped. My mood was rapidly deteriorating to the point where I was at throat-punch level anger.

"Not going to say anything about your aunt pulling Jackson down the hall like a chew-toy?" Flynn was walking backwards as he spoke.

"No. I'm not." I turned and strode away.

"Fine. Fine... be that way!" he shouted at my back.

I flipped him the finger; it really was the best way to deal with him.

****

I had been standing in the shower long enough that the water was cooling. I was as clean as I could get. I had washed my body and hair multiple times until I finally felt like I was fit to be around others, but not sure that I wanted to be. I shut off the water and stepped out. I stood nude in front of the mirror and surveyed the damage to my body.

Starting at my feet I catalogued my injuries: first were my legs, striped purple with bruises; the cut on my left thigh was neatly stitched closed; then my ribs and torso which were also colored purple in large blotches across my ribs, waist, and chest. The fact that I'd been beaten was readily apparent. My neck had a small cut from Julio's knife, and I had a few finger-shaped bruises. My arms were ok also, other than my wrists that were raw from the rope.

Leaning closer to the mirror, I studied my face. Seeing it for the first time washed clean of blood and dirt, my left cheek and jaw were bruised nicely and a little swollen. I had a split and puffy lip, and of course; the slice across my right cheek. It was red, but not overly so. I touched it lightly, tracing the slight curve.

I tried to imagine what it would look like healed. I had enough scars that it wasn't hard to do so. It would be a little jagged at the top where the knife had cut deeper, then trail into a fine white line that curved near my mouth. I considered what Rook had said, that it wouldn't take away from my looks.

We shall see…

****

Jackson emerged from the shower wrapped in a towel to find Beatrice sitting on his bed, patiently waiting for him. His body was tired, but apparently not all of him was. The sight of her, fresh and clean, looking just as delicious as she smelled had his towel in a precarious position.

"Fisher, I was so worried about you." She stood and walked closer. He opened his arms, wrapping her close to his chest.

"I'll always come back, Beatrice." He pushed her back slightly so he could see her face. "Listen, I know this is really fast and we don't know each other that well, but we're both too old to screw around. I've grown to care about you, very quickly. It's fucking scary, but I'm no coward. We're going to talk to Mic after dinner. You're staying here... with me. Forever."

Tears softly fell down her face and she gave the most appropriate response. "Just try and stop me, soldier." Standing on her toes, she crushed her lips to his and then jerked his towel the rest of the way off.

"Oh boy...," Jackson groaned into her mouth before pushing her backwards onto the bed.

****

We were all gathered in the kitchen as we had been ordered, but Jackson and Aunt Beatrice weren't here. I looked at my watch for the tenth time in the last few minutes; we'd been waiting for over half an hour.

"Someone needs to go find them," Pierce said.

"I wouldn't advise that," Rook said, laughing quietly. "Sorry, Mic, but I don't think it would be polite to interrupt them."

"For fuck's sake. They are adults. There isn't anyone on this planet I would trust more to take care of my aunt than Jackson. If he makes her happy, then I'm happy. What? Did you guys think I would freak out or something?" I was grumpy that they had so little faith in me.

"I'm glad you approve, Bea," Aunt Beatrice said from the doorway where she was holding Jackson's hand. Her small frame looked even smaller next to his hulking body. Happiness radiated from her; she was glowing with it.

I stood and walked toward her and Jackson. I studied him. He, too, looked happier than I had ever seen him. He seemed relaxed and comfortable.

"I just want you to be happy. It's been so long since Uncle Henry passed; you deserve this." I turned to Jackson, looking up at his eyes which shined with what I suspected was the beginnings of love for my aunt.

"Master Sergeant, if you break my aunt's heart, I'm going to break your legs. Got me?"

He chuckled as he let go of my aunt and wrapped me up in a huge hug, being careful of my ribs. "Of that, I have no doubt, Mic."

"Okay, guys, can we freaking eat now?" Flynn asked.

"What did I say about your language in front of me, young man?" Aunt Beatrice raised an eyebrow at Flynn.

"Sorry, ma'am." He had the wisdom to hang his head and attempt to look chastised.

"Flynn is right; we're all exhausted, let's eat." Jackson sat at the head of the long table and Aunt Beatrice took the seat to his right.

We piled our plates high and dug in. The food was as delicious as I'd ever had. Then again, considering that I hadn't eaten in something like a day and a half, even an MRE would taste like a five-star chef creation to me right now.

"God, Aunt Beatrice, you make the best potatoes…" I groaned in pleasure as I took another bite. It hurt to chew, but thankfully the potatoes were soft and creamy.

"I know, dear. You've loved them since you were a little girl."

"Mic was a little girl once? Like with pigtails and Barbies and sh…stuff?" Flynn quickly edited himself.

"Yes, Flynn, I was indeed a child once. I didn't play with Barbies though, I had those little green army men."

"I would be surprised if you had played with dolls. Army men fit you better," Rook chimed in.

"Okay, that's enough about me. When we're done, let's all head up to the war room and I'll debrief you on what happened while Julio had me."

The table fell silent; I hadn't intended to be such a conversation killer. Just call me Debbie Downer...

"I need to hear this too. I need to know what happened to you, Bea," Aunt Beatrice said, clutching Jackson's hand tightly. That was a sight I supported, but it was going to take some getting used to.

"Just debrief here. We're all right here, no need to change rooms because of the topic of conversation." Jordon spoke for the first time since we got back to the Wonka House.

"Agreed," Jackson added between bites of the rich and creamy green bean casserole Aunt Beatrice had made especially for him. We were all going to need to log extra time on the track if she kept cooking like this.

"Well...," I forced myself to be casual and not let my volatile emotions affect the telling. "I got there and some thugs hauled me into the house. Julio came down and welcomed me, the smarmy bastard." I held up my hand to my aunt. "I know, I know, language. But right now, just cut me some slack." I didn't give her a chance to respond before I continued.

"Julio got irate about my language and apparent 'rudeness' and knocked me out." I gestured to the left side of my face with its swelling and pretty colors. "I woke up in a small cell, hands tied behind my back and feet tied at the ankles." I related the story as if it had happened to someone else. I needed to distance myself from my emotions or I would never get through it.

"Big surprise there, Mic was rude to someone," Flynn whispered loudly to Pierce.

"Anyways," Rolling my eyes, I continued. "I kept at him. Trying to stall until you guys got there. He, *uh*... he put a knife in my mouth, and said that if I swore at him again he'd cut out my tongue and force me to eat it." Aunt Beatrice gasped and covered her mouth with her hands. "That's also when he broke my rib, by kneeling on my chest. He left after that and a small girl brought me water. She was one of the girls we rescued. The water was bitter and I should have known better than to drink it. He'd spiked it. I woke up on that table." I decided to spare Aunt Beatrice the details of how I was tied.

"He taunted me a little; admired my hair, the weirdo. That's when he sliced my face and leg. Soon after, the cavalry arrived." I shrugged, realizing I wasn't fooling them with my nonchalance, but appreciating that they weren't calling me on it.

"Then I killed him as he was getting ready to knife Jones," Rook added. "Bastard died too quick in my opinion."

"Agreed," I added, going back to eating.

"Bea Annabelle Michaels," Aunt Beatrice said in *that* tone, the one where you knew you were in trouble.

"Holy shit, your middle name in Annabelle!" Flynn was bouncing in his seat, he was so excited. Jordon caught my eye and smirked.

"Thanks, Aunt Beatrice, that's just what I needed."

"I told you your potty mouth would get you in trouble one day," she said, not looking up from her plate of food.

"Really? That's what you're going to say?" Irritation sharpened my tone.

"Don't take that tone with me, young lady. My heart breaks for what you went through, but you are the one who left here alone. You are the one who delivered yourself into the hands of that madman. I'm glad he's dead and I'm happier than I can express that you made it home safe, but I'm also very upset with you for being so foolish. You were raised to be smarter than that."

Flynn had both hands over his mouth. His face got darker and darker red, as he tried to hold in his laughter. Jordon just crossed his arms over his chest, looking very satisfied with my dressing-down.

"What she said, Mic," Pierce added, raising his hand.

"For fucks sake...," I snapped, getting up to take my plate to the sink. "Did you see those photographs, Aunt Beatrice? Did Jackson let you see what that fucker did to those innocent people? To those children? *Did he*?" She had the gall to look embarrassed. "I had no other choice. I *refused* to have the lives of more innocent people on my hands when I could stop it. Any one of you would have done the same." I threw my plate into the sink where it broke cleanly in two. "Thanks for saving my life, guys. I appreciate it. I'm sure the girls we saved are pretty grateful too. Compared to them, I got off easy. Did you make that call Jackson, or were you too busy fucking my aunt?"

He stood so fast his chair fell over, anger tightening his face. I remained firm, daring him to come closer.

"If you ever again imply that I am putting personal matters before the lives of innocent people, you *will* be gone. I will not speak to you about your insubordination again, Staff Sergeant," Jackson snarled in my face.

"Fine." I didn't bother to add his rank. I turned my back on all of them and left the room.

I let the kitchen door slam behind me and smashed the button for the elevator, pressing it over and over as if that would get it here faster. I felt entitled to my anger. I felt justified to be pissed the fuck off at the world right now.

"Well, Mic, you're in rare form today," Jordon spoke from beside me. I glanced at him, but he was staring straight ahead at the elevator doors.

"I'm pissed off. Leave me alone." My hands curled into fists, I was nearly shaking with rage.

"I see that; and no, I'm not leaving you alone. I think that's the last thing you need right now. What Jackson and your aunt don't understand is this..." He paused as the doors opened and we stepped in. He hit the button for Level Three without needing to be told. "You died... in your mind anyways. You let yourself die. Being brought back to life is rough on anyone."

I glanced at him sideways from the corner of my eye. *Intuitive, wasn't he?*

"Just what do you plan on doing down here?" He asked as the doors slid open again. I didn't answer, but instead hobbled down the short hallway to the pool.

"I can't run or lift weights. Water is okay, so I'm getting in the pool."

"Okay then." He stripped off his shirt and toed off his shoes. Neither of us had suits, but that didn't seem to matter.

I slipped off my shirt and shoes also, hesitating at the button of my pants. Jordon didn't have such reservations; he shucked his pants and more or less ignored me as he stepped into the pool. I was frozen by the sight of him in tight, navy blue boxer briefs; they clung to every sweep and curve of his ass and thighs.

This should be illegal...

I stripped my own pants off and joined him in the shallow end. The water shrunk my bra and panties tight against my skin. I looked down, grateful I hadn't worn white. The black material looked the same as a bathing suit would.

"I have to keep my face dry," I said, wading to the side of the pool where I propped my elbows and let my legs float out in front of me. The water felt amazing on my skin; it was warm and was doing wonders for relaxing my stiff muscles.

Jordon laughed. "I'll make a note not to splash you."

"Why are you here?" I asked, as I leaned my head back and closed my eyes.

"For you. Why else would I be here?" He sounded genuinely confused.

"Many reasons."

"It's like I said; I don't think you need to be alone right now. You don't have to talk to me or even look at me, but just know that I'm here with you... *for* you. Maybe it will be enough to help you feel a little better."

"Maybe, or maybe you being mostly naked in a pool with me, while I'm mostly naked, is too much of a distraction." I opened my eyes, enjoying the look of shock on his face.

"Is that what you want to talk about? Us... being naked... together?"

"Right now? No. But soon." I closed my eyes again and went back to ignoring him.

"The way I see it, if Jackson can be with your aunt, why can't we be together?" He'd moved closer to me, now sharing my bit of poolside.

"My aunt is not under Jackson's command."

"No, but she's a civilian."

"True." His hand touched my face, turning me to look at him. "This is going beyond simple want, Bea, this is need." He kissed me softly, a quick brush of lips that took me back to our first kiss in the jungle of Colombia.

"Chris... I just don't know what to do with you." I sighed heavily.

"Oh, Bea, I could think of a few things...," he said, wiggling his eyebrows at me.

"Not that, ya jerk. That, I have no trouble with. It's very

complicated. My feelings for you and my duty to this team are at war with each other and I don't know who is going to win." My heart was heavy with its burden.

"Well, I'm not going anywhere, baby. When you figure it out, you let me know." He brushed a piece of my hair off my face, tucking it behind my ear. I secretly loved it when he did that. "Rook said I should just pin you against a wall and have at you."

"Rook's an idiot." I tried to hide how my heart jumped at the thought.

"Maybe, maybe not. One day soon, we're going to settle this between us. Now isn't the time. When I finally get you under me, I need you healthy and healed. You're going to need to be, to keep up with me." He kissed me again and climbed the steps. I didn't bother trying to pretend that I wasn't watching the water slide down his golden skin.

"Just think. You could have this view every day," he said over his shoulder as he ran a towel along his arms.

"*Umm...*" was the most intelligent response I could muster.

He left the room without saying anything further.

My thoughts swirled and mingled in my head in the same way that the water was swirling around my body. Exhaustion pulled at me, but it didn't stop me from worrying about the girls we saved, or my aunt, or myself and Jordon, for that matter.

The Russian girls were my primary concern. I needed to know how they were brought into Mexico and who was doing it. How many more girls like them were there? If I could stop even one girl from going through a fraction of what I had experienced, then it was something I had to do. I *had* to.

Holding my wrists in front of me, I stared at the rope burns encircling them. How many other girls were tied or chained right now?

How many girls were suffering unspeakable cruelty at the hands of their self-proclaimed masters? Steel was powerful; we had the skills and resources to track this down.

A plan began to form in my head. To bring it to fruition, I would need help from both the U.S. government and those in the Eastern bloc. I stepped from the pool, drying quickly as thoughts raced through my head. I needed to find Jackson and Jones.

I pulled my clothes on over my soaking underwear and ran from the room as quickly as my leg would allow. Pressing and holding the elevator button, I considered using the intercom to confirm where they were, but the doors slid open just then. Rising quickly to Level Two, I bounced on my heels impatiently.

As soon as the elevator stopped, I hurried out, sliding across the floor in my rush.

"Jackson!" I yelled, startling everyone. They jumped up and began checking weapons. Shit.

"No, no. Everything is okay. Well, it's not, but there is no threat to us. Not right now, anyway."

"Shit, don't fucking do that! You scared years off my life," Flynn said as he re-holstered his weapon.

"I said I was sorry. Jackson, where are those girls?"

"As far as I know, they're still in the hospital in Mexico. Why?" He was standing now as well, picking up on my urgency.

"We have to find who bought them. I mean, how Julio bought them. Where are they coming from? Who is moving them from Russia? We have to find the trafficker and whack his fucking ass."

"Mic, slow the fuck down. This isn't something we're going to roll out on in the morning. First of all, you need to heal. If the girls are Russian, chances are the Russian mob is at least partially responsible. We can't just waltz into fucking Russia of all places. Not if we don't want to start a war. Let me make some calls in the morning when we get back to the compound." Without further comment, Jackson left the room.

Pierce gently gripped my shoulders in his hands. "Mic, I know you want to help those girls, especially in the face of what you've just been through; and we will help them, but we have to do this the right way. You need to go get some rest. None of us, you more so, have had a decent night's sleep in a few days. We can look at this problem with fresh eyes in the morning." He patted my shoulders before he, too, left the room.

"He's right. We need rest and we need to research this." Rook nodded as he followed Pierce out. Flynn and Jones left without a word. Only Jordon and I remained.

"Screw them. Rest? Who needs that? Come here and we'll watch a movie and make out." Jordon patted the couch cushion next to his hip.

Laughing, I took the seat next to him. I decided as I slid closer to his side, that Jordon was good for me. He was a balm for my very battered and damaged soul.

****

He watched the sun rise over the mountains as snow softly began to fall. He wouldn't be able to hide here much longer. His tracks would point out his location like a homing beacon. Observing a special operations team was challenging to say the least.

Snugly fitting his binoculars onto his eyes, he tracked the progress of the Suburban. It parked in the same spot it was always parked in. The one they called Flynn stepped from the driver's seat and the leader, Jackson, got out from the passenger side. The rear doors opened and one-by-one the team stepped out. The newest man, Rook, was someone he would need to be careful of. He saw things that most did not.

She emerged last, limping still. He was shocked when she helped another woman step from the vehicle. A woman who looked remarkably like her, only older.

She's got a relative? His heart skipped a beat at the tasty treat she made. Jackson surprised him further by putting a giant arm over her shoulders and pointing to his cabin.

What the fuck? She's Jackson's?

This was going to be good. Two Michaels' women within his grasp. His hands shook with anticipation. Again, he had to adjust the front of his pants to accommodate his growing excitement.

This winter would bring many changes to Steel Corps... ones that he couldn't wait to begin.

About the Author

J. B. Havens lives in rural Pennsylvania and is a wife and mother of three. When she is not spending time with her family, she is researching and writing her next novel.

Connect with her to learn about new projects and future release dates. She loves to hear from readers, so feel free to contact her and tell her what you think of Mic and the boys.

www.jbhavens.weebly.com is her website where you can find character bios, photos, and an exclusive short story, A Steel Family Christmas.

Find her on Facebook at

www.facebook.com/jbhavens

And Twitter @havens_b.

Email her at www.jbhavenauthor@gmail.com

Made in the USA
Lexington, KY
19 February 2019